# THE DEVIL'S RANGERS

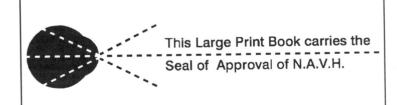

# THE DEVIL'S RANGERS

## JIM GRAND

**THORNDIKE PRESS**

*An imprint of Thomson Gale, a part of The Thomson Corporation*

Detroit • New York • San Francisco • New Haven, Conn. • Waterville, Maine • London

Copyright © 2006 by Otisburg Company.
Thorndike Press, an imprint of The Gale Group.
Thomson and Star Logo and Thorndike are trademarks and Gale is a registered trademark used herein under license.

Thorndike Press® Large Print Western.
The text of this Large Print edition is unabridged.
Other aspects of the book may vary from the original edition.
Set in 16 pt. Plantin.

LIBRARY OF CONGRESS CATALOGING-IN-PUBLICATION DATA

Grand, Jim, 1951–
   The devil's rangers / by Jim Grand.
      p. cm. — (Thorndike Press large print Western)
   ISBN-13: 978-0-7862-9771-9 (hardcover : alk. paper)
   ISBN-10: 0-7862-9771-9 (hardcover : alk. paper)
    1. Mexicans — California — Fiction. 2. Outlaws — California — Fiction.
3. California — Gold discoveries — Fiction 4. California — History —
1846–1850 — Fiction 5. Large type books. I. Title.
PS3568.O8894D48 2007
813'.54—dc22                            2007016708

Published in 2007 by arrangement with The Berkley Publishing Group,
a member of Penguin Group (USA) Inc.

Printed in the United States of America on permanent paper
10 9 8 7 6 5 4 3 2 1

# AUTHOR'S NOTE

*The Devil's Rangers* is a work of fiction inspired by historical figures and events. Several characters have been combined and the time frame and locales have been compressed, but the events and the fundamental truths of the tale — including the conflicts, many of which are ongoing — are unaltered.

■ ■ ■ ■

# PART ONE:
# JUNE 1849

■ ■ ■ ■

# 1
## LOVERS

The sun was rising but Carlos Murrieta didn't feel like getting up. The mountain air was still very cold, if mercifully still, and he was warm beneath his dusty deer-hide saddle blanket. Wrapped around a bundle of weeds, his wool shirt made a comfortable pillow that he did not want to leave.

But a new day was like a woman. There was no arguing with it.

The nineteen-year-old opened his eyes and peered into the rising sun. "Why don't you wake up too?" he murmured at the small stone circle that marked the boundaries of the dead campfire. It would be nice to have heat just waiting for him, like those steaming springs they had passed in Trincheras.

Carlos Murrieta lay there and watched the fast-brightening skies above the distant mountains, their silhouettes a deep blue against the paler yellow-blue of the sky. His eyes drifted down to the birds circling for prey. Behind him, he listened to what sounded like a large herd of deer moving through the fruit trees that grew further down the slope. The creatures of day were all up. It was time for him to rise too. He was helped along by a gust that scudded up the mountainside. It swept ash from the campfire and carried it toward him, under his nose.

It was like the smell of a small, old grave, the kind they occasionally unearthed while plowing the earth back home. He didn't like it. The stone-white branches that had fueled the campfire sounded like little bones rattling in the brief gust. The real bones nearby, the remains of last night's dinner, still had some meat on them. Within the ring of stones, tiny red mites and big black ants crept over the legs and ribs of what used to be a rabbit. Above, in the branches of a nearby oak, the dark gray fur of a hare still moved as the breeze stirred its surface. The pelt had been peeled from the raw meat and hung like a cloak. When dried and scraped and turned inside out, it would make a fine covering for one hand. Juanita had begun working on it the night before. The sinew still had to be cut away before it dried. Otherwise, the strands would tighten and cause the skin to become permanently wrinkled.

Carlos stretched. He could hear his sister-in-law moving behind him, packing her own bedroll. Juanita's husband, his older brother Joaquin, was already gone. Carlos slid from under the blanket. Throwing it off would only stir choking dust from the campfire, carrying it toward the mule, which was tethered to the oak. He kept his back to the young woman as he rose. He would go beyond the ridge to relieve himself before greeting her. He paused only long enough to pull his alpaca jacket from a branch beside the fur and slipped it on. He buttoned it against the stirring winds.

"Good day, Carlos," Juanita said.

"I hope it will be," he replied over his shoulder. He glanced toward the spot where Joaquin had made his bed. It was already cleared. "How long has Jo been gone?"

"Only a few minutes," Juanita said.

Joaquin had said he wanted to go ahead at the first glint of sunrise to find water, something they had not seen during their ascent. He hoped that deer droppings would lead him to it. Their pouches were nearly empty and travel to one of the lakes to the east would take two days' travel in the wrong direction.

As Carlos walked into the fast-rising sun, he passed the remains of an unlucky road-runner a coyote must have caught during the night. They were silent, those little killers. From the scarcity of prints he suspected the killer was a transient rogue. The sickly or injured members of a pack were eaten, but the wild ones were driven off. The dead bird reminded him of some of his earliest childhood memories. He recalled finding the remains of a wild turkey or quail just outside their stone hut. He asked his grand-father what they were and he said, *"Huesos de un ángel,"* "Angel bones," because there were still feathers attached.

Carlos asked how it was possible for angels to die.

"Devils," he had told the boy. "They hide in the bright light and jump out at them. That's why you should stay in the shadows."

His grandfather was either a joker or loco. Carlos and Joaquin had never figured out which. The Murrieta patriarch died when they were both very young.

As he made his way down the slope, Carlos saw a patch of grass that had been burned by a lightning strike. The blades were blackened and bent in a circular patch about the size of a well. The earth below and around it was charcoal-gray. The only things that had contained a potential brush-fire were the boulders that surrounded the area. He wondered why vegetation did not die like other things. Carlos also remembered, as a slightly older child, coming upon a cactus that had been split by a bolt and then sun-baked, burning off any water that was left inside. It looked more like sun-dried flesh than plant. In the field, dead cows or deer still looked like what they were in life. In time, when the rabbit bones were gone and the insects had fled, even this campfire would be as identifiable as the carcass of a longhorn in the plains. Why not green things?

*Maybe it is God's punishment for reaching toward the heavens,* he thought. If so, what must He think of the Murrietas climbing to such heights as they made their way north? In their village, men had always respected and feared the mountains. Could that be why?

Carlos reached the edge of the ridge. He found large stones lying side by side to use as a "necessary." They were ideal for a comfortable sit. It seemed more civilized than facing a tree and holding tight while he squatted like an animal. Carlos opened his hemp drawstring, dropped his cotton trousers, and sat partly astride both rocks, facing the valley. Surely God would not be angry at them for trying to improve their circumstances. He thought of the life he and Joaquin had led since leaving their home in Villa San Rafael de los Alamitos.

For the past two years and four months, Carlos and his brother had made their home wherever they were when the sun went down. Sometimes it was in the high grasses of a lonely plain; sometimes it was on the scrub of a dusty plateau. Once, two or three months ago, when the brothers found themselves high in the foothills of a southern range, they were forced to spend the night in a place where it was high enough for rain to become snow. It was the first time they had ever experienced icy rain and it was like being awake in a dream. It was also very cold. Breathing that frigid air reminded Carlos of the time he'd been kicked in the chest by a wild pony they'd tried to catch in a canyon. Each time he filled his lungs even a little bit, it hurt. But it was worth the pain to experience the beauty of the snowfall, and the blinding beauty of the mountains white and aglow in the morning sun. Both brothers felt as if God had allowed them to witness a tiny glimpse of Heaven.

This time, their camp was on the top of a mountain at a much lower elevation. The clouds were below them, but just barely. The travelers had come to this summit late on the previous afternoon in order to study the cut of the valley and plan their travel for the next few days.

The wind felt good on Carlos's skin. He undid the two buttons of his jacket and let the air move around his chest. In the absence of a river or lake for a shower, an airing was better than nothing. He heard movement above him and peeked back around the boulder. Juanita was on the ridge. There was a nest in the tree where she had hung the rabbit pelt and she was gathering eggs. If the eggs had chicks inside, she would leave them. If they were infertile, she would take them. At their next campsite, somewhere in the valley, she would mix the eggs with the flour they carried to make a paste. Dried, they would make tasty biscuits, *galletas de huevo,* which would stay fresh for days. In the short time they had been together, Carlos knew this much about his new sister: Any eggs and fruit they encountered rarely escaped her mixing cup. Whenever Juanita found grasses they could use, such as barley or clover, she picked that to supplement the flour they carried.

Carlos smiled as his new sister began to sing. She did not have a *fiesta* voice, one that would cause revelers to forget about the roasting pig and jugs of sweet red wine and dance. But Carlos could picture her smile as she sang, and she did have a wonderful smile. Juanita Juárez had only been with them for three weeks, but in that time she had become like blood to him.

The brothers had met the sixteen-year-old woman before they left Mexico. They had stopped in the small, sun-bleached town of Esqueda to find work, hoping to save enough to buy at least a horse to replace their aging mule. Instead they found Juanita, the daughter of a physician who went from town to town in the Distrito de Altar. The graceful but resolute young woman wanted to see the world beyond the foothills. Joaquin wanted a wife to join him in California, where they were headed. They joined their goals and solemnized their relationship immediately. The small dowry her father gave them was used to buy goods Juanita would need on the journey.

Juanita was not as convenient as a horse would have been. The men still had to carry their bedrolls and gear. But her cooking and sewing and even medical skills were exceptional and her eyes — and smile — took the edge off the hard land and even harder journey. Especially for Joaquin, who was far

16

more serious about their goals than Carlos had ever been.

Carlos buttoned his jacket and pulled up his trousers. He looked back out at the thick morning clouds spread below to the horizon. He had never seen the ocean, but he imagined it looked like this, only blue. A proud expanse with bulges and ripples moving slowly toward him. To the south he saw the clouds literally creep up one side of the higher foothills and spill over the other, like slow-moving water. He wondered what the ocean smelled like. Probably much different than the ledge, which smelled like wet straw. He enjoyed the feel of the sharp, warm sunshine above. Most days they were below the clouds when they woke, the world damp and gray. The view was worth the climb and he took a moment to savor it. This was another way he and his brother were different. Joaquin preferred to do his business and move on, whatever that business was. Carlos liked to take private moments to linger over things that gave him pleasure.

Joaquin was back by the time Carlos returned. He had brought three calfskin pouches filled with water. Two of them were plain and one was covered with small red beads. That pouch was one of the things Joaquin had purchased with Juanita's small dowry. He had bought it for her.

"I'll bet all you had to do was swing them through the clouds to fill them," Carlos said with a laugh, moving his hand over his head.

"There was a small pool about two hundred feet down," Joaquin replied humorlessly. "It was an outpouring from an underground stream."

Juanita winked at Carlos, who frowned. He did not bother to tell his brother he had been joking.

Joaquin set the pouches beside the dead campfire and hugged his wife hard. Juanita had to stand on her toes in order to put her slender arms around his broad back. For most of his twenty-one years Joaquin had been a field worker, cutting irrigation ditches or digging wells. Water was something he knew and understood. That was why the brothers had made their way north. They wanted to put his knowledge to use, to find land they could farm for themselves rather than work for some absentee landowner in France or Spain or a soft retired *caudillo* who needed strong arms to tend his holdings and plump his thick purse.

The embrace was a moment that seemed much longer. Carlos had looked away. Though it gave him joy to see his brother happy — which was uncommon enough —

the couple deserved a moment of privacy.

Joaquin moved away from his wife. He pushed the long black hair from her forehead. "Did you sleep well?"

"Like a lamb," she said with a laugh. "I never imagined I would have a bed so close to the stars."

"An angel deserves no less," her husband said.

Carlos felt a chill as he thought of the dead bird on the slope.

Juanita took a long drink of water, then began piling their few belongings in two separate blankets. When she was finished, the men would tie them tightly and compactly with well-worn leather straps. As she packed, Joaquin retied the plain white bandanna he wore around his own long black hair. He walked over to Carlos.

"I have to go back down," Joaquin told him.

"Why?"

"I couldn't see the valley from the pool. I need to go lower."

"We know we have to go north," Carlos said. "Why don't we just go in that direction?"

"The gullies on the south side were steep. I don't want to spend days picking our way through. If there is level terrain I want to try and find it."

"If you wait, we can finish packing and look together," Carlos suggested.

"No. The slope is very steep. I want to try and find a trail for the mule."

"The mule is very surefooted," Carlos said. He glanced at Juanita. "But I understand."

"I will find a trail and mark it for you," Joaquin said. "Follow as soon as you are able."

"Is something wrong?" Carlos asked. He knew his brother's moods. Joaquin was being unusually aggressive. "Did you smell a fire last night?"

"No, but we are downwind of the valley. There is always a chance someone may have seen or smelled ours," Joaquin said. He moved closer. "I saw horse droppings to the east. Not fresh, but there are plenty of pastures in the southern valley. Wild horses would not come up unless they were brought. Finish packing and follow my trail quickly."

"Of course," Carlos replied.

Joaquin picked up one of the water pouches and drew his knife from its leather sheath. He would cut X-shaped notches in trees or on rocks to mark his passage. Carlos knew how to spot them.

Joaquin stepped up to his wife. He nodded toward Carlos. "Because Carlos is Carlos, he will try and beat his big brother down the mountainside. If you're unsure of the descent, let him know —"

"Your wife does not like to lose either." Juanita grinned and cast a challenging look at Carlos. "If this is a race, I am also in it."

Joaquin smiled. He kissed his wife on the forehead. "Your safe passage is the only victory I want," he said. With a last look, he started back down the slope.

Juanita watched her husband go. "Has he always been like this, so very serious?" she asked.

"Yes." Carlos walked over to help Juanita with the blankets. The woman had a new one, which Joaquin had purchased from the local Pechanga Indians. It had a dark sawtooth design and was dyed the color of a pumpkin with tassels made of untreated wool. They caught the dirt when it was on the ground and made it easier to keep clean. Carlos took over binding the first of their five bundles. This one contained his brother's belongings, which included a hatchet, a second pair of leather boots, several maps they had bought from a retired American soldier, and a Bible his mother had given them when they left. Neither brother was devout, yet their mother had given them life and love. Any gift from her was an extension of that, and precious. Next, Carlos turned to the bedrolls. He would carry them for both men until they met up with Joaquin. He would offer to carry Juanita's — again — though she would refuse. The woman might be small and slender, but she was made of the same hard, stubborn clay as his brother.

"Has Joaquin been more determined since I joined you?" Juanita asked.

Carlos nodded.

"Perhaps I should have waited in the village, had him come back for me," Juanita said.

"No," Carlos told her. "He wants to reach the northern valleys quickly, settle in a place where you can be contented and safe. But you have made him very happy, and he needs that too."

Juanita smiled and picked burrs from the bottom of her ankle-length dress. Beneath it she wore moccasins with leather toppings that covered her shins. Though the stiff leather chafed, they offered protection from snakebites. "Then he has always been in a hurry?" she said.

"For as long as I can remember," Carlos said. "He always wanted to build a place where our parents and young sister and grandmother can also live. Somewhere without an *alcalde* deciding that our land belongs to him." Carlos chuckled as he secured the blanket to the mule. "But he competes with himself. Once we have built a ranch, he will want to establish a community, and then he'll decide that Heaven itself is not good enough for our dear *abuela,* so he'll have to create one here —"

"Hush!" Juanita said.

"Why?"

"God will hear you."

Perhaps He would, Carlos thought. But God, at least, could be forgiving. That was a concept Joaquin did not understand. He still growled whenever he was reminded of the bullies who once tripped their little sister on her way back from the well. Joaquin stopped what he was doing, went to the well, and threw each of the larger boys in. Then he waited nearby to make sure they stayed down until dark. Patience was something Joaquin lacked, except in the prosecution of wrongdoers. Or perhaps that was something different — perseverance? Joaquin had demonstrated that quality over and over when he mastered the skills he used to hunt — and protect his loved ones. He had spent years studying knife-fighting with his mestizo friend Tutul from the Oaxaca region. Though Joaquin used knives to hunt, the way he handled a blade — flipping it here and there as though he were a performer in *el carnaval* — was enough to discourage confrontations. Carlos smiled. He wondered if that had helped Dr. Juárez reach his decision to let his daughter go off with them — knowing that she'd be safe, or fearing what Joaquin would do if his wishes were denied. Joaquin had also taught himself to use a whip. He didn't like killing rattlesnakes unless they attacked, and had decided the lash was the safest way to drive them away without getting near. Sometimes his anger had a practical, even humane side.

"Do not avenge the wrong, but strengthen your sister so she can protect herself," the elder Murrieta had counseled.

Joaquin taught her a trick he'd learned for dealing with pests like flies and mosquitoes. They found river reeds and slit the ends to fine, fanlike threads. When the reed dried, it could be used to rake the eyes of anyone who threatened her. No man, however strong, could fight with blood in his eyes. She always carried her *rastrillo* in her sash or worn on her back.

"Anyway, I hope your grandmother does not see Our Lord for many long years," Juanita remarked.

"That is my hope as well," Carlos agreed. "I was only saying that you have married a man of vision and ambition."

"And as I told him, he will find me *very* determined to keep up," Juanita said with a flourish. She finished securing her flour and pans on the back of the mule. "Are you ready to catch our hero?"

"I am," Carlos said.

The clouds were beginning to thin below. They could see the brilliant white of a distant lake, the green of treetops, the piles of boulders shaken from the hills by some ancient tremor. Carlos wondered about the different kinds of trees and animals they would see here. It was exciting to contemplate.

When the bedrolls were packed, Carlos helped Juanita hoist one onto her back. Her wool blouse shifted slightly, and he saw the red marks where the leather straps had rubbed her flesh raw. She did not wince and she did not complain. His brother was a fortunate man. For himself, Carlos wanted a woman who was plumper, not so small-breasted or lean at the hip. But when he found his own wife, he hoped that she had the spirit of this *señora*.

The winds had picked up as the air

warmed. They blew up the slope, whistling loudly in his ears. At least they knew there were no animals ahead of them. Predators knew enough to keep upwind from other predators. As long as they watched out for nests of rattlesnakes, it should be an easy walk. Carlos slid his belt through the water pouches and tied it tightly at the side, on his left hip. The knot had a natural resting place there. His knife was at his right hip. Then he shouldered the other two bedrolls, one over each arm.

"What the hell're you Mud Bricks doin' here?"

Carlos looked behind them. Four men were just coming up the ridge where Carlos had recently been standing. The men were about thirty feet away. Carlos did not understand English and he did not know most of what the man had said. All he knew was that "Mud Bricks" was an unkind reference to people of his race and that the man's tone was unfriendly.

"We were resting," Carlos said. He maneuvered sideways so that he was between the men and Juanita. As Carlos passed in front of the young woman, he gave her a gentle push, to urge her down the slope. Juanita didn't move.

" '*Des*-can-*samos,*' " the man snorted,

repeating the Spanish word.

"What's that?" asked another man.

"He says he was takin' it easy. What the hell makes ya so tired? You Bricks don't work much." He glanced at Juanita and grinned. "Never mind. I can figger out what you were doin'."

The men continued to approach. They were all wearing firearms, and the man who spoke was carrying a coiled whip. They were all bearded and long-haired, with knee-length coats and wide-brimmed hats. They wore leather gloves so dirty the leather looked like spun coal. The men were obviously cowhands. That meant there must be a ranch somewhere nearby. If so, it was possible that Carlos and Juanita were on someone's property.

"We are sorry. We are leaving," Carlos said, bowing apologetically.

The men continued to approach. They smelled of sweat, coffee, horse, and no-good. The speaker looked down at the campfire as he passed. He toed some of the bones with his boots.

"We saw yer fire last night. You all are trespassin' on the Veehall Ranch," the cowhand said. "Now we see ya kilt one of Mr. Vee-hall's rabbits." He nodded toward the pouch strapped to Carlos's hip. "Josiah, see if they stole some of Mr. Veehall's drinkin' water too."

One of the men broke from the group and approached with a short, bowlegged stride. Like his brother, the Mexican youth had faced ruffians at home. But Carlos had always tried to talk them out of a violent confrontation and Joaquin was usually nearby to back him up.

Carlos stood his ground but did not stiffen his shoulders. He did not want to do anything to provoke these men. He suspected they were going to look for gold or silver or something of value. They wouldn't find any. He hoped the men would not be too disappointed and simply let them go.

That was what he hoped, not what he believed.

Josiah stood a head taller than Carlos and was broader by a half. He did not draw his gun. Instead, he drew Carlos's own knife and put his other hand on one of the water pouches. He cut the rope with a hard upward slice. Carlos's pants dropped from the weight of the other two pouches.

"Ya lost yer sheath," Josiah said.

The men laughed as Josiah tucked the knife in his own belt. Carlos remained as he was, the wind blowing through his bare legs. The long hem of his shirt kept him from being embarrassed in front of Juanita.

Josiah pulled the cork from the pouch. He raised it over Carlos's head and emptied the contents. The water washed over his dark hair and into his ears and eyes. He blinked involuntarily.

*"Stand still, Brick!"* Josiah yelled.

Carlos understood the tone. He shut his eyes and took the humiliation. The cowhands were bullies, no different from bullies everywhere. Hopefully, that was all they were.

Josiah shook out the last of the water into his mouth. He touched his tongue to it. "Yep. It's Veehall water," he said. The big man remained standing beside Carlos. He looked at Juanita, who ignored him.

"So ya took food and our drink without askin'," the other cowhand said. He shook his head deliberately. "That means a fee plus a interest, like they sez in the bank. Ya got money?"

Carlos understood the word "money." He shook his head once.

"That's too bad," he said as the other men reached him. "And ya know what else? Now ya owe us two bits for the shower."

Carlos moved his hands slightly, palms up, and shrugged. He didn't know what the man was saying. He only wanted to show him that he was no threat to them and was sorry for what he'd done.

"Step outta yer pants," the man said. He pointed to the fallen trousers and motioned Carlos to one side.

Carlos hesitated.

"I said step outta yer damn pants!" the man screamed, using the pouch to cuff Carlos on the side of the head.

Reluctantly, Carlos did as he was told.

"Too bad," the man said. "If yer lady here was older, we'd take her back to the ranch. Old Mud Bricks is good for keepin' house."

"And cookin', Mr. Rawth," Josiah said.

The other man looked back at him. "What, you sayin' you don't like Stool's cookin'?"

"I like it well enough for a man's cookin'," Josiah said. "I'm just sayin' old Bricks is better."

"I agree," said Hank, the third man to speak. He was the tallest of the group, bigger and broader than Josiah.

Rawth looked at the last member of the group, a short man with a belly that hung over his leather belt. "Stool, I guess we better find ya an old Brick to learn ya."

"Well, awright," said Stool. His eyes were on Juanita and his mind was not on breakfast.

"In the meantime, what do we do with the young one?" Hank asked.

"I guess the same thing the Brick's been doin' to her," Rawth said.

*Josiah. Hank. Rawth. Stool.* Those were names Carlos was beginning to realize he would never forget. Maybe he did have that in common with Joaquin.

"Come here, *señorita*," Rawth said. He crooked a finger at the woman.

Juanita stood where she was.

"Dammit, I said come here, *señorita!*"

"*Señora*," she said defiantly.

Rawth laughed and regarded Carlos. "She got spunk fer a stupid, uneducated Brick."

"Mr. Rawth, I'm countin' three bedrolls," Josiah said, peering behind the girl. "Somebody prob'ly went off to piss or somethin'."

"Did yer daddy go off 'n' leave ya?" Rawth asked the woman.

"Maybe he saw what happened and he's hiding to keep his own trousers and their contents," Hank said.

"Well, let's see if we can't bring him on out," Rawth said. His tone was no longer playful.

The leader motioned with his whip hand. It was a small gesture, a cock of the wrist, but the men understood. They separated, forming a wide circle of four around the two.

"Y'know what's gonna happen, *señor* and *señora?*" Rawth asked?

The words were still a mystery, but Rawth had now communicated his intentions clearly. Carlos forgot his nakedness, forgot himself. Whatever the cost, he had to protect Juanita.

"You have to run down the slope, shout for help," Carlos said to her. "I will try and keep them away."

"They will kill you."

"Quit yer jabberin'," Rawth said.

"They will kill me anyway," Carlos said.

"They will not hurt you if I give them what they want," Juanita said.

" *'No!'* Carlos snapped.

" 'No' what?" Rawth demanded. "What the hell you pieces o' scat squawkin' about?"

Carlos didn't intend to discuss this with Juanita or anyone else. He saw what he wanted, what he needed, and there was only one way to get it. He ducked his shoulder and ran into Josiah hard. The man fell back and Carlos grabbed the gun from the cowhand's holster. Josiah grabbed for Carlos, but the younger man was able to pull away. He rose on wobbly legs and aimed at the others. Carlos's knife had fallen from the man's belt. Juanita recovered it.

"Get out of here!" Carlos told her.

There was a whistle, a crack, and Carlos felt pain rocket from his forearm to his shoulder. Rawth's whip cut through his shirt and his flesh, stinging like a nest of hornets and causing his hand to go numb. The gun fell to the ground. So did Carlos. He landed on his knees. He saw Josiah get up. The man kicked Carlos hard in the ribs, then rushed past him.

A second lash caught Carlos across the face. The right side of his face burned as though someone had pushed a torch to it. He whimpered involuntarily and fell backward as though his spine had turned to sand. His knees were still bent and that forced him to roll to his left side. He looked behind him. Through tear-filled eyes he saw Josiah wrestling with Juanita. The big man was laughing as he twisted her wrist. Carlos's knife fell from her hand. Then he put his big left hand on her too-small shoulder and pushed her to the ground. She was wriggling back and forth and up and down like a mouse in a snake's jaw, trying to get away. She was snarling, but she did not scream.

Juanita did not want to bring her unarmed husband into this struggle — and to probable death.

Two other men rushed past Carlos and joined the battle against the slender woman. Carlos tried to get his left elbow underneath him, but a third crack of the whip made that impossible. The lash cut through the side of his chest, exposing rib and causing his entire body to convulse. The blow did not leave enough wind in his lungs to cry out. He whimpered softly as blood seeped from the ragged wound. The sticky dampness streamed along his waist, backbone, and shoulder. He tried once again to push off the ground, but his elbow folded and he dropped onto his back.

"Stay put, Brick!" someone yelled.

The whip shrieked again and struck diagonally across his bare legs from knee to thigh. Then again. Then a third time. Carlos's entire body quaked. Flame crept from each long gash, moving outward in every direction. The spilled blood cooled quickly, offering some relief to his hot flesh.

Carlos could not move, except for involuntary twitches as his body recovered piecemeal from the actual blows and began responding to the pain. Carlos heard the last man move past him. He felt something hard and powdery drop on his face. It stuck there, clinging to the water Josiah had poured on him. Or perhaps it was the blood from the cut on his face. He couldn't be sure.

"Ashes to ashes," one of the men laughed as he clapped glove to glove, cleaning off the dust he had scooped from the campfire.

Carlos knew he wasn't dead. He hurt too much. And he could still hear the hard beating of his heart as well as the grunts of the men. Occasionally, he heard the defiant bleat of his proud new sister. He tried not to imagine what these animals were doing to her. The only hope he had was that his brother would not come back until the men were gone.

"Ya got her?" one of the men asked.

"Yeah. Want me to pluck?"

"Not yet," said the man. "Where's his knife?"

"Here."

A moment later, Carlos heard footsteps crunch on the dirt. They were coming toward him. He heard breathing beside his left ear.

"I know ya don't unnerstand me, you dumb Brick, but I need somethin' o' yours," the man said. Whatever he was saying, there was cruel mockery in his voice. "I figure I'm actually doin' you a favor. I'm about to bleed ya out."

Carlos felt his shirttails pulled roughly from his belly. The air no longer felt good on his skin. A leather glove groped the inside of his legs and pushed them apart. Carlos felt something hard and cold pressed against his thigh.

"Not much of a man-sized helpin'," one of the men said.

"He won't even miss it," said another.

Carlos knew what was going to happen but there was nothing he could do. He remembered a few psalms from church and he began reciting them. The man pulled his own fist as far as it would go and then applied the knife. The blade moved upward in a single harsh slice, as it would through the flesh of a wild colt. Carlos sucked air hard through his teeth and arched his back. He screeched on the exhale as the sharp pain punched through to his brain; the voice didn't even sound like his. For a moment the agony became his entire being.

Carlos moaned and slumped back as the footsteps moved away. He felt something hit his side.

"There's yer trousers." The man laughed. "Ya may find it a little drafty down there."

Carlos lay on the ground, motionless except for the shallow, gasping breaths he drew. The severe pain below the waist was gone. It was replaced by a dull ache between his legs and a swirling sickness in his gut. He coughed and vomited what little was in his stomach, turning his face to the side to let it out. He saw swimming black circles in front of his eyes as he bled his life away. But he was not ready to die. Not yet.

The backs of the young man's legs grew moist with blood. It reached all the way down to his knees. The drumming pain in his forehead and temples seemed increasingly distant. Carlos would lose consciousness soon, he knew, and there was something he had to do first.

Carlos flexed the fingers of his right hand. He could do this. He *had* to. His arm was lying across his face. He moved it toward his side, toward the trousers. It was like hefting a sack of grain. When his hand was near his legs, Carlos spider-walked his trembling fingers to his bloody flesh. Then he stretched a shaking index finger toward the trousers.

*This isn't going to work,* Carlos told himself. *Not this way.* He had to be on his side.

Carlos didn't so much move to his right as roll there. He got onto his right side though his left arm stayed behind, as if it were asleep. He had to try again. Breathing heavily, he rolled over to the right to drag the left arm ahead. It flopped over his side and landed beside the right arm.

"Hey! Yer boy is tryin' ta run!"

The men all laughed at whatever had been said. They had obviously seen Carlos move, but they did not seem concerned. Carlos didn't care what they said or did as long as they stayed where they were. Only one thing mattered.

Carlos coughed, vomited more, fought to stay conscious as his head grew light. He tried not to be distracted by Juanita's involuntary gasps. The poor girl. The poor, brave little bird.

The dying man was on his side now and used his left hand to stretch out a section of the leg of his trousers. His vision was beginning to blur as he dragged the bloody index finger across the trousers in small, uncertain strokes. He could not afford to take too long. And he had to make certain that when he was finished, the men did not know what he had done.

Carlos scratched the fabric, forming lines the way his mother had taught him not so many years before. He could almost feel her small, steadying hand on top of his, helping him move a pencil across lined paper they had obtained from the church. As he wrote, she taught him what the letters sounded like, what words they could form. He had always meant to learn more words.

The pain in his body now seemed as far as the sounds of the men and the soft sobs of Juanita. Carlos finished his work and rolled onto the trousers, covering them with his body. He felt a sense of satisfaction, as though his suffering was not without purpose. He convulsed again and vomited what little was left in his mouth and stomach. His vision grew rust-colored, then black, and his head swam with thoughts of other times, of his grandmother's voice and prayers he had forgotten. He thought, for some reason, of the dead campfire, white with ash and brittle.

And then he grew cold and began to shiver.

Then the shivering stopped.

# 2
## SAVAGES

The neckerchief they stuffed in Juanita's mouth was awful. But it gave her something to think about other than what was happening.

Josiah had pushed Juanita on her back, straddling her at the waist and pinning her arms, while the fat man stuffed the foul-tasting cloth deep in her mouth. She gagged and tried to cough up the cloth, but the fat one slapped her hard in the face, then again, until she stopped trying. She was forced to breathe through her nose, every breath tainted by the awful smell of the fabric. At least it allowed Juanita to scream without fear of being heard by her husband. The young woman continued to wrestle against Josiah and kick her feet behind him, but she was unable to dislodge him.

"This is gonna happen," the fat one said, leaning close to her ear. "We're gonna have fun with you. You might as well stop kicking."

The third man arrived, and then the leader. The gang closed around her. The leader was winding his black whip into a tight coil. He used the tip to tie it tight. Juanita looked at the whip rather than into their dark eyes or at their shoulders or hips, which were the only other things she could see.

"Someone get her feet so's I can switch around," Josiah said.

The man called "Hank" went behind him. Juanita felt his thick, gloved hands on her ankles. He leaned his weight on them. Sharp stones dug at her flesh from underneath. She could no longer move her legs. Without releasing her wrists, Josiah shifted so that he was behind her head. He pinned her forearms to the rocky earth. She felt more vulnerable now than when he was on top of her. Juanita did not want to see the clear, open sky and the freedom that could not be hers. She shut her eyes. The leader kicked her red cheek hard with his boot.

"Don't take a *siesta*," the man warned. "We want to see your purty eyes. We also got somethin' to *show* you."

She understood what he wanted. She opened her eyes and looked up defiantly, but only for a moment.

The third man, Stool, moved a finger as though he were ringing a triangle. "Ding-a-ling-aling! Chow time!" He smiled.

"I don't think she's hungry." Rawth chuckled. "Too damn bad." He kicked Juanita's cheek harder. "Open yer eyes, woman!"

Juanita knew what he wanted and looked up. She wished she could spit at these men.

"Let's get the rest of her out," Rawth said impatiently. He pulled Stool back. "Ya still got the knife?"

"Right here." Stool patted his belt.

"Get on it."

The leader moved away. Stool drew the knife quickly. Grinning a wide, near-toothless grin, he got on his knees beside the woman. She looked away, but Rawth kicked her again, this time hard in her side. She turned her hard gaze on the cook as he put the bloodstained point of the knife into the neck of her blouse. He cut down slowly, holding each of the three stone buttons in turn. They popped away and he palmed them, tucking them in his shirt pocket.

"Souvenirs," he said to her as he opened the blouse wider.

Juanita was wearing a white silk brocade vest beneath. There were two hooks in the front. Stool jabbed the knife into the ground. He opened them slowly by hand. He peeled back the sides and exposed her breasts.

"Firm as little red apples," Stool commented.

The only sound was the wind and the rapid breathing of the men. Juanita tried unsuccessfully to move her limbs. The men laughed as she struggled.

"Lookit 'em go!" Stool chirped, pointing to her breasts.

"Maybe you should bob for 'em," Hank said with a laugh.

Stool cupped his hand over one to stop it from moving. The men laughed again as he took up the knife again and slashed quickly through the sash around her waist. There was nothing careful about his actions now. Removing the sash revealed the three large buttons on the side of her dress, from waist to hip. He pulled those apart. Rawth dropped the whip to the ground and walked behind Stool. He grabbed the dress at the bottom and yanked it off, revealing a flimsy petticoat.

"How'd she walk with all that shit?" Hank asked.

"Them Brick bitches protect their virtue from the eyes of strangers," Rawth said.

"But we ain't strangers no more, are we?"

Impatient now, Rawth roughly tore the undergarment away, knocking Stool back in the process.

"Somebody got the horns," the cook said.

Hank snorted. "After ridin' with you for three days, even a Brick starts to look good." He helped the others by unlacing Juanita's leather leggings and tossing away her moccasins.

Juanita lay naked beneath the sun, save for the neckerchief that filled her mouth. Rawth quickly began to undo his suspenders and pants. He smelled rank, like a ram, and he was full of sharp, aggressive moves like a bull in heat.

"Hank, Stool, show me the promised land," Rawth said.

Juanita tried to think of how strong and sweet her Joaquin had smelled, how loving her new husband had been.

Rawth dropped his pants to his boots and stood between the two men as they roughly separated the woman's legs and pinned them to the earth in their new position. She did not struggle. The coarse earth and rocks beneath her would only cause her additional pain.

"Lift on three," Stool said.

The cook counted and, on three, the men

pulled Juanita's legs straight up. Her lower back was barely touching the ground as Rawth dropped to his knees, using his trousers for padding. He spit into his palm and rubbed the saliva on himself. Then he straddled her. She tightened her body and tried to close her legs as he tried to enter her. The attacker pinched her nostrils between his strong, gloved fingers. Juanita drew hard with her lungs and managed to wheeze just a whisper of air around the neckerchief. Her eyes teared and the muscles of her neck cramped.

Perhaps it would be good to lose consciousness, she thought. She continued to fight her captors until her mind blurred.

Rawth released her and she sucked air through her nose. She was instantly alert and determined to fight, but he had already pushed inside her, grunting low in his throat as he ground his hips against hers. She felt his hands on her breasts, digging into her buttocks, and then he pulled the neckerchief from her mouth so he could push his lips to hers. He groaned and salivated into her mouth and then he cried out once, twice, before falling limp on top of her. Breathing heavily, he stuffed the cloth in her mouth, backed off sluggishly, and stood. He pulled up his pants and took Hank's place holding her leg. Then the second man dropped between Juanita's legs and fished himself from his trousers. He guided himself inside her. This time she didn't struggle. She wanted them to finish and be gone. If Carlos were still alive, he would need her help.

The first attack had been short, the second one shorter. When Hank finished, he was replaced by Josiah, who wrapped his arms under her legs and held them himself while the other men stood around watching. Stool held the woman's hands. He had his face above hers, looking down, aglow with anticipation. When Hank was finished, Rawth walked over.

"Hold her arms down, Stool," Rawth ordered. "By the hands."

"What's up?" Stool asked.

"Just do it."

The cook pushed hard on her hands, pinning them to the ground. Raising his foot, Rawth drove the heel down hard on her right wrist. The bone shattered and she screamed into the neckerchief. He broke her other wrist the same way. Juanita screamed into the neckerchief.

"Don't know why I didn't think of that sooner," the leader said, still sweating from his encounter with the girl. "Now yer hands are free to ready yourselves for the second go."

"That's why you're the boss," Stool said admiringly.

Rawth kicked the young woman again in the ribs to make sure she stayed still. No one at all had to hold her as Stool opened his pants and mounted her with giddy laughter. When he was finished, Hank returned, pulling the neckerchief from her mouth and sitting himself on her chest. He positioned himself between her lips and pushed on her cheeks, encouraging her to open her mouth. Tears fell from her eyes as each movement of the man caused her arms to shift and her wrists to hurt. She tried to move so her wrists would hurt less. When she didn't respond immediately, the man pulled the knife from the ground where Stool had dropped it. He pushed the tip against the lower lid of her right eye. She blinked reflexively, cutting her flesh.

"Suck it, you lazy piece o' dirt, or it'll be the last thing you see!"

Juanita understood his tone and did as she was told. His flesh had smelled foul, but it tasted worse. As he grew inside, she wished she could hurt him, make him suffer for whatever they had done to poor Carlos. But Juanita knew they would only hurt her more, perhaps kill her. It was easier and wiser to cooperate.

She worked hard to be done with him and choked when he finished. She was barely able to draw a breath before Rawth took his place. He rested his knees on her arms, causing her broken wrists to send fire through her arms and into her brain. More than anything she wanted that pain to stop.

When Rawth was through, one of the other men came over. She shut her eyes and they didn't tell her to open them. She concentrated on the pain, on getting through that. She thought of Carlos and her dear husband.

She felt the next man enter her mouth and tried to do what she had done for the others. But he did not respond, did not feel the same. Nor did Juanita feel the weight of anyone on her chest. She opened her eyes. The men were gathered around her laughing. The cook whistled as though this were a celebration. After a moment, Juanita realized what was in her mouth and let out a guttural cry that came from the darkest corner of hell.

# 3
# HATE

The world below the cloud line was dreary and close. Sounds that he knew were far above the mist seemed right behind him — the squawk of the birds, the buzz of bees, and the strange, brief whistle that sounded like the wind moving through an aphid-hollowed branch. It was as though the droplets of moisture that composed the clouds were carrying the sounds to him, like buckets in a fire brigade. Yet they were all sounds that were on the northern side of the cliff. He could hear nothing from the camp, which was blocked by outcrops of rock and thickets of trees.

At the same time, every sound below seemed magnified. Wherever they went in their travels — Carlos and Joaquin, and now his precious Juanita — the richness of nature was astonishing and humbling.

One aspect that didn't change was the flow of human nature. From the villages in

Mexico to the outposts in California, Joaquin had seen people eat and drink, sleep and wake, laugh and hate, love and lust in the same way. That was why he had hurried Carlos along. The white men of California had not shown much liking for Mexicans. If ranchers were grazing their horses or herds in the grassy hills of this region, he did not want to meet them. Mexican *vaqueros* were renowned for their skill on horseback and willingness to work for less wages than cowboys from the north and east. Joaquin did not want to give anyone reason to imagine that their livelihoods might be threatened.

Joaquin picked a path down the slope. He was following the natural path cut by runoff from the gully-washers that obviously tore through this region. It did not rain much in the desert, but when it did it was a torrent. The jagged ditch was actually wide enough for him to walk through, and as deep as the midpoint of his shin. It would not help them with their mule, however. He needed to find a better way down.

His eyes moved to the left and right, searching. As he moved, he was aware of every sound that was truly close by, like the field mice who disturbed the grasses with a distinctive flutter as they dashed under rocks, or the quail that flew away in loud, flapping batches. He had to stay alert for the telltale hiss or rattle of poisonous snakes. He heard the singing mouth of the underground spring from which he had pulled the water for the pouches. Throughout Joaquin's life running water had always been among the most welcome sounds. It meant relief from the heat, satisfying thirst, a bath, or a place to play with other children or their dogs.

Joaquin thought often of the past. Life had been hard for the Murrietas, which is what kept him going now when comforts were scarce and dangers many. His father was a carpenter whose specialty was building or fixing wagons, wheels, and yokes. He often had to travel a hundred miles to get the wood he needed, especially during drought years, and even then people did not always have money. They paid for repairs with eggs and milk. The elder Murrieta was often forced to supplement their income by working as a day laborer at one of the remote farms. The work would take him away for weeks at a time, leaving Joaquin's mother to raise the three children. The two boys went to work as soon as they were able, taking odd jobs around the village and learning how to do everything from building wells to making adobe bricks. To this day, the smell of straw automatically brought Joaquin back to those shallow pits where he walked back and forth for hours, crushing the stacks into the cold, muddy clay, then scooping it out into wooden troughs to form the bricks.

Joaquin wanted his own children to know how to do all of that, but only so they could build their own home or assist a neighbor. He wanted his old family and his family yet-to-be to build a new village where agriculture would flourish, where it was a livelihood and not a constant challenge.

Joaquin was just below the spot where he had found water. He paused and cut an X in the trunk of a sapling before moving on. Carlos would see it and probably smell it. His brother had a very good nose.

It was funny. When they left, Joaquin's mother accused him of "chasing a cloud." And here he was, walking through them. When he sent Carlos back to get her, he would show his mother that the only barrier between man and cloud was the willingness to climb.

*Or descend,* the young man thought as he stopped suddenly. Just below him, the narrow rocky outcropping was covered with young scorpions. There had to be thirty or more of the scuttling red creatures. He did not want his wife walking through these, but he dared not anger them by dusting them away. There was probably a colony under the ledge. They were swarming over a dessicated gecko, pulling away pieces of flesh and sinew with their strong pincers. The animal had apparently chosen this spot to sun itself. That was probably why the colony lived here. It was nature's own trap for the unwary lizards.

Joaquin moved to another ledge that jutted from the cliffside. He looked to the west and then the east, trying to pick out another passage through the rocks and sparse trees. It was difficult to tell where the ground was navigable, since the underbrush was densely tangled. He decided to try the east, since deer might be grazing in the rising sun. They knew the slope and, with luck, he could follow their prints to the base of the mountain.

Joaquin made a mark on the rock ridge, then edged along above the ridge, toward the sun. He moved past a long line of large ants that were moving bits of leaves and tiny slices of animal matter to their own colony. The odd tarantula moved slowly through exposed roots, indifferent to fellow creatures large and small. Joaquin had always felt these regal little creatures possessed as fine a wardrobe as he had ever seen on something that crawled. He had also seen snakes with majestic skins, which made him question the Bible's prejudice against any swarming creature that God had set apart from men. Compared to men he had known, *los bichos* he had encountered here were elegant and unthreatening unless hungry or provoked.

The route to the east did not look promising. There was a deep, deep ravine that had been invisible from the north. Discouraged, Joaquin went back to where he had cut the X, crossed it out, and cut one in the opposite direction. There was a very steep slope, but the section below might be navigable. He edged over, surprised that he did not hear his wife and brother moving above. Certainly the mule would be complaining by now about the steep descent.

After walking down part of the slope on his heels, Joaquin was able to stand as the angle softened. He took out his knife and climbed back, cutting a series of footholds for Juanita and X's on rocks and tree trunks. With Carlos's help, she and the mule would be able to make it down here.

Joaquin continued down the slope. The valley below grew quickly, like a rose opening under the morning sun. The clouds parted, the sun came through, and he could see colors and life, contours and textures invisible from above. He made marks on the larger trees and boulders as he descended, pausing only by a small grove of orange trees. He pulled a fruit from a branch, peeled it, and bit into it as he walked. The juice was invigorating. He knew that Juanita would see these and probably pick more than they could carry. But he would find a way to keep them for her. That was what the Murrietas did. They encountered challenges large and small and beat them.

It was not long after that Joaquin reached the bottom of the mountain. The smells here were as rich and varied as the colors. There was the musky scent of the lilacs mixed with the powdery tickle of the bear grass. Back home, his grandmother used to clear off the fine, dusty flowers and use the stalks to make watertight baskets. He saw fleet roadrunners zigzagging through the conelike stalks of giant horsetails. It was a place of quiet beauty, fed by runoff from the underground water sources. This was much like he had always pictured Eden to be. He looked around as he finished the sweet orange. Perhaps it would not be necessary to go further north, where they had heard the farming was best. This valley might provide them with everything they needed to build a home, a community. He wondered if the mornings were always damp and chilly here. He hoped so. The moisture and cool air helped keep the flies away. It would be nice if the family could have breakfast without hordes of pests trying to share their meal.

Joaquin wiped his hands on his trousers, then turned and looked back up the mountain. He wondered where Carlos was. He could see up to the cloud line and there was still no sign of his wife or brother. They should have been below it by now. He sat on a flat rock, looking up the mountain, and waited. He watched as the clouds continued to break and blue sky became visible. He watched as the circling eagles moved from the eastern slope to the top of the mountain.

This was not right. Joaquin could feel it under his skin. More concerned than annoyed, he rose and started back up the slope. The young man stopped and called their names every few steps until nearly the halfway point, when he gave up shouting. They couldn't hear him. Instead, he put all his energy into scaling the slope as quickly as possible. He used his voice only to pray, silently, that nothing had happened to them.

There were so many dangers in the mountains, in the desert, yet there was really just one that he truly feared.

Joaquin cleared the deep slope where he'd cut the steps for Juanita and hurried up the last stretch of mountainside. He didn't speak, but he listened and was alarmed to hear nothing from above. His only hope was that Carlos had somehow missed a mark and gone down the eastern side of the mountain. Perhaps he was confused by the two marks on the rock.

When Joaquin finally scrambled over the northern ridge, his gloveless hands raw and bloody, he saw that wasn't the case. He stood motionless, save for the insistent wind that stirred the hem of his shirt and his long hair. It took him a few moments to understand what he was looking at.

The shapes on the ground did not resemble the people he knew. They resembled bodies he had once seen lying on the banks of the Río Aprisa after a flood. The limbs were haphazardly arranged, the hair matted, the clothing ripped away. Life seemed very far from both people.

Joaquin was unable to scream or cry. He was here, this was happening, but his brain did not admit that. He took a quick look around. There was no one here. Not any longer. He ran to his wife first and fell to his knees beside her. Her head was tilted to the side, her eyes shut. The odor coming from her was not his wife's scent, it was animal spoor. Human beasts. Ranchers camped in the valley, or perhaps men who had come from Mexico or elsewhere and happened upon their campsite. Whoever they were, the attackers had moved quickly. Joaquin had not been gone that long.

He bent close to the ear of his young bride. "Juanita, my love, can you hear me?" he asked urgently but gently.

There was no response.

The young man put his index finger in his mouth. He spit out the dirt that had stuck to the juice of the orange. He held his moist finger below her nose. He almost wept when he felt her faint breath. From the corner of his eye he saw her bloodied legs, the stains on her mouth, the many sets of boot prints in the dirt. He knew what had happened, but at least she was alive.

He noticed something lying in the dirt beside her. At first he thought it was her tongue; attackers who left their victims alive, out of cruelty often mutilated them so they couldn't talk. He was about to check her mouth. Then he recognized what the object was and wondered if she had taken revenge on one of her attackers. Yet he saw no blood leading from her face.

Joaquin suddenly realized why. It hadn't come from one of her attackers. An involuntary cry rose in his throat and Joaquin clapped both hands over his mouth. He didn't want the attackers coming back. Not yet. Shouting into his open palm, he scrambled from the dismemberment. He turned and rushed over to his brother.

Carlos was dead. Joaquin could see that right away. His eyes were staring at a rock. The young man's legs were lying in a pool of red mud that was thickest around his waist.

Travelers from the north occasionally came through their small village with tales of horrors inflicted by hostile natives. But those were typically acts of retribution, deeds so horrible that transients would not think of hunting tribal herds or molesting women as they cleaned clothes by the river.

Who would do such a thing as this for amusement?

Flies circled Carlos's waist and darted along his bare, sweat-covered legs. Joaquin didn't bother to shoo them. They would only return. Instead, he pulled Carlos's trousers from beneath him and laid them out across his legs. As he did, Joaquin noticed what looked like red marks on the pale fabric. It was writing.

He looked at his brother's right hand. There was blood on the tip of his index finger. Tears formed in Joaquin's eyes now. Carlos had used the last moments of his life to leave his brother a message.

Joaquin used his knife to cut the section away. He folded the cloth carefully and tucked it in his belt. Then he laid the remaining fabric over Carlos and began grabbing rocks from the surrounding terrain to cover him. He pulled them up with his fingers, pulling them from the hard earth, fighting with the ones that didn't want to move, pushing his fingers until the flesh was flayed. He wanted to hurt, to share his wife's pain. He finally used his knife to dig up some of the deeper ones. It was not a proper burial, but it would protect his body from animals for now. He needed to tend to his wife and could not do so if he was fighting off wolves or hawks. Joaquin sheathed his knife when he was done. He vowed the next time this blade was drawn it would be for revenge. Three Murrietas had bled today. None would bleed again.

He walked back toward his wife. He wanted to hit something, someone, anything, anyone but his poor stricken lamb.

He wanted to scream until he had no voice; he wanted to tear at his hair with his bloodied fingers. *Why had he left them?*

He was angry at the attackers, but he was also furious with himself. Joaquin had feared that others might be nearby. When they climbed the southern slope the previous dusk, he saw patches of grass that looked as though it had been eaten to the root. That was how horses grazed, fearless and unhurried. During the night he thought he smelled horses on the wind and wood burning in a campfire that was not their own. He couldn't see smoke or a ruddy glow because of the clouds. Even if there were others on the mountain, he had no reason to believe they were dangerous. Besides, it would have been impossible to leave in the dark, and he still felt it would have been more dangerous to stay in the valley. Here, at least, they would have heard someone approaching. He would have anyway. He should never have left them alone this morning. Carlos had heart, but he was not a hunter or fighter —

*No!* Joaquin told himself. *This is not the time to think of that.* His wife was gravely injured and he had to care for her. There would be time to find the men who had done this.

Joaquin was no longer enraged as he knelt beside his wife. He took the water pouch from his belt. He spilled a little warm liquid in his hand. He poured it carefully along her forehead so it would wash down her temples and not sting her eyes. Then he dribbled some along her cheeks and emptied a few drops into her mouth. He spilled a little on his fingertips and lightly cleaned her lips. Juanita's mouth responded to his touch, but she still did not open her eyes.

"Rest, my love," Joaquin said softly. He choked up again and had to push his face into his shoulder after he spoke. He did not want her to hear him crying. Then he sniffled down the tears and smiled at her. He knew she couldn't see him, but he hoped she could feel his love, hear it in his voice. "You will be well again very soon. I will see to it. And when you are, we will find that valley we have been seeking. We will have our family. We will be happy."

His eyes shifted to her bloody thighs. He wondered if they could still have children. Or if their first child would be the offspring of a monster. Whatever it was, they would face it together. That was the vow they had taken. He looked at his knife. Joaquin always kept his promises.

Joaquin knew he could not negotiate the

slope while carrying Juanita. He went to where their mule stood, a mute observer to the horrors that had transpired. He arranged the blanket to carry his wife and removed his shirt and laid it across to soften the cushion. Then he went back to Juanita. He was about to lift her when he noticed the woman's hands. Her fingers were no longer delicate and smooth, they were swollen and red. For the first time Joaquin noticed her bruised and bloodied wrists. He snarled involuntarily. There was no end to the savagery of these monsters. He used torn pieces of her dress as bandages, then collected several straight and sturdy sticks to use as splints. He secured them firmly using what was left of the dress. Carefully sliding his strong arms beneath Juanita's shoulders and knees, he raised her from the earth.

She winced when he moved her, and groaned slightly.

"I'm sorry, *mi mariposa*," he whispered. Her butterfly wings were torn and there was nothing he could do. He wondered if she might also be hurt inside, in a place he couldn't see. There was no way for him to know that. All he could do was sit with her and feed her and care for her.

Joaquin laid his wife athwart the animal's

back, on her belly. The ride would be difficult, but the blanket would provide some comfort. He carefully laid her arms out along the side of the animal, a counterweight to her legs. He placed them so that her shattered wrists would hang as still as possible.

Joaquin kissed her on the temple. With a lingering look back at his brother's temporary resting place, he turned and led the mule down the slope. The animal did not complain as it had coming up. It seemed to know better.

The young man's arms were swinging forcefully, his breath drawn hard through his teeth, his eyes staring. He was not looking at the dry grasses or scurrying wildlife but into the future. Not at the valley they would find or the ranch they would build or the community they would establish.

Against his better nature he was looking at something much closer.

Revenge.

# 4
## NAMES

The sun was well up by the time Joaquin reached the valley. The heat was climbing and the dusty winds were scalding. He had covered Juanita's exposed neck and head with Carlos's blanket, but he knew he had to find proper shade for her before noon. There were no caves in the foothills, just crags that provided temporary relief from the direct sunlight. He did not know in which direction native encampments might be located, nor whether the inhabitants would be friendly. Still, he would risk it. The boot prints suggested that white men had been responsible for the attack. Perhaps local tribesmen had suffered as well and would be sympathetic.

But he heard no one and saw no one. The countryside was dusty and barren due to the absence of aboveground streams or ponds and the constant exposure to the sun. If there were settlers, they were over to the south by the lakes Joaquin and his companions had seen from the mountaintop. That was where they had encountered the Pechanga natives. It was where the richest farms and ranch land would be.

Joaquin finally had to settle on the best place he could find, a small citrus grove in a small dale by the foothills. There was a natural dip in the earth that allowed runoff from the mountains to collect here. The presence of the fruit, like the orange tree on the hillside, indicated that Europeans had indeed come through this region, bringing seeds with them, and had planted them before moving on. The climate had allowed the trees to thrive on their own.

There were carpets of thick, cool ground ivy amidst the trees. Leaving the mule to fend for itself, Joaquin placed his wife here, on her back. She was still unresponsive, save for an occasional wince when her wrists moved suddenly. This was the first time they'd stopped, and Joaquin used the opportunity to examine her wounds closely and to clean her. He rubbed the ivy on himself, making sure it wasn't too rough or an irritant, before using the leaves to wipe the blood and sweat from his wife.

Shadows moving beside them caused him to jump. He spun, shielding his wife protectively as he did. They were only hawks, riding the air. They shifted their wing tips here, then there, as they rode stationary on the wind. He wondered if they were watching for field mice or waiting for him to leave.

*At least they mean no harm,* Joaquin thought. *They are only doing what birds of prey do.* He turned back to his wife.

*Her poor, broken body,* he thought as he wiped away the grime. She was still bleeding between her legs, and he used his shirt to try and stop the flow. Sometimes, it seemed as though he had succeeded, and then it would begin again. In the meantime, he repaired her clothes as best he could, punching holes with sticks and using roots to bind the torn pieces together. He tried feeding her a piece of orange, but she did not respond. He squeezed the juice into her mouth. Her tongue moved a little and for a few moments she appeared to swallow deep in her throat. Then she stopped. He thought the tartness of the fruit might wake her.

Joaquin reset the splints around his wife's wrists, then cleaned the burrs that had caught in her hair when she lay on the mountaintop. He continued to stroke her hair long after he had suspected that she was no longer breathing. Joaquin was afraid to check. He wanted to have her until they were old and stooped like his *abuela.* Finally, he wet his finger with a tear and held it under her nose. There was no air, no warmth from her breath. He lowered his finger in front of her mouth. Nothing stirred from between her still but lovely lips.

His finger trembled as it hovered there. He touched her chin. For a moment this flesh had been his, and his had been hers. They had shared a time of sweet uncertainty and loving discovery, a journey just begun.

Now it was ended.

Joaquin sobbed, his tears landing on Juanita's forehead, on her cheeks, on eyes that could no longer cry for themselves. He rose slowly, his legs unsure. His dream was empty, his own life barely different from death. Happiness had been taken as suddenly as it had come.

*"Mi mariposa,"* he said sadly.

Despite everything that had happened, Juanita looked peaceful lying on the bed of greenery. Perhaps, in her last minutes, she knew her husband was there, knew he was caring for her.

Joaquin did not have a shovel. He had only his knife and he had vowed not to draw it yet. Kneeling beside her and tearing at the ivy with his hands, the young man cleared a patch of rich soil and began scooping it away. Already bloody from the climb, his fingers stung as they encountered tough root and sharp rock. He tore them away with increasing anger as he dug.

*You are burying your young bride.*

And when he was finished, he would climb back up the mountain to add more rocks to his brother's tomb, protecting his remains. He would also add a cross so the angels would know to watch over him.

*Why had they died?* he asked himself.

There were good reasons to die. Joaquin had seen men die defending their property and their honor, their families and their livestock. He had known others who passed through their village on their way to battles against the federal republic and the oppressive regime of Antonio López de Santa Anna.

For people to die because they were not white or because they were strangers, or for the amusement of men — these were not reasons. They were sins. In Mexico, government officers were stationed in outposts to arrest wrongdoers. Every village had a jail cell with iron bars to hold these criminals. Provincial magistrates traveled the land to pronounce judgment on those who had been accused of serious crimes. Here, in the territory of California, there were no such men and no such laws.

He continued to claw at the earth, his heart drumming, his eyes swollen with tears. His mouth was twisted into something bitter and angry as he thought about what he was doing.

*You are digging a grave for your wife.*

He grunted, he wept as he pulled at rocks made slippery by the blood from his fingertips. He wiped them on the back of the cloth he had taken from his brother and continued to dig. His arms moved swiftly, despite exhaustion, sweat blinding him as he worked by feel. Then he was inside the hole, burrowing like an animal as though the goal were not to inter his wife but to bury his humanity. He was breathing like a storm wind, his arms thrashing like branches in that tempest, and suddenly, finally, he fell back against the far edge of the grave.

He stood there drawing long, deep breaths. It was done. He pulled himself from the pit and crept to his wife's side. He wiped his hands on the ivy before he took her red hand in his.

"I said . . . I would make you . . . a home," he panted through tears as he looked at his wife. "I have done so, *mi mariposa.* And now I make you this promise. I will also make homes for those who did this to you. Only they will not share your blessed grace and eternal radiance. They will dwell in torment where the only light is the flames of the devil."

Joaquin remained beside his wife, weeping until his eyes were dry. He shuttled between sadness and rage, apologizing for not having been there and promising to avenge this atrocity. At times he invoked his brother's name, lamenting their loss and declaring his enduring love and begging the angels above, *their* angels, to avert their eyes from what must be done.

He rose, and with a heart far heavier than his bride's slender body, Joaquin Murrieta scooped Juanita Murrieta into his loving arms for the last time. Then he stepped back into the grave. He laid her at his feet, an unfitting place for so fair a lady. He crouched in the tight confines of the grave and said a prayer, nothing he had learned but something he felt, praying that God watch after her until Joaquin could join her.

"*If* you see fit to permit me that privilege, *gran Dios,*" the man added humbly. Making the sign of the cross, Joaquin raised himself up so he was sitting on the edge of the grave. Then he swung his legs around. He did not want his back to be the last thing he showed his wife. He stood for a moment and smiled down at her, then stepped to the side, where he had piled most of the dirt. He knelt, as if in prayer, and used his palms to push the soil in with slow, firm thrusts. It helped him to think of the earth flowing over the side like water, not dirt. His butterfly was being caressed, not covered. She was being washed, not shrouded.

He was putting her to rest, not entombing her.

When he was finished, Joaquin tamped down the soil and covered it with large rocks. He did not fashion a cross, which would be knocked over by wind or water. Instead, he used a small rock to etch a mark in a large stone he'd placed by the head. Then he wrote her name, and the years that embraced her brief life. Joaquin cried again when he realized that he did not even know his wife's birthdate. She was born in the spring, that was all he knew.

Still kneeling, he scratched below the years: *una mariposa de la primavera.* A butterfly of the springtime.

When he was done, Joaquin rocked back onto his feet and stood. Though his nose was full from crying, he smelled fragrant scents on the wind. They made him angry because his Juanita couldn't enjoy them. Nor could she feel the warm sun, nor see the rich blue sky.

The men who attacked her, who killed and mutilated his brother — they still enjoyed these things, along with food and drink and fellowship, as well as sleep from which they could wake.

Joaquin stepped away several paces before turning from the grave. He drew from his belt the piece of fabric on which Carlos had written in blood. He looked at it, saw names his brother had written in his dying moments.

*Josa. Hanc. Rath. Stul.*

His eyes were drawn to the blood from his own fingertips. On his wrists was blood from his wife. He wiped it with the cloth and then walked to where he had left the mule, just outside the small grove. Juanita had a small sewing kit in her bag, which included a set of tiny shears. He took those out and cut the fabric into a large triangular shape. He left enough cloth so that he could knot the ends. Then he went through all the bags to create one bundle of necessities and a few mementos. He saved the Bible, some utensils, the little bit of jerky and bread they had, and his brother's "rock," a small stone he had packed from beside their home in Mexico. He'd wanted to place it beside whatever new home they built in the northern valleys.

Joaquin did not repack the blankets. He removed everything else from the mule, picked up a branch, gave the animal a sharp whack in the hindquarters, and jumped back as the animal kicked.

"You have worked hard the many years I've known you," Joaquin said. "But you are slow. I cannot take you with me and this looks like a good valley. I wish you a long life here, and a contented one."

Joaquin knew the animal would be challenged by local predators. But the mule was large and loud. A mountain lion or a pack of coyotes would not come away from an encounter uninjured.

The mule galloped away. It was a different world from the one in which Joaquin had woken just a few short hours ago. Then he was surrounded by loved ones. Now he was alone.

The animal stopped a short distance away and brayed several times. Joaquin knew the animal's sounds. The cry was one of happiness, that of a creature celebrating its freedom. It was strange: That was all they ever called the animal, *la mula.* Maybe they sensed that it was destined to be its own master.

Joaquin wondered if he himself would ever

be free or happy again. He didn't even know how this venture — or this day — would end for him. All he knew was where it must go. He would finish his brother's interment and then follow the boot prints to the north.

The young man turned and headed toward the mountain he had to climb.

# 5
## SCALPS

The ranch founded and run by sixty-two-year-old Edison Veehall — formerly of western Pennsylvania, where he became bored with lumber, sold his mill, and moved his family west — was established in 1840. Veehall's passion was horses, and he negotiated a contract to capture and raise them for settlers throughout the southern region. As a sideline, he began corralling and raising cattle, anticipating the population growth of the region. After the abortive Bear Flag Revolt of June 1846 — when oppressed settlers tried, unsuccessfully, to follow the example of Texas and revolted against Mexican rule — it was widely expected that the United States would be drawn into a war with Mexico. When that happened later in 1846, Veehall was well positioned to provide not just horses, but beef to the cavalry. Hostilities ended two years later, with Mexico surrendering thirty-five percent of its territory, including the bulk of California. The war, and now the peace, left Edison Veehall one of the wealthiest and most powerful men in the territory. He was a champion for statehood, an early proponent of a transcontinental railroad — despite the seemingly insurmountable impediment of a towering mountain range between the coasts — and he was determined that one of his two sons would one day be president of a greatly expanded United States of America.

With peace secured, settlers began moving from the East. Most were attracted by land grants in a region blessed with nearly perpetual sunshine and abundant waters, and by a great ocean to facilitate shipping and trade. Reports of gold and silver drew a smaller, more independent breed of immigrant, not just from the Atlantic Coast but from Europe and Asia.

Apart from the arduous journey, the greatest hindrance to growth in California was the inconvenience of natives who lived on land being offered to settlers. Unconcerned by legality, local, state, and federal governments tacitly — sometimes openly — offered bounties for the scalps of men, women, and children. Veehall himself encouraged his ranch hands to ambush tribesmen who lived beyond his valley. These cowboys, forty-five in number, had been responsible for the recovery of more than seven hundred scalps over a two-year period. Veehall had a hands-off policy regarding the small, agrarian tribes that dwelt on the edge of his land. He liked the fact that there was a "Redskin wall" between himself and tribes passing through the fertile region. Chiefs who enjoyed both the bounty and protection of Veehall and his valley — and who had ancient blood feuds with many local tribes — sent riders to the ranch with information about the presence, size, and location of migratory bands.

Fees were not paid for Mexican dead. "Mud Bricks" were useful for labor or entertainment. Veehall used them to help manage the herds on the outer reaches of his eight-hundred-square-mile ranch. When the Redskin wall failed to detect hostile natives, it was the Mexicans who suffered at their hands.

Randy Rawth was one of four deputy foremen of the sprawling ranch. His charge was the western rim of the valley. It was nearly a two-day ride from the ranch itself. Because that region was farthest from the inland desert, it had the most temperate climate and attracted the greatest number of squatters. Reward or not, they were dealt with harshly by Rawth and his field team. Bricks had a way of chattering among themselves, and actions against the few had an impact against the many.

The men usually spent seven days making a circuit of the western valley and the surrounding foothills. They would kill or drive off trespassers, measure the height and expanse of the grasses for future grazing, then return to the ranch for two or three days before repeating. They had already been in the field six days, and Rawth was eager to get back. He had grown up on a small farm in New York State and gone west via the Erie Canal when he was seventeen. Rawth didn't like milking cows and he had no mind for business, reading, or writing. He liked herding steers. He found that in Texas, which had just won its independence from Santa Anna. There were thousands of stubborn, free-ranging longhorns he could rope and wrestle for the growing number of ranchers. Things started to get crowded in 1841 when the Republic of Texas empowered the Texas Emigration and Land Company to recruit settlers. It was about that time Edison Veehall sent his foreman Dave Battat to hire experienced hands to work on his new spread. Rawth didn't know much about horses, but he told Battat he could learn. He also promised to find whatever cattle were out there and bring them in. That sounded all right to the foreman and Rawth was hired.

Rawth liked California more than he did Texas. It wasn't as dusty and it wasn't as flat. He liked going into the cold mountains with a whiskey bottle and companions, hunting, hunkering down around a fire, and doing his job. The climate at the higher elevations reminded him of his childhood in New York, only without the bumpkins who pulled cow tit to survive.

*Not that there was anything wrong with pulling tit,* he thought as he and the boys made their camp before the early nightfall. He preferred Brick or Redskin to Jerseys, and he liked Mrs. Toothe's white girls in San Diego over them all.

Texas and California did have one thing in common, though. Texas had become a state of the Union and California would be made one as well. Rawth had always wanted to be there at the start of something big.

The sun dropped swiftly behind the mountains to the west. The valley was thrown from bright colors, to a carpet of green-gray, brown-gray, and gray-gray, and then in a moment it went black. The only light came from their campfire. The ranch itself was so far from them that its lights were invisible. Stars appeared in a splash of white, some of them alone, some of them a curious red or yellow, and some clustered in a spray that ran through the night like a river.

Rawth had thrown his blanket against a large, sloping boulder. He leaned against it as the men shared three wild turkeys Hank had shot and Stool had cooked. Rawth's riata was looped beside him. He used it as a weapon and also as a pillow, preferring the hard feel of the coiled leather to the soft embrace of down.

There was movement in the high grass nearby. In the distance, coyotes snarled at prey or each other — they were scruffy, unfriendly dogs that hunted in packs out of need, not liking. The campfire would keep them away, though Rawth and his crew always camped away from the high grasses. Solitary hunters were known to prowl the foothills after dark. Venomous serpents had no cause to attack a sleeping man, but a loco coyote or wolf might.

Then there were those flying bugs he just couldn't figure, the ones who killed themselves. He watched as moths of all sizes and colors circled and dropped into the campfire. He never understood why they did that. You see something die, you get the hell away. That was common sense, even for a flying pissmire.

Rawth tossed a stone at the grasses and the sounds stopped. The only sounds were the lively crackling of the fire and the gentle whisper of the winds. He went back to eating, then tossed the leg bone into the fire. It flared slightly and the musky smell of the burning marrow filled the campsite. It was better than the dusty smell of the air that blew from the desert.

Stool wrapped his hand in a cloth and pulled the coffee kettle from a spit above the fire. He came over and refilled Rawth's tin cup. Though it had been a miserably warm day, the valley cooled quickly when the sun set. It was now close to freezing. The hot coffee felt good going down.

"Anyone for poker?" Hank asked. He was resting against his saddle, not far from where the horses were tied to a tree.

"I wouldn't mind takin' some of yer wages," Josiah said. He was lying on his bedroll smoking a cigarette.

"I'm shot," Rawth said. "I'm gonna turn in."

"You just shit at cards is all," Stool said.

"I don't like 'em."

"That's 'cause y'ain't got a poker face." Stool laughed. "Ya open a hand and ya smile or frown like yer lips was a dog's tail, all waggin' or hangin'."

"Crud, Stool. I just got more sense than to spend my money on *nothin'*," Rawth replied.

The cook chuckled as he offered the others more coffee. They declined.

"I don't wanna go off pissin' in the dark like Randy does," Hank said. "This ole snake don't hold what it used ta."

"Too many Bricks," Josiah and Stool said in unison.

"Ya can't say the Brick tired you out," Hank snorted at the foreman. "She wasn't as wild as some."

"She was one o' those noble gowns, like a nun," Josiah said. "You could almost hear her prayin'."

"Maybe two spunks first thing after sunup wore our boss down." Spool laughed.

"Go fuck your mouth," Rawth snarled. "And when'd you ever pop a nun, Josiah?"

"I didn't. I just think they'd be like that."

"You fuck a nun you go to hell," Stool said soberly. "That's why God gave us Bricks an' Redskins."

Rawth had had enough of this. The men usually chucked barbs at the big man; it was how they built their own self-respect and he let them have it. He finished his coffee and then set the cup aside. Then he turned his back on the campfire, pulled over his whip, and laid his head on the side.

The other men laughed and decided not to play cards but to turn in themselves. The climb up and down the mountain had tired them to begin with, checking out the Brick campfire. Their own duties had added to the men's exhaustion. Leaving the campfire burning, the other three ranch hands rolled themselves in their blankets, talked for a few minutes, and then fell asleep.

The night quickly enveloped the campsite, a sea of constant yet unseen motion, of faintly heard predators and their cautious prey.

Some, perhaps, were not cautious enough.

In the small hours of the night, Randy Rawth woke. Half-asleep, he threw off his blanket and got his feet under himself, and moved a few steps downwind from the camp. He stopped short of the grass, near the barely glowing embers of the fire. He undid the buttons at the front of his trousers and relieved himself in the wind-stirred grasses. When he was finished, he didn't bother to rebutton his pants. He stumbled back to his bedroll with his eyes half-shut, his face downturned.

For a moment, less than a heartbeat, Rawth thought he saw shooting stars below him. They flashed toward him, then vanished. He didn't have time to wonder where they had gone or whether they were really there. They were followed by a hard punch just below his chin. The blow woke Rawth fully, but only for a moment. His throat immediately grew warm and wet and he reached for it. He felt the flowing dampness and then the hilt of the sharp metal that had caused it. A moment later, he couldn't think at all as his vision rusted and his head began to swim. His lower legs wiggled and weakened and he tried to fall to his knees.

The knife held him up. It had dug painfully through his lower jaw and was pricking the back of his tongue. His jaw trembled but he couldn't cry out. A hand also held him up. Fingers grabbed his vest and pulled him forward and the side of a forearm pressed against his chest helping to keep him upright.

*"Para mi mariposa,"* a voice said softly in his ear. *For my butterfly.*

Rawth tried to say "Huh?" but all that emerged was a low gurgle. He thought about the moths that had died in the flame. He wondered if this were some kind of Redskin guardian spirit of bugs coming to avenge their destruction. *Then why would he use a knife? Why not just piss rain on the campfire?*

But that was all Rawth thought, all he wondered as the wound continued to spill his life onto his clothes and his brain went to sleep and finally his large body was allowed to drop to the ground with a heavy thump.

# 6
## GUARDIAN

Joaquin withdrew the knife as the foreman fell. He wiped the blade on the dying man's pants. The rapist's legs twitched. Joaquin found it brutally appropriate that this man's day had ended as it had begun: with violent spasms that spit life essence from his body. God's design for life was as simple as it was great.

The young widower didn't linger over the body, but walked a few paces to the west. Joaquin had noticed a whip while watching the campsite from a peak directly overhead. He wanted it. He walked quietly, on the balls of his feet, as he always did when approaching a potential meal. More often than not he had secured whatever he sought. Then, as now, it was a matter of survival. Reaching the boulder, he felt for the whip, found it, and slipped his arm through the loop. Then he went to the campfire and slid his knife into the dull embers. Tiny orange specks rose from the charred wood. This was the only reason Joaquin had wiped away the dead man's blood. He didn't want the smell to wake the men. Otherwise, he would have been happy to mingle it with those of his brethren killers.

Joaquin crouched beside the ruddy ash and waited for the blade to be ready. He was numb inside, his soul asleep. He could not let himself dwell on his loss or he would be distracted by sorrow. He needed to focus on what had to be done. Unlike his heart, his senses were very much awake, his muscles coursing with power.

Joaquin removed the knife when he saw the telltale glow from beneath the embers. He rose quickly, allowing the red-hot blade to serve as a torch. He approached the other men, quickly noting where they were sleeping. He stood beside the nearest man, the one who was called Josiah. Joaquin looked from him to the man beside him, Hank. In the fast-fading glow of the blade, the young man stabbed them both in the throat, one and then the other, quickly and deeply. It was the same as killing an animal for food except for one thing: He enjoyed this.

The men coughed out weak, bubbling screams, which woke the last man. The cook bolted upright and Joaquin stepped back.

He laid his hot, bloody knife by the stones of the campfire and let the whip slip from his shoulder to his hand. He undid the strap near the base that kept the whip coiled and shook out the lash.

"Hank, Jos, what is it?" Stool asked.

Joaquin listened carefully to his voice. He swept his arm gracefully around his head and snapped the lash forward. The crack was loud, but not loud enough to cover the cook's cry.

*"Jesus Holy Christ!"* Stool screamed. "Randy, what's goin' —"

The whip howled and snapped again.

"Shit! *Shit!*"

Joaquin heard the man stumble. Stool stayed down, crawling among the gear and muttering in pain. He whispered the names of his two mortally wounded companions. He must have come upon them because he fell silent.

Joaquin sent the tail of the whip flying once again. Once again, it found its target, causing the cook to shriek.

*"Stop! What's wrong?"* the man screamed.

Joaquin used the toe of his boot to kick up the fire. The stirred ashes flared, throwing a deep orange glow over the campsite. The cook looked over. He was on his knees, tightly gripping his bloody right arm. There was also a gash along his back and wrist. Stool's expression went from confusion to terror.

Joaquin kicked the fire again. Flames licked upward, casting more light on the camp and illuminating the bodies of the other three men. Rawth was sprawled in a deep pool of his blood and the other two killers were writhing slowly in red puddles of their own. Stool just now noticed them and screamed.

*"Usted mató a mi esposa y a mi hermano,"* Joaquin said. His voice was low and flat, made even more so by the mask he wore, made from the bloody remnants of his brother's trousers.

*"Mi esposa . . . hermano,"* the cook muttered. "Something about your wife and brother." He seemed perplexed, but only for a moment. "Sweet God. The third bedroll we saw. Let me explain — I had nothin' to do with that. It was all Rawth's idea, his doin'. Him an' these others."

The cook spit at Hank, who was nearest, and tried to rise. Joaquin cracked him in the ear with the whip. The man screeched and fell to his forearms. The young man did not want this murderer off his knees.

"Listen, *please*," the man said, crawling forward. "I'm just a cook. *Un cocinero,* you gettee?"

Joaquin whipped him again, snagging his forehead and dropping the man to his belly. He lay there shaking from the pain. Joaquin picked up his knife, stirred the dying fire with the point, and walked over. He pulled off his mask and showed the man the names.

"*Usted lea,*" Joaquin said, thrusting it toward him.

The man raised his sweat-covered face from the dirt. He took the fabric and looked at it. "Our names — written in blood."

"*Mi hermano Carlos!*" Joaquin hissed.

"Your brother Carlos wrote these," Stool said. "I — I understand. But I didn't do anything. I tried to stop them."

"*¿Cuál es su nombre?*"

"*Nombre* — name? What is my name?" He shook his head. "It isn't here — *mi nombre no está aquí.*"

Joaquin looked down at the pathetic husk of a man. He pointed to his own ears, then pointed up to the ledge. "I hear," he said in English. "You Stool."

"No, no!" the man said. "Stool is — it's one of the horses. My name is —"

"*Un hombre muerto,*" Joaquin said as he reached down and grabbed the back of the man's collar. He pulled the struggling, clawing cook to the campfire, hoisted him over the rocks, and dropped him face-first in the embers. Then he put his foot on the back of the man's head and held him there.

"Here is a taste of the hell that awaits you!" Joaquin screamed.

Stool made a sound like nothing Joaquin had ever heard before, a cross between a trapped hog and a chicken on the chopping stump. Though he was enraged at this coward for what he did, and for having lied about who he was, no man would bring Joaquin to the level of torturer.

The young man knelt on the killer's back, along his spine. He raised his knife high and plunged it into the back of his neck. Stool died instantly, his shoulders relaxing and arms spreading out as though his flesh were stuffed with mud. Joaquin rose, dragged the body from the fire, and dropped him on the ground. Stool's face smoldered in the dirt, sending wisps of smoke skyward. It was the only part of this devil that would make its way toward heaven.

Joaquin suddenly felt the strength leave his limbs. His arms and legs shook weakly, uncontrollably, as he contemplated what he had just done. He had never killed a human being. It was not like taking down a buck for food. He understood the sounds, the gestures, what was happening, what they were experiencing. However necessary it may have been, it was not a pleasant thing to do.

Joaquin looked around the campsite as darkness once again encroached. He had avenged the deaths of his brother and wife. He hoped that by stopping these men he had protected the lives of others.

He started toward the horses, then looked back before the fire had completely died. It would be right to leave these men in the open where the wolves and coyotes could feed on their unchristian remains. But Joaquin was not like they were. Turning, he kicked the fire and used the glow to find more wood to feed it. When it was alive again, he climbed up the side of the foothills and began rolling rocks down the side, toward the camp. When the large stones had gathered in sufficient numbers, Joaquin laid the men side by side and covered them in a tomb of rock.

He etched a small cross over each body, not for the dead but for any who might wander by and wonder what the pile concealed.

Joaquin went to the horses. He would not steal a saddle, but he would liberate the three steeds and borrow the fourth, a pinto, for himself. Joaquin had ridden the Spanish breed before and knew their high-mettled moods. He had ridden them bareback for three years running in the *carrera a campo traviesa* during his region's annual corn festival. Joaquin had never lost a race because he did not try to control the horse, merely tried to guide it.

Holding the animal's white mane, he swung onto its back and gently nudged it onto the plain. The horse started at a spirited gallop, then slowed once it was outside the reach of the campfire's glare. Horses were intelligent beasts when it came to navigation. They knew not to run when they couldn't see.

Joaquin wondered if *he* were that smart.

The young man knew that these dead men worked for a large ranch. They were out here patrolling the western reaches of pastureland. Steer and horses were rotated throughout the season, and they had to protect the grasses from interlopers. Joaquin had seen boundary markers as well as fences across narrow glens. All of them were marked with the VR brand. Joaquin suspected that what had happened to poor souls like Carlos and Juanita was not unusual. The ranchers here were undoubtedly as ruthless as they were ungoverned. Water and grazing lands were life itself.

But his brother and his wife had not been a threat to the ranch. It was clear to Joaquin that bored or aggressive cowboys were victimizing Mexicans and small, nomadic bands of tribesmen. These blameless souls needed someone who would watch out for them. Men would come looking for these others. They would seek to inflict retribution on others. Someone had to prevent that as well.

Joaquin turned and went back into the foothills so he could watch the plains and the grave site. He was determined to be that man. He had nothing else to live for. He wanted to free this land of fear so that when he returned to Mexico to collect what was left of his family, he could tell them, "Carlos and Juanita gave their lives for a reason."

To that end, unlike the mule, Joaquin gave his new horse a name. He called it Libertad.

Freedom.

He also gave himself a new name. Since his campaign had begun in fire and blood, Joaquin would think of himself as an emissary of justice. It was his job to send the souls of evil men to their just fate. Henceforth he would think of himself as *El Guardabosque del Diablo.*

The Devil's Ranger.

# 7
## DAWN

Veehall's teams did not contact the foreman when they were on patrol unless someone were injured. In that case, one of the men would be sent back. If they were close enough, a large campfire would be lit. There were eight field teams, four of which were scouting the perimeter of the ranch at all times. They were due to report back at a certain hour of a certain day. If they did not, a pair of riders was sent out on a reverse course, assuming the team was nearer to the end of their sweep than the beginning. If something had happened, one of the riders returned for help. Typically, that round trip took a full day and night.

Rawth's crew was due back at noon. They were rarely late, and never by more than an hour or so. When there were no signals by one o'clock that afternoon, a pair of riders from the replacement team went out. The two men rode the plains until sundown.

They discovered the graves the following morning, shortly after sunup. Rather than separate, both riders returned to the ranch. They reached the Veehall compound well before sundown. The short, balding foreman, David Battat, rode out to meet them. Judging from the dust the men kicked up, they were riding hard.

Expressionless as he chewed tobacco, Battat listened while the men described what they found.

"What killed 'em?" Battat asked.

"Three o' the boys got their throats cut," said rider Fletcher White, an aging deputy foreman.

" 'Cept fer Stool," said his companion, young Flynn. "It looked like he was tortured. His face was all burned up and he was stabbed in the back."

"Redskins?" Battat asked calmly.

"I would say yeah. They still got their scalps, but the horses was took," Fletcher replied.

"But not the saddles," Flynn added. "Skins ride bare."

"Can't figure why they'd take time to bury the bodies and cut a cross on the rocks, though," Fletcher said. "It wasn't like they *hid* what they done."

"Who knows why those savages do what

they do," Battat said. "Mockin' a proper Christian burial, I'm thinkin'."

"That's prob'ly it," Fletcher agreed.

The foreman looked past them. The forty-year-old Battat was a calm man who rarely raised his voice. Just the intense conviction that sometimes settled on his dark eyes was enough to bring a man around. It didn't hurt that he was fast as a striking diamond-back with the twin Colt revolvers he carried in well-worn holsters. And he rarely missed. Not by enough to matter to the target.

"I'm gonna put you boys out with another team. We gotta make sure our borders are secure," Battat said. "I'm gonna talk to Mr. Veehall about taking another team out to find the ones who did this."

"The hoofprints was headed south, so I'm thinkin' they was goin' down Pechanga ways," Fletcher said.

"Those Redskins ain't never attacked us," Flynn remarked.

" 'Ain't never' might be 'Now they has,' " Fletcher observed.

"Fletch is right," Battat said. "Chief Ao-ti has been scratchin' at the barn door since his daddy kicked it."

The Pechanga tribe of the Luiseño Indians had lived in the valley of Exva Temeeku — the place of the union of the Sky and Earth

— for over ten thousand years. Nearly twenty years before the coming of Edison Veehall, the Emigrant Trail had been established between Mexico and their holdings in the north. The wide passage ran through Pechanga territory, causing the tribes to suffer deprivation as their food sources were hunted and their agriculture pillaged. The popular tribal leader Pablo Apis took their cause to Governor Jose Figueroa, who appointed the brothers Pio and Andres Pico administrators of the region. Instead of helping the natives, they imprisoned Pablo. After four years of legal struggles, Pablo was released and was granted sole jurisdiction over the region. He organized security forces composed of local braves and they enforced the laws protecting Pechanga land. However, when the Mexican-American War ended in the region with the signing of the Cahuenga Capitulations, virtually all of the accords between Mexico and the natives were negated. That opened the area to fresh immigration, this time from the east. Veehall became the new owner of the valley and decided to honor Pablo's arrangement, with one important distinction. The Pechanga tribe was relocated from over a thousand acres to only a few hundred at the mouth of the valley. The fact that they wanted to remain near the graves of their ancestors did not matter to Veehall. The Easterner allowed the band to keep their herds of livestock, but not to hunt outside their holdings. Veehall insisted it would be easier for them to protect their new home. In fact, the settlement created a bottleneck so that interlopers from the south would have to pass through their lands to enter the area. When they did, Veehall would have to be informed.

Pablo and Chief Caliente did not like the new arrangement. But both men knew that resistance was unlikely to succeed. As much as they owed allegiance to their forebears, they owed a future to their children. The tribe settled into their new life and Pablo became more and more involved with the activities of tribes to the west and north, where white settlements were growing at a much quicker pace. When the aged Caliente died following a rare snowstorm that swept through the region, his son became chief and immediately pressed Veehall to return to their traditional home. His request was denied and the new chief vowed to work with Pablo to reverse the edict.

David Battat didn't have a personal gripe against the Redskins. But he did not like anyone telling his boss how to run his spread. The murder of Rawth and his field team would give Battat an excuse to remind the Pechanga band of that fact.

Returning to the ranch, Battat told Fletch to organize a posse while he went to see Mr. Veehall in the main house. The home was a large adobe structure with a roof of flat, light-colored stones to repel the heat and protect it from fire. The furniture had been shipped from the East, most of it elegant and handsomely finished. The walls were decorated with hand-painted wallpaper and tapestries created by Mrs. Willa Veehall and her Brick maids. Battat removed his hat and dusted off his clothes before entering. Mrs. Veehall kept a clean house.

Edison Veehall was a large, barrel-chested man with thick gray hair and a leathery face. He rarely smiled, which was not the same thing as frowning. There was no time for either, no time to relax. He always seemed to be too busy thinking about the next thing he had to do.

The men met in Veehall's study, a large room with specially built stands displaying all the saddles he had ridden in his life. The large six-pane windows were open, though Pechanga-made blankets were lowered to keep out the flies, hornets, and other insects. The walls were decorated with a variety of antlers from wild buck and the skulls of longhorns that were all different — some horns were straight, some curved, some twisted in odd ways. There was also a collection of cured lizard skins, all of them different patterns and designs and pressed under panes of glass.

Veehall already knew the team was late and had anticipated the worst. His trusted foreman stood before his large oak desk and told him what had been discovered and what he recommended.

"You won't find those horses with those Redskin," Veehall said, his voice gruff from one of the thick cigarettes he smoked. He wasn't smoking one now. His wife didn't like them being lit indoors.

"I don't expect to find the animals, sir," Battat agreed.

"Okay, I understand what you're getting at, David," Veehall said, preempting a lot of discussion. "You'll use this to teach Chief Ao-ti manners because he can't prove his boys didn't do it."

"Yes, sir."

"Meantime, if it wasn't the Redskins, what's your plan to find the savages who did the killings?"

"I'm assembling a team of Bowies and marksmen and we'll make the same circuit,"

Battat said. Among the hands were men who were skilled knife-fighters and gunmen. "They'll look for tracks and see where they lead."

"You got men you can bring in to fill for Rawth and the others?"

"When the posse is set up, Fletch will ride to the Lugo ranch at San Bernardino. He just had a battalion of Mormons come in from some-the-hell-where. He can't use 'em all, so we'll borrow what we need till I can get proper hands."

Veehall nodded. "If these fellas think they can get away with picking us off, they'll do it again."

"I know, sir. They won't."

"Good man," Veehall said.

A compliment from an accomplished and powerful man like Veehall was as good as silver to the foreman. The tracking team would leave before the sun was entirely gone, not just to put a mile or two under their hooves, but to plant eyes and ears in the field in case anyone tried to move through during the night. Battat and his group would leave before sunup.

Because of the high peaks, the sun set early and rose late in the valley. But the glow of dawn reached over and around the mountains early enough for riders to get a good jump on the day. Battat and his men made their way south through the valley. They did not hurry but they did not rest, save to water the horses at the freshwater lake midway between the ranch and the tribal grounds. They reached the Pechanga village by mid-morning.

The half dozen men rode in through the free-ranging cattle and then the rows of tightly woven willow baskets that lined the northern frontier of the village. The nearly two dozen vats contained corn and acorns and were as tall as a man and nearly as wide. They rested on platforms the legs of which were coated with pitch, which the Pechanga band obtained in trade from the Chumash to the north. The foul-smelling tar, which bubbled from the earth in vast pits, was used to prevent mice from climbing the platforms. Tiny feet were often found clinging to the wooden stands. Owls pulled away the rest. There were deep talon marks above the pitch line.

The domelike homes of the tribe were also made of large stalks of wild-growing willow brush, layered like skirt upon skirt to keep out rain and wind. A coating of baked mud two hands high kept the abodes anchored to the earth during the strong winds and helped to keep out varmints.

The ranch hands rode in boldly, single file, at a canter. They did not stop or detour for anyone. They headed directly toward the hut of Chief Ao-ti, which sat alone, to the east. There was a ritualistic reason for the location. It was said that the sun rose at the behest of the tribal chief. However, the more practical reason was that the sun shined longest here. This enabled tribesmen to bring their problems and concerns to the chief while it was still light.

The chief was with his sons and two representatives of the Cahuilla tribe, which lived to the east of the mountains. They were negotiating a trade for fowl, which the Pechanga did not breed. The chief had been alerted when the riders arrived. Their hostile intent was signaled by the pace at which they rode and the composition of the team, all of whom were known to be expert killers. Ao-ti did not come out until the men had surrounded his home. It would have been considered demeaning and conciliatory to go forth and greet them. It was regarded as heroic to make them wait and then to face them unarmed.

The chief's two sons came out behind him. They were also unarmed, as was traditional when meeting representatives of other tribes.

105

Battat did not speak the tongue of the tribe, but his Pechanga deputy Stone Wolf did. The young native had gone to the ranch because he wanted an active life, something the agrarian tribe did not offer. He wore two hatchets in a specially made belt. He could throw them or fight with them equally well with either hand, and had been known to take down two deer at one time.

Stone Wolf parked himself to Battat's right. On his left was "Trench" Selby, a lean, tall gunman who could hide in any gully or fissure, wait along any branch, with the patience of a lurking cat.

"Four of our field men were killed and their horses were rustled," Battat said through Stone Wolf. "What do you know about that?"

"Less than you," Ao-ti replied.

"That doesn't help me," Battat told him. "When did your powwow buddies get here?"

"With the sun."

"That means they camped somewhere in the valley. Maybe they did it."

"They did not."

"How do you know?"

"They are Takic and Cabezone, men of peace."

"That doesn't help me either," Battat said. In fact, it did help the foreman. It gave him a reason to take on the chief. "Do the braves wear long knives? That was what killed our men."

The chief did not answer. He stared ahead.

Battat looked at Stone Wolf. "Do you speak the Cahuilla tongue?"

The native ranch hand's long black hair framed his grim features. He shook his head once.

"You see, Chief?" Battat said. "I need you to *ask* if the Cahuilla killed our men and took our horses. You don't know. Maybe they sent them back with riders who came with them through the mountains."

The chief didn't move.

Battat leaned forward. "You're shaming me, Chief. Don't do this."

The chief looked up at the foreman. "You shame yourself by requesting what cannot be given."

Battat snickered. "That's just stubborn-dumb. If I nod my head in your direction, you and that tent and everyone in it will cease to be."

"That would be your doing, not mine."

"No matter. It's the way you go from being a live philosopher to a dead Redskin. I'll give you a few seconds to think about it. Till then, anybody who tries to leave the tent dies."

After Stone Wolf translated, Chief Ao-ti motioned to his sons to go back inside, then turned his back and went to enter his tent. The foreman pointed to Trench and told him to put a hole in the man's head. That would be regarded as an execution, instead of a back-shot, which would be regarded as cowardly murder.

Trench slid a Colt Dragoon from his holster. The gun had a blue finish that was less likely to reflect the sunlight and give his position away. He was close enough so that he wouldn't have to aim, only fire from the hip. His horse knew well enough not to rear when the gun went off.

Trench hesitated as the chief ducked back into the hut.

Battat looked at him. "What're you doing?"

The big ranch hand didn't answer. His right arm began to tremble and he seemed puzzled.

"Trench, what the hell is it?" Battat asked.

"I got — feel strange —"

The trigger guard spun around his finger and then the revolver dropped to the dusty earth. Trench himself sat upright a moment longer and then his upper body twisted to the right. It fell over, dragging the rest of him with it. He landed on his face. There was a long knife sticking from the back of his cowhide jacket. Blood was beginning to stain the white-and-black-spotted fabric.

Battat rose in his saddle and looked back. He saw a man about thirty yards distant. The bastard had a kerchief of some kind over his mouth and was riding toward them, hard, on his horse —

*No. Not his.* He was riding Rawth's pinto.

Battat spun his horse around, toward Stone Wolf, and yelled for the other men to follow. But the lone rider had kicked his horse to a gallop and was on them before they could pick up any speed. The Pechanga scattered as the intruder tore through the circle of ranch hands. He was swinging a whip over his head snapping at riders to the left and right as he swung his horse in a tight circle. The lash too was Rawth's. Ranch hands fell all around, none of them able to draw because they were too busy trying to get out from under their panicked horses.

Because he had not drawn a weapon, Battat was the last to feel the sting of the whip. Before striking, the attacker turned on him and the foreman got a good look at his mask. It was tan hide covered with either dark red paint or blood. That was all he saw before the black leather coiled in a tight S and cracked out at him, catching him in the forehead. His face felt as though it had been struck by lightning and his entire body shuddered from the shock. He fell back-first, and had the wind knocked from him as his spine struck the rocky ground. He was aware enough to roll from under the rising and falling front hoofs of his horse, tucking himself into a ball and protecting his head as the animal and the one beside him reared several times and then ran off. It was several long moments before Battat dared peek out from behind his arms. By then, the rider, like the horses, was racing into the valley.

The foreman's brow was burning and bloody. It throbbed hard as he pulled his feet beneath him. He looked around at the other fallen men.

No shot had been fired, nor a hatchet or knife thrown. It was not just a humiliating defeat but a decisive one. By a single rider.

Stone Wolf walked over, his hatchets in hand and his eyes intense. He was watching the rider. The native had obviously decided the assailant was too far to hit and had too much of a head start to chase — even if they could get to their horses in time, which was doubtful. It would take an hour or more to collect them. Battat ordered the men to get started with the roundup. He told Stone Wolf to stay with him.

The Pechanga returned slowly when they were sure the ranch hands were not going to attack. Chief Ao-ti himself emerged from the hut. It had been slightly damaged by the panicked horses, but no one inside had been hurt.

"Takic and Cabezone are men of peace," the tribal leader repeated decisively through Stone Wolf. "They are also not Mexican," he added.

There seemed to be the hint of a smile in the chief's proud mouth. Or perhaps that was Battat's imagination. They had just been mortified in front of men they had threatened to punish. Battat was tempted to shoot the chief out of sheer displeasure. But that might turn the rest of the tribe against them. Clearly, the men no longer had a chaw to chew with Ao-ti or his guests.

The foreman tapped the barrels of his guns to make sure dirt hadn't gotten inside. As he looked down, he noticed that at some point the Brick demon had swung down and recovered his knife from Trench's back.

Two men came to pick up Trench, while the others had Pechanga braves mount up and help them recover their own horses. Battat walked away from the hut, toward the north, to supervise. His body hurt in places it hadn't for years, when he'd first come to the ranch from Oklahoma and broken wild horses for Veehall. He looked to the west as he walked.

There was something troubling about the attack. It was more than the fact that the man had come at them unafraid. And it was more than just his skill with a whip and knife, both of which were considerable. Those could be dealt with by an organized posse. What bothered him was the example of resistance a lone fighter had demonstrated against overwhelming numbers of better-armed men. To tribesmen, that was the rich soil in which legends grew. It was a deed that could inspire others to do the same, not just individuals but bands of individuals. And not just Redskins or Bricks, but a union of the two. Battat briefly considered turning his men loose on the tribe, killing as many braves as possible to keep the story from ever leaving the settlement. What stayed him was the realization that he couldn't kill all of the four hundred or so Redskins and would lose men himself, men he needed on the ranch and to hunt down this villain; and the fact that, in the end, capturing and executing the lone rider would have a greater impact on the minds and spirits of the savages.

Battat had gotten a good enough look at the killer to know what would bring him to them.

*You're going to die,* Battat thought as he studied the shrinking cloud of dust. *Very unpleasantly.*

And very, very soon.

As soon as the horses were collected, Battat shouted orders to his team. They left Trench's body with the Pechangas for now. While two rode west to stay on the murderer's trail, the rest rode south to get what the cowboys needed.

# 8
## FIRE

Racing across the floor of the valley, Joaquin felt like air and lightning were packed inside his body. He was excited, he was scared, but most of all he was satisfied. Everything had gone the way he had hoped. Perhaps astonished was more like it. The young man had galloped into the crowd of hostile ranchers not certain he would be coming out.

He had gone up into the foothills to wait and see who came looking for the missing men. When the two riders left, Joaquin followed them back from a safe distance — if there were such a thing in a valley where the wind changed from moment to moment and the sun could cause a spur to gleam from half a day's ride away. He had watched as they met with the man from the ranch, then followed that man and his killing party to the Pechanga settlement. Just a few days before, Joaquin had been there with his wife and bought her a blanket.

Joaquin didn't know what his next move would be, only that he had to get far enough away from the men so they couldn't follow. He had crossed a creek some two miles away — seasonal, he suspected from the erosion high along the banks — and would bury his hoofprints there. Then he would return to the foothills. There were defensible crags from which he could watch the valley and see, smell, or hear anyone who might come looking for him. He did not own a gun nor have any use for one. He had only fired a few rounds during his life, when his Uncle Juan came to visit. His mother's brother was a traveling salesman, with two horses and a fine-looking covered wagon. He always had cash and coin, silver and gold, and a great many goods on his cart. He needed to be able to protect himself. To Joaquin, however, guns were loud and their use either scared prey or warned others that a hunter was in the region. If men were pursuing you, firing a gun would bring them to your hiding spot. It was better to retreat, regroup, and attack when the advantage was yours.

After crossing the creek — where he paused to refill his water pouch — Joaquin allowed Libertad to slow slightly. They moved due north. The ranchers had gotten a good look at Joaquin's clothes, at his swarthy face above the mask. They had to know he was Mexican. No doubt they would assume he was a bandit who had killed the four cowboys to steal their horses. They probably reasoned he would head south in an effort to get "back" to his homeland.

When they came, Joaquin would be watching for them.

Joaquin followed a well-worn grazing trail into the foothills. He could see the mountaintop where the Murrieta family had camped. He felt a welling of rage when he noticed hoofprints in the sand where boulders protected them from the wind. This was probably the same route the killers had taken to reach them. He trampled the markings to dust as he passed, and continued some five hundred feet up to a spot that overlooked the valley. Leaving Libertad in a small natural cove formed by three massive boulders, Joaquin went to the edge. He turned his back to the valley, withdrew his knife, and rubbed it on the grasses at his feet. As much as he wanted the dead man's blood on his blade, he did not want the metal to rust. He was content knowing that the sheath had absorbed a little of what his grandmother called *la sidra putrefacta,* the "rotten cider" that had powered the killer. She felt that some people were born that way, like bullies in the village or some of the soldiers who passed from one killing ground to another — men who didn't have the weariness of death on their shoulders, but the joy of killing in their expressions. Until this land was safe, Joaquin wanted that stain on his person, the smell in his nostrils, the tint before his eyes. He sheathed the blade so it would not reflect the sun, then turned and looked out. He could see the entire valley floor and, in the distance, the Pechanga settlement. It pained him that those good and peaceable people should be subjected to the cruel whims of these ranchers. That had to be stopped. If Joaquin needed to take the fight to the ranch itself, it *would* be stopped.

Sniffing among the grasses, he detected rabbit droppings and found a small warren. He killed one of the young animals with a twist of its head; if he killed the parents, they would all die. He cut an opening in the back of the neck and stripped the skin, then sliced off strips of meat. He did not dare light a fire, but laid the meat on a rock to let the sun dry it out. He actually preferred jerky to cooked meat since it retained the taste of the animal from which it had come. When that was done, Joaquin lay on his belly at the edge of the cliff and watched the valley. He tried not to think of the loved ones he had lost, but of the others he would save as he had today.

The sun threw longer shadows and darker hues across the fertile landscape, and finally took its light behind the mountains to the west. The valley was gray and the only lights Joaquin saw were campfires in the Pechanga settlement. The men would not be coming for him. Not today.

Joaquin ate a little of the jerky and wrapped the rest in a thick, greasy cloth he carried for that purpose. He had not eaten more than a little fruit during the day, but he did not want to gorge himself. He did not know when and where he might be able to eat, and he wanted to make sure his stomach got used to that. The young man hung the cloth from a tree limb where varmints couldn't get to it. Then he lay on his back at the mouth of the cove. He did need sleep and the horse would whinny if anyone approached. The animal would not leave in the dark. Joaquin drew his blade and slept with it on his chest. If someone did come up, he wanted to be ready to defend himself. Even a man on his back could be deadly when he was armed, like a snake.

The night passed entirely without incident. It was cool, but the boulders protected Joaquin from the wind. An owl woke him briefly with its sweet, lonely, one-note song. Its presence in the trees indicated that nothing else was nearby. The bird was not a carrion-feeder, and left the packet of jerky intact.

Joaquin secured his knife, flipped over, and belly-walked toward the ledge. He looked into the valley, which was dark beneath the low layer of clouds. He did not see or hear anyone. He went to his bag of jerky and chewed on a slice while he led his horse to a patch of grass. He stroked the animal along its side for a moment, then went back to the ledge, where he crouched behind a large black rock. The jagged surface of this boulder was different from the tawny smoothness of the other boulders. While he squatted there, he wondered why God would make rocks differently. Or why He would make men so different.

He knew the answer to the last question. If we were all the same, we wouldn't learn from one another. We wouldn't grow. He had learned knife skills from Tutul and had taught his mestizo friend how to read, something a priest had taught Joaquin. Juanita would have loved to learn weaving from the Pechanga people. Perhaps one day she might have. Skills and experiences were mastered by pockets of people who passed the essentials to others. Yet hate was also relayed from person to person. What was to be learned from that? How to defend yourself, and when? Why did God feel that was necessary? Why not just smite the men who did evil? It had to be more than just the sin that cost Adam and Eve a home in paradise.

*You cannot appreciate smooth rocks without the jagged, the warmth of light-colored rocks without the chill of the darker ones,* Joaquin told himself. Men who do not know hardship deep in their heart, who do not learn how to survive it, cannot endure colder weather or crippling heat, drought or famine, devils or false gods. Perhaps what Joaquin was being forced to endure would inspire others to strengthen themselves against man and nature.

The village where Joaquin had grown up did not have many black rocks, nor were any of them this large. The young man just now noticed that this one was layered. It occurred to him that the rock could be broken with a wedge to make long, flat stones for walls or roof tiles. Everything had a reason. It was not for him to question God but to understand Him.

In the meantime, he had to decide what his own immediate move would be. If the men pursued, as he knew they must, then he would let their attack dictate his response. Joaquin had learned that tactic from a Chinaman who worked on a farm outside the village. The older gentleman had studied a form of fighting he called "circles." Simply by moving his arms or hands or legs in a wide or small circle, he could block any blow that came toward him and turn the force against the attacker. The younger, more powerfully built man had once tried to punch the Chinaman at his own invitation. Joaquin literally started the strike from behind his head, aiming at the smaller man's face. The Chinaman intercepted Joaquin's forearm with the slender edge of his own hand. It was just a light downward chop, part of a circle the Chinaman described around his chest, from the outside in, like a hoop. Yet it redirected the blow down. Joaquin ended up punching his own groin.

The Chinaman was not keen on sharing his secrets. He did not want everyone to know what he knew or he would have no defense. But Joaquin understood the concept, which could be applied to every kind of situation.

It was strange to think these forgotten thoughts in a situation he had never imagined, in a place he had never seen, fighting people he did not even know. This must be the way all soldiers felt when they were sent into battle. Yet they one had disadvantage that Joaquin did not. Soldiers in foreign wars killed to survive without necessarily hating the men they slew with cannon or shot, arrow or blade. Joaquin Murrieta cherished the opportunity — the obligation — to send these wicked men to God for His final, damning judgment.

The air was still and the sun grew very hot. Joaquin stayed behind the rock and watched throughout the morning, but there was no sign of the cowboys. Perhaps they were waiting at the ranch or outside the Pechanga settlement hoping to draw him out. He would not oblige them. At least, not during the daylight. Without surprise, an attack like the one he had made the day before could not succeed. The only souls Joaquin saw were a group of eleven settlers who were crossing the near side of the valley from the south. They were probably immigrants like himself, looking for work or a small square of land they could farm. Many people probably came through this natural corridor looking for new opportunities in the north. Joaquin was tempted to ride down and ask for their help in making the land safe for Mexicans and other native inhabitants. But he did not have the right to challenge them to make that sacrifice. If anyone ever joined him, it had to come from their soul. For now, he was content that the ranch hands had not seen these people. He did not imagine that the owner of these lands would permit anyone to pass through unmolested.

The sun had passed overhead and beyond when, to his surprise, Joaquin saw smoke from the northern end of the valley. He did not imagine that the immigrants had camped with so much daylight remaining. Also, the smoke was black. Wood fires started white and changed when greasy meats were being cooked. Joaquin decided to take Libertad and investigate.

He rode along the ridge instead of descending into the valley. That enabled Joaquin to watch the entire region while he traveled north. He saw nothing from the south, which surprised him. He really did expect the cowhands to come after him in force. After riding for an hour or so, he understood why they hadn't.

The small Mexican caravan had been

stopped by mounted men. Five horses stood side by side. Their reins were tied together and held by one man. Four other men were standing among the Mexicans, who were arranged in a circle around them — save for one poor soul. He was staked to the ground with his left hand tied to a spit above the fire. His burning flesh was what caused the black smoke. As Joaquin approached, he could hear the man scream.

Joaquin recognized two of the horses from the Pechanga attack, an Appaloosa and a paint. He didn't know whether this vile act was intended to draw him out or whether it was simply more cruel fun for these demons. In either case, he could not allow it to go on. He also couldn't ride down without a plan. Charging into the group as he did before, in the open, would certainly mean his death and probably the death of the immigrants. The young man pulled on his mask as he looked across the valley floor. There was nothing to use nearby as a hiding place, no defensible position for whip or knife, no shortcuts he could employ to outrun the men if he tried to get away. Save for the high grasses, there was only the emptiness of the flat, verdant field from here to the distant Pechanga settlement.

Suddenly Joaquin realized there was one

thing he could do. Something else Tutul had taught him.

The young man unsheathed his knife, held it along his waist, and stood facing the south. He caught the sun and flashed it toward the native lands. He did not know their language, nor they his. He flashed five times, then stopped. He flashed five times again, then stopped. He hoped they saw and understood. After a moment, he saw glints from the eastern side of the camp. There were five flashes, then nothing. They had seen him. He watched expectantly. It was difficult to stand here and do nothing while that poor man howled below. After a moment the natives flashed once.

*Five flashes followed by one flash. Yes,* Joaquin thought. There are five men against one.

Joaquin signaled back with one flash to indicate that he was the "one." The Pechanga did not signal again. The young man hoped that was a good thing. He looked back at the terrible scene below. He looked south and studied the terrain as best he could from this distance. There were gulches where rainwater ran off the foothills and thick patches of grass with dirt paths between them, worn to the pale earth below by the passage of men and animals. The ranchers would probably divide their force to pursue him. He might be able to slow the men by jumping a shallow ravine here or moving into the high grasses and turning in a different direction. That might give the Mexicans a chance to overcome whoever stayed behind. It was unlikely he could stay away from them before the braves from Pechanga could come to his aid. And what if they didn't follow him at all? He could try scattering their horses, but he would still be an easy target for their guns. Or they could start shooting their prisoners if he tried to run. What would he do then? There was only one possible solution, the most difficult of all. He had to offer them the one thing he was sure they wanted.

Himself. But it had to be done in a way that would guarantee the freedom of the others — and take time.

Joaquin rode Libertad down the slope on the northwestern side where the men would not see him. He left the horse in the shade of an oak tree, and hurried around the boulders piled high at the base of the mountain. He carried his whip and his knife and also his pride. Whatever these men took from himself or his countrymen, they would not get that.

Joaquin also carried something else. Something he had put together after leaving the horse.

The young man strode through a long patch of waist-high tule grass. It was fed by the underground waters from which he had filled his pouch a lifetime ago. Those waters were low now and the grass was dry. He strode confidently toward the men. They didn't see him at first. They were standing in a dusty clearing, too busy laughing at their shrieking victim and smacking back those of his companions who tried to help. Their fire was more heat than blaze. Now and then one man would sprinkle water on the flames to keep them down. This was the kind of dry weather and gusty wind that would turn an ember no larger than a fly into a wildfire.

Some of the water would also land on the man's palm. Heating, it caused him additional pain.

Joaquin was finally close enough so that one of the men noticed him. He tapped the arm of the man beside him. In a moment they were all looking over. They drew their guns but hesitated.

Joaquin knew they would not fire. He was carrying a lit torch fashioned from a large branch and dry grass. He had used roots from wild grape vines to tie down the grasses. The roots were dormant and dry enough to smolder without burning. He had used the flint he carried to strike the initial spark. If the men shot him, the torch would fall and set the tule grasses ablaze. All the grazing land from here to the southern mouth of the valley could be destroyed in less than a day.

"Look who joined the pilgrims," one of the men shouted.

"What the hell you think yer *doin'*, ya dumb goddamn Brick?" another of the men yelled.

Joaquin had no idea what the man had said. But he could guess. "Let those people go," he shouted back.

The men conferred among themselves, then turned to the Mexicans. One of the men was pushed forward.

*Good,* Joaquin thought. *Perhaps he speaks their words and can translate —*

One of the men shot the Mexican in the back of the head. He fell, propelled by a spray of blood.

*"Put the damn torch out!"* the cowboy screamed. He pointed at the flame and then dragged a thumb across his throat.

Joaquin understood what he meant.

One of the Mexican women was screaming and reaching for the dead man. A ranch hand shoved her forward. The girl fell to the ground beside the corpse and hugged it, wailing pitifully as the trigger-friendly ranch hand pointed his gun at the top of her head.

"I'm gonna splash her brains on her daddy if ya don't *lower that torch!*" the man shouted.

Joaquin believed that the men would shoot her and the others anyway, or worse. He had to remain strong. He lowered the torch toward the tops of the grasses. The tule blackened and curled. Without these grasses herds would perish.

The ranchers stood there for a moment. Then the man with the gun, apparently their leader, lifted the Mexican woman up by her hair and pushed her forward.

"Tell him to surrender and we'll let everyone go," the cowboy said.

The sobbing woman raised her face. She was standing about twenty yards away and he couldn't see her clearly. But she couldn't have been much older than his dear Juanita. The dead man was either a father or uncle, Joaquin guessed.

She told Joaquin what the man had said.

Joaquin did not move the torch. "Tell him to release the man from the fire. I will lower my torch and surrender to them when you have all been set free."

The woman half-turned and told them what Joaquin had said.

"How do we know he'll keep his word?" the gunman demanded.

"Because I am a man of honor," Joaquin replied through the woman.

"You knifed Trench in the back!" the gunman shouted. "Men of honor don't do that. They don't wear masks either!"

"Do men roast poor boys in a fire?" Joaquin asked. "Do they rape women in the hills? Those are the acts of beasts, not men. What I did was the only way to save the chief's life."

"It ain't civilized to trade a white life for a Redskin," the gunman said. "You had no cause."

Joaquin listened while the woman translated. It was all he could do to keep from dropping the torch in the grass. There was no pain in her voice, just acceptance. That made it worse.

"I want you to untie the man in the fire," Joaquin said to the woman.

"They will stop me."

"They won't."

The woman turned, hesitated, then went to the fire.

The man with the gun grabbed her arm. "Where you goin'?"

She nodded toward Joaquin. "He said I should release my cousin Esteban from the fire."

The gunman looked at the masked intruder. Strands of grass were beginning to fall from his torch. Any one of them could trigger a flash fire. The man released the woman and glared at Joaquin. "You're a dead man. But you betray us and we'll hunt them like the sick dogs they are," the ranch hand warned.

The girl didn't bother to interpret what had been said. She hurried to where her cousin lay moaning. She untied him. Two other members of her party helped him to his feet and carried him off with his arms around their shoulders.

"Keep going," Joaquin said to the woman.

"But my uncle —"

"I will see to his burial," Joaquin promised.

The woman was too busy to cry. She smiled gratefully as the remaining immigrants gathered their belongings and followed the others. The woman joined them, pausing briefly to look back at Joaquin.

"You will always have the gratitude of the family of Donato San Julian," she said.

"Go into the mountains," Joaquin said. He did not take his eyes off the ranch hands.

"Move as quickly as you are able. It will be difficult for them to follow on horseback."

She thanked him again.

The wind was growing louder and the rustling of the grass was like a waterfall. Joaquin continued to face the ranchers.

"Put it down now, Brick," the gunman said, motioning downward with his free hand.

"When they are safe," Joaquin replied, cocking his head toward the San Julians as they headed toward the foothills behind him.

Both men understood each other. They stood with the dead man between them as buzzards and crows began to circle in the sky above. Flies had already begun to collect on the bloody hole that was once the back of his head. It was strange for Joaquin not to be worried about himself. His only concerns were for the girl and her family and, if possible, to punish as many of these vile men as he could.

Setting a fire would help to accomplish that, but Joaquin had given his word. Even if it cost his life, he would uphold that vow. The San Julians must witness that sacrifice and carry the ideal forward.

Sweat covered every part of his body, a combination of the sun and the heat of the torch. He had, he believed, another five to ten minutes before the grass and the last of the vines had burned away.

"Hey, Brick — give it up!" the gunman shouted. "You gave your word."

Joaquin did not think the men would shoot him. He expected they would beat him, but he could endure that. Then they would certainly bring him to the ranch for praise, perhaps for a reward. That was where he would die.

The young man raised the torch before him. He began walking toward the men. Concealed by the grasses, he uncoiled the whip from the sash around his waist. Joaquin had said he would surrender, but he did not say he would do so peaceably. As he neared the edge of the field, he found it strange that something so fragile as dry grass should afford him such protection. He was reminded that nothing in nature was without a purpose nor its own unique strength.

The gunman walked forward with his free hand outstretched. "Hand the torch here, you dirty bastard."

Joaquin waited. Time was against him. Every moment he could buy worked in his favor.

The men stood in a line. They were not

stupid enough to encircle him. If it became necessary to use their guns, they did not want to risk hitting each other. Joaquin emerged from the grasses with his heart racing. His mouth was the only part of him that was dry. He stopped at the edge of the clearing and set the torch at his feet.

"Put that down, dirt!" one of them said, gesturing at the whip.

Joaquin declined.

"I gave you an *order!*" the man repeated. He drew his handgun and pointed it at Joaquin's left leg. "You drop it or I drop you!"

Joaquin shook out his whip. He circled toward the horses.

"If he gets within ten paces, cut his legs off," the leader said to the man holding the horses. "The boss'll be just as happy to hang half a man."

The man with the horses held a double-barrel shotgun under his arm. He pointed it at Joaquin's knees. All the young Mexican had wanted was to scatter the animals. A whip crack would have done that. Now he didn't dare. He might be able to endure a beating. He would not survive twin shots from the steel barrel. Reluctantly, Joaquin dropped the whip.

"Shit, that was Randy's hog-tamer!" one

of the men snarled, pointing.

The leader shook his head. "We're gonna hurt you from top to bottom, Brick. We're gonna shove that mask down yer throat and shove the whip up yer ass." He grinned a wide smile full of brown teeth and empty spaces. "But first we're gonna soften you up and drag you back to Veehall."

Now the men formed a circle around Joaquin. One of them stomped out the remains of the torch as the others moved closer. The leader stepped close and struck him hard in the belly. Joaquin bent so hard, he felt as if someone had pushed him down by the shoulders. He was brought back up by a strong left hand around his throat. The man who had hit him looked in Joaquin's eyes and spit at him, then released him and knocked him back with a fist to the nose. Joaquin felt a sharp pain race along his cheeks and down his neck as he stumbled back. Another man caught him, held him up, and Joaquin took a second blow to his gut. His legs wobbled and he fell to the dirt. The men kicked him as he knelt there, blows landing on his thighs and against his arms and ribs. He bent over to protect his chest and took several kicks to the head. He had decided not to try and fight back, but to conserve his energy and protect himself as best he could. And at some point he stopped remembering anything, until he opened his puffy eyes and saw blue sky above. He realized that he was lying on his back. He felt dull aches on most of his body, and the men were doing something with his hands. They were kicking up dirt as they worked. It landed on Joaquin's face and clung there, sticking to perspiration and probably blood, if the metallic taste in his mouth was any indication. He winced as something pulled hard on his wrists.

"Is he ready?" a man asked from somewhere above and behind him.

"Nearly."

*What are they doing?* Joaquin wondered. He tried to turn around, but his arms were pulled taut behind him and blocked his head. He lay back, trying to think beyond the pounding against his temples and forehead and the bloated ache in his cheeks. He smelled the men nearby, a mixture of musk and campfire smoke that was a part of their clothes, and there was also a horse. The young man became aware of feet scuffling the dry earth, but also hooves. He heard bugs buzzing, but also the distinctive whoosh of a horse's tail nearby.

"He's set," someone said.

"Let's get him to the boss," another replied.

Someone chuckled. "He'll do that air dance with one chewed-up ass," the man said.

He heard the men move in different directions, then mount their horses. The animals whinnied and hooves moved again. As Joaquin lay there, momentarily unattended, he paid less attention to the pain in his face and torso and realized that his arms were lifted behind him.

And then Joaquin cried out, involuntarily and hard. There was a raw red pain in his wrists and a hard, terrible pull against his shoulders, all at the same time. It was followed by a sharp stab in both hips as he began to move backward. He understood now that he was tied to a horse and being dragged behind it. He was looking toward his feet and noticed that his shoes were gone and two large boulders had been tied to his ankles with heavy rope. The rocks kept his legs stretched along the ground and he felt every bump and rock, every rut and clump of grass, from his heels to his backside and along his spine. The bonds quickly tore his flesh raw. He remained conscious for every punch, every stab, because the upward angle of his arms prevented his head and neck from being dragged along the rough terrain. The horse did not move quickly and there were few lacerations — just the constant, bruising pain and a choking cloud of dust kicked back by the animal as it trotted south. He remembered falling down a slope as a child. He had been climbing to pick a flower for his mother and lost his footing. He had bounced from arm to back, sliding and wailing and scraping himself from cheek to elbow. This was like that, but on a hill without end. Joaquin's only cushion was the knowledge that this was not an act of God but the work of man. He was being tormented for what he was. This had not begun over anything he had done. That strengthened his resolve to remain true to what was being attacked: the proud, unbreakable character of his people.

But strength was a finite quality. *Dear God and Juanita,* he thought as the unending torture tested that.

Joaquin shut his eyes. The clear, sharply blue sky somehow made the pain worse. His heart would grab the beauty for a moment, and then have it harshly torn away by the next jolt on his backbone or raking along his side. It was better to see only rusty blackness, to brace himself for each fresh torment.

Joaquin was grateful, at least, that his attackers had contemptuously pushed his mask into his mouth. Perhaps they hoped to make it difficult for him to breathe. But it gave the young man something to bite in those moments when the agony became unendurable.

At some point long after the pain had become a constant blur, along with the moan it elicited, Joaquin felt it subside. The horse that was pulling him slowed, then halted. He heard shouts and gunfire, but that was not in the forefront of his thoughts. All he cared about was that the animal had stopped moving. The pain was everywhere, but it was not everything. Joaquin could breathe without dirt flying into his nostrils. Lying still, he could shift his leg here or his arm there to alleviate pressure. Best of all, the rattling along his entire lower body had stopped. He felt as if he were floating on a lake instead of riding a barrel down a hill. Even though backbone and pelvis still hurt, the absence of constant knocking was pleasurable.

There were more shots. They were followed by screams, then distant whoops, then silence. Even the wind seemed to have left. There were only the aches and the sun and the horse that was now moving restlessly at the other end of the ropes. It started to turn and pull Joaquin with it, but stopped after just a few moments. There was another horse beside it. Joaquin could hear someone jump from its back. Footsteps moved toward him and something momentarily blocked the sun. Joaquin opened his eyes. There was a dark shape above him. It looked like a man.

*An angel? Could it be his Juanita?*

Joaquin shut his eyes again. There was a gentle tugging on the young man's wrists, and then his arms were lowered gently to the ground. His arms were moved slowly from above him to beside him. They were placed carefully on the ground. The cloth was removed from his mouth.

"You safe," he heard someone say in broken Spanish.

Joaquin wasn't sure who the speaker was, and it didn't matter that the language was crude. All he cared about was the sentiment.

That was the last thought he had before he slept.

# 9

## ALLIANCE

It was night when Joaquin opened his eyes again. There was a bright orange campfire to his right and a woman squatting to his left. She was touching a cloth to his face. It had a fragrant odor, like lilac. It didn't sting, but even the light pressure hurt. He would have raised his hand to move her away but his arm was too heavy. He just lay there looking up, savoring the cool night and the new companion.

The woman said something he couldn't understand to someone he couldn't see. A man walked over. Joaquin recognized his strong face in the glow of the fire. It was the chief of the Pechanga tribe.

"We equal," the chief said in Spanish.

"Equal?" Joaquin said. What came from his mouth didn't sound like his voice. It sounded like a pig in slop.

"You save me. I see message, save you."

"Oh." Now Joaquin understood. They

were *even.* He remembered flashing the knife in the direction of the settlement and asking the Pechanga for help. The tribesmen had responded.

"Ranchers dead by spear and arrow. We cut wounds with knife so they not say Pechanga kill," the chief went on. "They will think you did."

"I hope so," Joaquin said through his swollen mouth. "I wouldn't want to get your people in trouble."

"Nor Ao-ti. Don't like Veehall but cannot fight."

"Why?" Joaquin asked.

The woman carefully raised his head and gave him water from a calfskin pouch. Joaquin had not realized how thirsty he was until he drank.

"We have not men and guns to defend valley from other whites," the chief replied. "If they come, not all would let us stay."

Joaquin nodded as the woman laid his head back down. He had noticed other fires in the distance. He was obviously some distance from the settlement. He understood why. If Veehall riders went searching by torchlight, and found him there, they would punish the village for what they had done.

"They hurt you," the chief said.

"I know."

"You need while to heal. Daughter Lokani do."

"Thank you," Joaquin said to the chief, and then smiled weakly at his daughter.

The young man shut his eyes and thought of how Juanita used to smile, and the next thing he knew it was morning. He hurt a great deal more than he had the last time he was awake. Every part of him was sore, even areas that had not been in contact with the ground. He dimly recalled the ranchers beating him before he went unconscious the first time. But the early morning sun felt good and the touch of the slight breeze was welcome. Joaquin forced himself up on his elbows and looked across the valley floor. The fire beside him was out and he was alone.

He noticed that Libertad was tied to a tree well behind a row of boulders. The Pechanga must have gone looking for him to remove any evidence that Joaquin was still in the area around the killings. The natives were thorough, honorable, and loyal. Their efforts touched the young man. Would that the ranchers were worthy of such good-hearted neighbors.

Lokani came by with a paste made from water and bread. She was dressed in a long jacket made of deer hide with rabbit-pelt lining. Her long black hair was tied back with vines that had been sun-dried into hoops. The young woman looked as though she might have been spawned by the ground itself, a part of all things that the land provided. She propped his head atop several blankets, knelt beside him, and fed him using a long reed, putting the meal past his swollen lips.

"Thank you," he said when she was finished.

*"Noto-ma,"* she replied with a little bow of her head.

Lokani left a water pouch behind and returned to the village. A short time later, her father rode over. It wasn't a long walk, but Ao-ti was evidently in a hurry. He dismounted and helped Joaquin to his feet. The young man stood very unsteadily; it had been the first time he had been off his back since arriving. They walked carefully but with some urgency to where Libertad was tethered.

"Pechanga scouts in north signal as you did," the chief told him, motioning with his hand. "Ranchers come. You must go."

"I understand," Joaquin said.

"My son Kunga go with."

"That isn't necessary —"

"You weak. Need help to travel, hunt."

Joaquin couldn't dispute that. The chief was carrying Joaquin more than he was carrying himself.

"You go south," the chief continued. "They not think to follow that way."

"I'll go north," Joaquin told him.

The chief shook his head. "They find you."

"They will try," Joaquin replied. "A band of my countrymen was moving through the valley the other day. I want to talk to them."

"Why?"

"They saw what life is like here," the young man said.

"You save them?"

Joaquin nodded. "Maybe they will help me to change the way things are."

"You cannot change," Ao-ti said, shaking his head emphatically. "I try to make tribes join, fight. Takes time. Patience."

"All of these killers will die eventually. There was a time when I was patient. No longer. My wife and brother were murdered here. I will not let others suffer as I have."

The chief considered this. Ao-ti did not speak again until they reached the horse. The Pechangan helped Joaquin climb to the blanket the natives had provided. Saddlebags made of pigskin lay across the front of it. "I understand your words. Where you ride, Kunga ride."

"Thank you," Joaquin said. Though Libertad was gentle, it hurt to sit up on the horse. The young man refused to show the chief any pain. "Tell me, Chief Ao-ti. You speak Spanish but not the white English. Why?"

Ao-ti smiled. "I have nothing to say to white."

The chief walked in front of the horse as Joaquin reacquainted himself with its back. He had to find a way to sit that didn't hurt. It wasn't possible, and he sought a way that hurt least. Leaning forward slightly, holding the horse's mane, kept the pressure off his badly bruised thighs and buttocks. He still had to hold tight with his lower legs, but Lokani had lotioned and bandaged them where the rock-ropes had ripped away the flesh. The pain was not as harsh as it had been.

Kunga rode out to meet them. He was a tall, powerfully built young man with his dark hair worn in a pair of braids that reached to his shoulders. The grim-faced young man was bare-chested save for a large necklace of talons from eagles, hawks, owls, and other predators. He wore a long cloak made of leather. It was tied to his back by a strap around the neck and waist.

146

Joaquin looked down at the chief. "Thank you for all you have done."

"Thank you for what you will do," the chief replied. He pointed to the saddlebag. "Your mask there. Your brother's blood?"

Joaquin nodded.

The chief made marks across his own cheeks. "We do same. When we cry, tears mix with blood of dead, become one. When we fight, no tears. Only blood."

"There will be no tears," Joaquin promised him. "Not until this land is free of savages."

The chief reached up and clasped Joaquin's bandaged wrist. "The spirits look on you with favor. They will protect. So will son. He speak Spain too, though not as well as I do."

Joaquin tried to smile. His swollen face had to look more like a grimace. He hoped the chief understood.

Ao-ti spoke to his son in their tongue. Kunga's expression did not change. He nodded once when his father was finished. Then he touched two fingers to his lips and put them to his heart, under his necklace. Ao-ti did the same. Joaquin later learned that because they were parting for what could be an extended period, Ao-ti passed the sharing of the title of chief to his son. If something happened to Ao-ti during Kunga's absence, Chief Kunga would be the tribal leader. Ao-ti may have been expecting retribution from Veehall. It was a short and sweet ritual that touched Joaquin deeply.

Ao-ti said he would leave soon to ask the valley spirits for their protection. Kunga turned and headed toward the northwest. Ao-ti had obviously told him what Joaquin wanted to do. The young native looked back to make sure Joaquin was following. Joaquin gave Libertad a little knock on the ribs to start him out. The horse set off at an easy lope. It was as though the stallion sensed the uneasiness of the rider sitting upon its back and moved accordingly. Horses were like people in that respect. If they were treated with respect, they repaid that kindness.

Joaquin looked at Chief Ao-ti as they rode away from the settlement. The young man did not say farewell as the natives had done. Instead, he raised an open hand in peace and friendship. Ao-ti did the same. When Joaquin lowered his hand, he grasped Libertad's mane tightly in his fist. He did more than just hold on as they rode. He was marshaling his will to do what he had vowed — not just to the chief but to his murdered family. He would make this precious land safe for all people or he would perish in the attempt.

The horses moved toward the foothills on the opposite side of the valley from the ranch. This area was watched by the Pechanga tribe. There would be no Veehall patrols. By following the foothills north, Joaquin hoped to catch the slower-moving San Julians, who were on foot with a wounded man.

Though most people he had known would rather dwell in fearful peace than risk their lives for security, Joaquin hoped that some would be willing to fight — perhaps among the San Julians or others who had been abused.

Whenever and however it happened, Joaquin would find men and women who believed as he did, that the right to be free comes from God. Even if no man came forward, Joaquin would not be alone.

■ ■ ■ ■

# PART TWO:
# JULY 1849

■ ■ ■ ■

# 1
## LOVE

Captain Harry Love was always happy when a fracas interrupted a card game. That was because he stank at poker and always lost too much of his wife's fabric-buying money. He played to be sociable and to hear what people were thinking and doing. He had no choice. If he went to the bar as the deputy sheriff–elect of Los Angeles County stationed in San Bernardino — Los Angeles had not yet ratified or funded the position — no one around him said much of anything.

The forty-year-old former cavalry officer was always too busy listening to mutterings at the table or paying attention to what went on at the bar of the Last Stop House or out in the street to mind the game. Unlike his fellow deputies or even the sheriff himself, Love did not believe in the prevailing lynch law. Deputies in Ventura or Orange were happy to hear the noise of the accusers

153

against the accused and step aside. Not Love. If a man were accused of a crime, he believed in immediately assembling at least eight diverse members of the community — twelve, if the accused insisted — so they could hear the evidence. If a man were found guilty, sentence was carried out within the hour. But not every man was guilty all the time.

The Last Stop House — so called because that was where the stagecoach from San Francisco stopped before turning around — was typical of the saloons that had come to the territory over the last few months. It was four wooden walls, a pair of wood-burning stoves on the windblown east and west sides, a long highly polished bar on the north side, and rickety tables everywhere else. They were only covered with black-and-white-checkered tablecloths when people ate. That was a rule Love himself had established. Otherwise, gamblers tended to hide cards in laps that were covered by the hanging edges. The temptation was great and it wasn't worth dying for.

It had only been a year since Love left the 1st Dragoons and came west with his young new wife, the daughter of medical officer Perry Bruce at Fort Leavenworth. After serving in Company B and helping General

Kearny beat the Mexicans, Love was ready for something different. The Army wanted him to help lead the newly formed 2nd Dragoons, but he just didn't want to do that. He was tired of muddy forts and leaking tents, of vicious sunburn and ice-burn alike. Unlike those who followed Love to California, he was not looking for bucketfuls of gold or huge tracts of land. He wanted a little house in a quiet town where there was clement weather, a respectable schoolteacher, and an environment friendly to the children they hoped to have.

So far, the captain and Diana hadn't managed to have the children or find that quiet town. Over one hundred thousand men, with and without their families, had come from around the globe to settle in the newly liberated territory. Towns were thrown together, overrun, expanded, and overrun again — most without many laws to govern them or lawmen to enforce what regulations there were. The town that had grown up around the fringes of the 37,700-acre Rancho San Bernardino was one such place. It was a mixture of hardworking, hard-drinking laborers, merchants, Eastern bankers, and newly arrived Mormons. There were land and silver speculators, hunters — of both buffalo and bounty — and itinerants who couldn't make a living doing any of those things and tried to steal or con their way through life.

Lately, there were gunmen who were looking to hire on as guards or Indian killers. It was a mix of friction matches and gunpowder and it called for someone who was ready to put his foot on the fuse, hard. Deputy Sheriff Love had a big foot.

As usual, he also had a bad hand.

It was just after ten p.m. The hanging oil lamps had been lit for over an hour and most of the people who were coming to the saloon were already there. The few stragglers who arrived closer to midnight were men who knew that the whores in the attached shack out back were just getting ready for their third go-round of the evening. The men liked coming at that hour because the girls were a little tired and let their guests stay a lot longer so they could rest. Midnight was also the time when the first and second round of clients had been back at the bar long enough to get seriously intoxicated. The ones who passed out were rolled or carried to the street, where they stayed until sunrise or they were stepped on by a horse. The ones who didn't shut their eyes often became belligerent and needed to be thrown out.

No one was outlandishly drunk when Love threw in his five cards. He ordered his second whiskey of the night and nursed it past his graying handlebar mustache. He didn't believe in shots. He didn't have to prove his manhood by gulping his liquor. Love had a rule that he never broke: Pleasure was always to be taken slowly. As long as his wife didn't complain, he wasn't going to change that.

Anger, on the other hand, was served hot and fast.

The deputy sheriff didn't get angry about his "skunky hands," as his Dutch friend Barend put it. The boot-maker would have been the worst player there if not for Love. But he was grateful when he could get off the hard wooden chair and stretch the cramped muscles of his backside to help with the dragging, carrying, or tossing out. Usually, he stretched for a while before going back to his game. Talked to townspeople who were there, found out who was causing trouble and needed a watching, or who was new in town and needed a watching-after. That was easier to do when you were losing hands. People felt bad for you.

Tonight, though, things would be different.

The pale orange glow of the lamps was

diffused by the thin cloud of dust that hung in the room, sand kicked up by a day of horse and cart traffic moving along the wide dirt street. Love stood with his whiskey, took a sip, then put it down and arched his back. He picked up the glass, walked toward the bar, and acknowledged the nods of the ranch hands who stood at the far end of the bar. As he took another sip of the drink, the batwing doors at the front of the saloon swung in. Two men entered carrying a third between them. The doors were constructed without handles so drunks could easily be heaved in the opposite direction. Love had never seen a man brought *in* with assistance. The men dropped him. They were big men. One of them was Victor Eugene, the town blacksmith. The other was a well-dressed man Love did not know. The room went silent when they entered.

The man on the warped wooden floor was a white man in his early twenties. He was bloodied about the face and hands. He was breathing but his eyes were shut. He said nothing. Love did not recognize him either.

"We caught him on a mount weren't his," Victor said.

"Whose horse was it?" Love asked.

"Nadler's," Victor said. He looked past the deputy sheriff at the bar. "He was on your mount, Carl."

"Is he okay?"

"Got a little spooked, but no harm was done," Victor said.

Love looked down at the man. "Turn him over."

Victor did as he was asked. The man was bleeding from his nose and left cheek. A front tooth was missing and the youth was breathing very heavily through his bloody gums.

"Who knows him?" Love asked.

No one answered.

The sheriff slowly looked around the room. "Somebody must."

"Never seen 'im," someone said from the bar.

"We told ya what he did," Victor said. "Just run him out o' town or I'm gonna move we lynch him."

"On what evidence? What'd he do, just walk into town after sundown and decide to rustle himself a horse?" Love asked. The silence was incriminating. He recognized it from the stony faces of his cavalry unit whenever someone snuck into the covered chuck wagon and grabbed an extra helping of cheese or liquor. No one bled out the truth as long as it was somebody they liked. Or someone who could hurt them. The sheriff looked at the bottoms of the young man's shoes. "Not too worn out. This boy ain't done a lot o' walkin'." Love stood tall at the entrance to the saloon. He peered at the group. "Who is he? Or do I gotta sit up all night and hope he comes to?"

"He'll come to and lie," Victor vowed. "He's a horse thief."

"Maybe. But until he can defend himself o' those charges he ain't," Love replied.

The deputy sheriff went to the bar and asked for a glass of water. He poured it on the boy's face. The young man moaned and moved his arms a little, then went back to sleep. Love shook his head. Something didn't feel right here.

He crouched beside the boy and looked the body over. He smelled flowers and traced the odor to the boy's hands. But there was no green on them, no dirt under the nails. In fact, his hands were fair.

Then he recognized the smell. It wasn't flowers. His wife wore the same scent. This man hadn't been with a horse. He'd been with a woman.

He rose and faced the blacksmith. "Who is she, Victor?"

The blacksmith said nothing and his expression did not change. He would have made a good poker player.

Love looked at the other man. "Who are you?"

"Albert Angel, Victor's brother-in-law from Fresno," the well-dressed man told him.

The deputy sheriff looked the man over. His eyes settled on the man's tan gloves. There was blood on them. Victor's hands were clean. "Let me see that," Love said, pointing lazily toward Angel's hands.

"My gloves?"

Love nodded once.

Angel handed them to the deputy sheriff.

"What the hell're you doin', Cap'n?" Victor asked.

Love didn't answer. He smelled the leather, then looked at Angel. "Same as his hands," the deputy sheriff remarked.

"Ya wanna smell mine too?" the blacksmith demanded. "We wuz holdin' him, that's how we got the stank!"

"You're sayin' *his* smell rubbed off?" Love asked. "I got a wife. She puts stuff on her to smell good. I don't. You don't. I'm betting Angel don't either. You didn't beat this fella bowlegged over a horse. Who'd he get friendly with? Your daughter, Victor? Or does Angel here have a wife?"

"Let it be," someone said from the bar.

Love turned. "Who had a contribution to

this investigation?" he asked.

"I did," Carl said, shifting his big self toward the deputy sheriff. "This fancy boy came to town early this morning looking for women and trouble. He didn't have no money for whores so he tried to take hisself a decent gal."

"By force?" Love asked.

No one answered.

"Do I have to go to the women at this indecent hour and find out?" Ladies were not permitted in the saloon except those who worked there. "Who saw him here? Which of the ladies did he approach?"

The room remained silent.

"He's Katie's brother," someone said at last.

Love looked through the crowd. One of the whores was standing by the entranceway to the back rooms. She was dressed in a shimmering but wrinkled red gown that reached to the floor.

"He came in early this morning to take her home," the woman said as she approached. "Katie didn't want to go. He said he wouldn't leave till she did. I don't know anything more'n that."

Love looked back at Victor. "You don't mingle with these ladies. What's this all t'you? Or you?" he asked, looking at Angel.

Then he glanced down at the unconscious man. "Katie's a brown-hair. He's blonde. He don't look a thing like her." Love walked up to Angel. "She his girl — or his wife?"

"Wife," Angel said. "But she doesn't wanna be."

"You send girls from north to here. Is that your trade?" Love asked.

"Ain't nothin' illegal 'bout that."

"There is about bearin' false witness and beatin' a man near to death for tryin' to take his wife home." Love looked at Victor. "I don't care if this man is your kin. You help him wrongly and I'll charge you."

"This is a family matter, Cap'n," Victor said. "Best let it be."

"This is a matter of law," Love replied. "I *won't* let it be."

Silence filled the saloon. It was as heavy as the tester of dust and cigarette smoke that clung to the air. The deputy sheriff told the barkeep and Carl to help the beaten man to a bed and tend to him. There was no doctor in the town. The whores took care of small hurts and the barber took care of amputations. The men did as they were told. Love remained with Victor and Angel.

"You I want out of here now," Love said to Angel. "You come in by horse?"

"I met him at the coach stop by Veehall

Ranch," Victor said.

"Take him back there at sunup," Love said. "He can wait there to get passage home. Victor, this boy's gonna stay with you till he gets better."

"Cap'n, the fella is loco," Victor said, pointing toward the bedrooms. "He wanted to kill Angel."

"Me too." Love looked at the fair-faced man from Fresno. "Maybe I oughta say I caught this dude stealin' my horse. Put his lousy blood on the saloon tab instead o' my own."

"That woman *wanted* to come with me," Angel insisted. The man was suddenly defensive and more than a little scared. "She said she wanted to earn enough money to move east, to New York. She didn't want to live on a wagon with a traveling rag-doll-maker."

"The lady shoulda thought that through before she married a traveling rag-doll-maker."

"Well, she didn't. She was lovestruck. He was gonna open a store but couldn't save —"

"Shuddup," Love told Angel. He looked back at the blacksmith. "If that boy don't heal, we'll have some talkin' to do. Make sure he does."

The room returned to life as Love turned and went back to the card table. He was not surprised to find that the cards were as he left them. The men enjoyed playing more when they could take his money.

Love picked up his cards but didn't really see them. He wasn't happy with what had just happened. A peace officer could serve the law without furthering the cause of justice. He had saved a man's life but he had also extended the suffering of two people. He couldn't imagine Katie would go back with him. She was a strong-minded little bobcat. Maybe the doll-maker would recover but be so overwhelmed with sadness that he killed his wife and himself. It could happen. Then Love would be responsible for her death, and maybe Angel's too if the steamed kid decided to take him along. And what if Angel's girls went belly-up because they didn't have someone to look after them? A few of them could go honest again, but not all.

These kinds of thoughts hurt his head. The deputy sheriff couldn't know tomorrow any more than he could know what the next card would be — though in the case of the cards they were usually bad. Maybe that was it. Maybe the future was too and he had to just accept that. Love used to think

165

that war was the serpent in the garden. But it was really just a concentration of the killing and hate that went on all the time, every day, over a larger territory.

He couldn't worry about that. His jurisdiction was here and it was now. His job was defined by a few laws and a lot of morality. What came from making lawful choices was in the hands of God.

Like these cards, hand after hand that he didn't throw in because there was always the chance that the next draw would be one that made everything better.

# 2
## HOME

Deputy Sheriff Love only played a few more hands. He asked to see Katie before he left. He wanted to make sure she was here of her own will and that she didn't want to leave with her husband. Angel may have been many unsavory things, from a flesh-peddler to a bullying thug, but apparently he wasn't a liar. Katie did not want to go back to Fresno. He didn't sense fear in her voice, as though Angel had threatened her. He heard conviction. Love promised to make sure that when her husband got well he stayed away from her. She seemed a little saddened to hear that he had taken a beating. But not so sad that she wanted to see him.

Then, beneath a spectacular sky of stars and shooting stars, Love walked home along the dark street. He sniffed as he walked, steering clear of the horse patties. They had someone who shoveled the streets during

167

the day. That wasn't possible after nightfall.

The Loves lived in three small rooms above the one big room that served as the sheriff's station and jail. It was a freestanding wood structure painted white with a sloping roof with long eaves that helped to block the intense sunlight. It was dark but not suffocating, with a hint of a cross-breeze from the high desert and floors that creaked because that same air kept them dry.

The rooms were a bedroom, a kitchen, and an attic for storage or guests — short ones, since the eaves limited the areas where someone could stand. Diana Bruce Love stood just under five feet and moved with relative ease up there. Her six-foot-tall husband did not. His broad shoulders barely made it through the opening where the ladder was placed.

There was always plenty of color and sweet aromas here. Diana literally made flowers blossom in the desert with native wildflowers as well as seeds she had brought from the fort. The window boxes contained roses and lilies, irises and honeysuckle, as well as spices she used for cooking. Diana usually didn't make dinner until after sundown when the temperature dropped considerably. The deputy sheriff had come home and had stew before heading over to the saloon. Unlike the open hearth used by most people west of the Mississippi, the Loves had a coal-fired stove they had obtained courtesy of General Kearny's military connections. He had it purchased in Philadelphia ostensibly for the newly renovated Fort Delaware, then had it sent west. Coils in the bottom of the stove enabled the Loves to heat water as well, which they used to fill the small bathing tub in the bedroom. The outhouse was located just behind the jail and was accessible by a staircase from the bedroom. The home was modern and luxurious by any standard of the day.

Diana was asleep when her husband came home. She was an early riser and he required very little sleep. He removed his clothes in the kitchen and left them in a pile beside the coal scuttle. The deputy sheriff liked wearing the smell when he was out. It reminded him of home.

He put on his long underwear and slid his large frame into the narrow bed. He and Diana slept on separate beds, but they were set side by side. Love considered it a good night if he came home unharmed and the squeaking hinges of the doors and springs in the bed didn't wake his wife. Tonight, he was a little less careful than usual. He wanted the woman who didn't mind staying with his big log of a self to know he was home. He made sure he sighed loud enough for her to hear, facing her, as he pulled up the covers. Half-asleep, Diana sidled into his big left arm. He drew her close.

"I smell rose petal," the woman said dreamily.

"Is that what it was?" Love said. He liked learning things, especially when it added detail to a crime or conflict.

"Who was she?" Diana asked.

"A saloon girl."

"Is she unhurt?"

"Outside she's fine," Love whispered. "Inside she's a little stirred up. Go back to sleep."

She curled in closer. Diana would never have asked if her husband had consorted with her. Everyone who knew him, who knew the couple, understood the bond they shared. She was the sun and he was the sky and nothing could separate them. Captain Love had always been an important part of something, whether it was a large Texas family or a regiment. Now he was part of this team and like those other relationships, it "bettered him," as he put it. That — and she — were dearer to him than whatever fast-forgotten flirtation he could have enjoyed. It was not like killing men in the war, and occasionally as deputy sheriff. Those were over and done with. Love had seen brief encounters with women become drawn out, difficult, and occasionally deadly.

"I was dreaming about the dog we used to have at the fort, Tafia," Diana said. "She was a big dog the color of molasses."

"Why didn't you just call her Molasses?" her husband asked.

"Daddy once drank Tafia in the West Indies and thought it was quite delicious, very special. So was this dog. It used to sleep with me when I was a little girl, right at the foot of the bed."

"Are you sayin' I should be there?"

"I like you better here," she said, digging in closer.

"What made you think of the dog?"

"I was going through the chest before and found letters my father had written to my mother when he was garrisoned in Baton Rouge," she said. "They were apart for two years. I'm glad we're not."

"Remote as this place is, I never feel lonely," he agreed.

It was a good sentiment on which to fall asleep.

The knock on the door came shortly after the sun. It woke Love up, and he went downstairs to see who it was. The village didn't have problems this early in the morning. Anyone who was awake had work to do.

The caller was a stocky man with a neatly trimmed beard and cold blue eyes. Love recognized him at once. It was Tim Parmenter, Deputy Sheriff of Los Angeles. They had met at a gathering in Los Angeles several months earlier when they tried to draft a code to present to the provisional government about organizing a standing posse to patrol Redskin territories. Violence between the races was on the rise in many regions, mostly — it seemed — in response to settlers and bounty hunters trying to keep Indians away from their new homes.

Diana was still asleep and Love stepped outside to shake Parmenter's hand. The man was wearing a long gray duster with a rabbit-fur collar and smelled of a familiar South Carolina cigar smoke. Love knew then that Parmenter had been an overnight guest at the Lugo ranch. The lawman would have been able to leave before sunrise because of the wide trail that had been cut through the acreage and the lantern cart that accompanied visitors. The open wagon was lit at both ends and gave visitors an hour or two start on daylight when traveling long distances. Love also knew that the deputy sheriff wasn't staying very long. His large black Morgan was still saddled and loosely tied to the hitching post.

"How are ya, Timothy?" Love asked.

"Toes still wriggling in my boots. How's the missus?"

"Unaffected by my flaws," Love replied. "She's asleep or I'd ask ya in."

"I gotta move on anyway, though I'm less fond of these long rides than I once was." The twenty-three-year-old peace officer laughed. "Nothing quite rankles your bee-hind worse than seating a cold saddle before sunup."

"I'm guessin' there's important business then," Love replied. "You still doin' the hurry-up-for-statehood reel?"

"That's part of it," Parmenter admitted. "The ranchers want to consolidate power before we petition Washington. Get the In-juns under control, get a constitution and some draft laws writ, make sure the ranch-ers and farmers and shippers got their corners of commerce all tidied up. They're even knocking around plans for a railroad that'll go from one ocean to the other."

"They better get the okay of the ranchers in Texas," Love suggested. "They're hospi-table as sunshine, but only fer people who're passin' through."

"Texas won't see a hint of iron," Parmenter told him. "These boys want to go through the midsection of the continent."

"They got some mountains might not agree."

"They're thinking to go over them, Lugo told me. That's part of where the money would come from. Developers back East who want to establish towns along the way. It's a big plan."

"What do they want you fer, to ride shotgun?"

"Wouldn't be so bad, my legs up in a warm car watching the plains. No — we got a problem down here I wanted to talk to you about before I head north."

"We can go to the saloon if you want to sit —"

"I really haven't got much to tell you. I just wanted to say there's a situation developing that you'll need to be a part of. Have you heard of that band of outlaws calling themselves Los Guardabosques del Diablo?"

"The Devil's Rangers?" Love said as he shook his head.

"Started about five weeks ago with the scalping of some ranch hands," Parmenter told him. "Buncha Mexicans and an Injun or two. Leader wears a bloody mask. They been goin' from ranch to ranch killing and tearing things up — they started with Vee-hall down south, then hit Gaynor and Lugo."

"Why?"

"We think they may be leftovers from the Mexican territorial authority. Could be insurgents working for payoffs, trying to scare people off and get regions handed back to Mexico City. Or they could be displaced settlers who don't want to go home and are on a vengeance ride. Either way they got to be stopped."

"By us."

"By someone," Parmenter said. "We aren't going to have a state until we have laws *and* the people to enforce them."

"I'm ready to enforce," Love said. "We just ain't got the folks to try who we bring in."

"That will come. What we need to do first is stop this band and scare off any shadow gangs who may try to do what they're doing. These superstitious savages may start to think the same killers are showing up in different places like they can fly or something. That's how legends get born."

"Also by killing them," Love pointed out.

"Not if you do it soon enough, which is

why I'm letting you know what's on the horizon. So far, all of this falls in your jurisdiction. Sheriff Drumseller may boot it down to you."

"Gonna leave it to me to deputize?"

"I honestly don't know," Parmenter said. "He may want men from all the local districts to represent a united California."

"We haven't even got a united town, let alone a state."

"They don't know that in Washington," Parmenter said. "That's why I figured you might want to start talking to people. See who's willing to ride and also who might know something."

"I will do that and I truly appreciate the alert."

Parmenter nodded and walked to his horse. Love stepped off the wooden stoop and went with him. Though the sheriff's station was in the center of town, it was a freestanding structure. That allowed air to circulate around the building. The shaded air in the alleys helped keep the structure slightly cooler during the ferociously hot, windless days of summer.

"I'm not sure how much of a bother this is going to be," Parmenter said as he untied his horse and mounted. "These people don't use guns, and they usually strike in ambush so their victims can't use 'em either. There's nothing to listen for. And if you're close enough to hear, chances are they'll getcha."

"Do we know where their hideout is?"

"In the mountains somewhere. At least, that's what the ranchers think. It's tough to track them. They move in water and on rocky terrain whenever they can. And nobody ever sees campfires so they know where to build 'em."

"Anybody tried baitin' 'em?"

"Veehall took the biggest bite from his work force. I hear tell he set out stray beeves and stallions with gunmen watching from cliffsides and gullies. All that did was cost him beeves, stallions, and two more men."

"Sounds like we have a little war going on," Love said. "Why didn't one of the ranchers let me know before it got outta hand?"

"They didn't want locals knowing they couldn't handle their affairs," Parmenter told him.

"Proud sons of bitches. Any of 'em tell you what started this thing?"

"Four ranch hands were cut up west of Veehall's place," Parmenter told him. "Horse thieves, they say."

"You believe that?"

"Got no reason not to."

"Got any reason 'to'?"

Parmenter grinned. "They pay the bills for the sheriffin' business. I'll send word when I know more."

"I'll do the same."

Parmenter threw off a little salute as he turned his horse toward the north and rode off. Love stood beside the stoop. He watched the sun rise on the other side of the street. It turned odd black shapes into the familiar general store, stagecoach stop, and barber. Love drew a long breath of the morning air. It was still fresh, free of dust from riders and carts, smoke and soot from cooking fires, and the scent of fresh waste from horses and dogs. He didn't mind those intrusions. Like crime and violence, jealousy and hate, wherever men collected, those things followed. That was one reason the news of an outlaw band didn't surprise him. California was the "new open," as Diana's father had called it. But there were already people living here, familiar with their old ways and former government. Like a cattle herd that couldn't be turned suddenly without a few broken necks and busted legs.

*And not just among the steers,* Love thought.

■ ■ ■ ■

He needed to go back inside to finish dressing and to heat the stove. Hot coffee was a necessity before the sun got too high and the town got too lively. It was also important to extinguish the stove before the day got too hot. Otherwise, the rooms became insufferably warm.

Love had not been out in the field since his military days. He was not sure how he felt about that. Part of him liked the idea of being out on a mission, a strike that would better the lives of more than just his fellow townspeople. Especially if things were getting as bad as Parmenter had said. The ranchers were not nanny goats. They didn't cry when their snouts got stuck in a tin. If Lugo and Veehall were squawking, then this was a serious matter that needed tending to. The idea that they were already in a war made him angry not just at the bandits but at the ranchers. They were an arrogant bunch, a law unto themselves. As long as they stayed that way, the territory would be under pressure. People had journeyed to this country from lands near and far to get away from the service of kings. They came for a little land, a little business, and a lot of freedom to work them. Love had always thought that was no less than a man deserved.

But part of him — an equal part — didn't want to leave his wife behind, his town un-sheriffed, or be away from the streets and sights and even the smells that had come to define "home." He had worked hard to make this region safe and generally well behaved. There were men he could deputize, who had volunteered for such service — mostly around the card table when fellowship was high and the hour was late — but they were untested. Too little attention over days and weeks and the town could start to reek of abuses like the one he'd prevented the night before. Too much attention and resentment could build and harden between people and groups.

Love wondered how life had managed to get so complicated.

He turned and went inside where things were warm and familiar, where change was not something he had to shoulder alone.

# 3
## TRIAL

It had seemed like a very good idea at the time.

Tim Parmenter of Hartford, Connecticut, faced with the prospect of years of study at Yale to become an attorney who fought for justice in a court, in a suit, opted to take the family money he was given, learn how to ride and shoot from Peter Jenkins, who had fought in the War for Independence as a boy, then buy himself passage west and test himself against real dangers. He would face wrongdoers and become the kind of hero he read about in the penny magazines.

He hadn't counted on spending most of that time on horseback getting to and from places that had problems — usually after the problems had been resolved with the spilling of blood. Sheriff Drumseller liked to hold the reins in the city proper and let his three deputies take care of the out-reaches.

As the newest deputy, with just under two years of service compared to the five and six years of his colleagues, Tim Parmenter got to visit the outermost of the outreaches. He had mastered living off the land and surviving in the wilderness, skills he hadn't thought to acquire from Jenkins, and had rarely gotten to use the talents he did learn. His mother wrote that no one would think less of him if he were to return to Connecticut, enroll at Yale, and join the family law firm.

Yet *he* would think less of Tim Parmenter. Being a cold, tired, and uncomfortable deputy was not enough reason to go back East and become a bored, unhappy attorney. He did not yet consider himself a failure. He was still young, only twenty-three. If he continued to work hard and pay his dues, he would get a promotion. And with statehood apparently near, new counties would be established with more cities and a much larger population to protect.

At night the titanic mountains were visible only in silhouette, marked by the stars they blocked. In the early morning, it was not necessary to imagine their size and features. The foothills to the north and west were rust-colored, with patches of dark green and silver-gray on their faces and upraised ridges. The morning was unusually clear, without the cloud layer he frequently encountered. Something else was very different today as well.

Tim Parmenter was not alone.

The deputy sheriff saw three people walking parallel to him about two minutes' gallop to the east. It was difficult to tell who they were because the sun was behind them. They were all adults, but they could have been Mexican or Indian. Either way, it was odd to see them more than a day's walk from water. It got hot out here once the sun cleared the mountains.

"*Señor,* if you would please stop."

The voice belonged to a woman. It came from his left. Parmenter turned as he reined his mount to a halt.

The woman was sitting on a small palomino. Two riders sat on either side of her. They had obviously come from behind a small incline in the plain. From where he was sitting it had looked like an unbroken stretch of land.

The riders that interested Parmenter — and scared him — were the ones immediately to her left and right. One was an Indian brave and the other was a Mexican. The Mexican wore a bloody mask that covered everything but his eyes. A black whip hung loosely from his right hand. The men on the far ends of the phalanx sat high in their saddles. Both of them held bows taut with arrows.

"I am Deputy Sheriff Timothy Parmenter of the Los Angeles County Sheriff's Station." The young man wasn't frightened. If they wanted him dead he would already be on the ground. He was angry that he had been suckered. The three "travelers" to the east were coming toward them now.

"You should stay in Los Angeles, Deputy Sheriff Timothy Parmenter," the woman told him.

"I would like nothing better," he admitted. His eyes shifted to the masked man. "I take it you're the leader?"

"What did Lugo want?" the woman asked.

"I don't know if I'll be telling you that, but I surely don't talk to people who point arrows at me," Parmenter informed her.

The woman informed the others. The man with the mask motioned for the two men on the ends to lower their bows. They complied immediately. That answered Parmenter's question.

"Answer now," the woman ordered.

"Mr. Lugo wants the killings to stop," Parmenter said.

The woman translated into Spanish. The

man in the mask remained impassive. He spoke.

"When the ranchers respect our lives, the death will end."

"Are you saying the ranchers are responsible?"

"They kill us. We defend ourselves."

"That isn't the story they tell," Parmenter said. "They say you live off their land, eat their food, and kill their workers."

"This was our land," the woman said.

"Maybe once but not now." Parmenter looked at the brave while the woman interpreted for the others. "It's the white man's land and you have to live by the white man's will."

The masked man spoke.

"His will is to rape women and torture young men," the woman told the deputy sheriff.

"That isn't true," Parmenter replied. "We want peace."

"You want slaves like the Africans," the Mexican said through the woman. "We will not be so."

The three wanderers from the east arrived then. They were all Mexicans, two elderly and one of them with his left hand missing.

"My cousin was tortured in a campfire," the woman said. "His hand was burned so badly it was lost to him. That is not peace."

Parmenter looked at the young man. He may have been short a hand, but there was strength in his remaining fist and steadfastness in his eyes. The deputy sheriff looked back to the others. Here he was, finally confronting the enemy, and what was he doing? Talking to them as an attorney would do. He had two six-shooters at the ready on his hips and a carbine holstered on the horse. He might be able to drop them all. That would guarantee a sheriffality. Then again, he might miss one. That might be all it would take to get him an arrow in the chest or back.

"Whoever started this, the ranchers intend to end it," Parmenter said. "They have more men than you do. And those men have guns."

"Men and weapons have not saved them so far," the Mexican replied through the woman.

"They're only just getting started," Parmenter said. "Call this off and go home. Elsewise you will all die."

"We are home," the Indian replied.

"No, you are on Lugo land. Right here, where we're talking, is his property. It goes on for another day's ride in that direction," he said pointing north.

"Lugo built a ranch on this land," the brave said. "That does not make it 'his.' "

"The U.S. government says it does."

"Where is this government?" the brave asked, holding his arms wide.

"I'm it," Parmenter said. "I'm the mouth. I speak its wishes."

"Speaking something does not make it real," the brave replied. "That is merely wind."

This was pointless. And insulting. He had foresworn a life of lawyering so he would be more than just wind. Parmenter took another look around, wondering if he could end this uprising himself. His mount had been trained to stand still when loud noises went off around him. His long coat was not buttoned from the waist down for exactly this reason. The deputy sheriff could drop the reins, turn both guns to his left, and kill or wound the men on that side. The people on the right were not carrying weapons as far as he could tell. If they did, he would have turned on them before they could reach under their serapes to grab them.

Parmenter's job was to uphold the will of the state. If he loped away like a scared dog, he would not be doing that. Worse, he would lose respect for himself. He wondered if the gang would even dare to attack him. There was always the chance they might hit their amigos on the other side —

Parmenter acted. It was the last thing he ever did.

The masked Mexican flung a knife from his side. It struck Parmenter in the right shoulder before his gun had been fully drawn. The deputy sheriff listed to that side and reached for the wound with his left hand. He dropped both guns and instinctively reached for the carbine with his wounded right arm.

An arrow punched through his breastbone and knocked him from the right side of the horse. He moaned as he fell, then cried out as his back struck the ground. He tried to get up but while his legs moved, he felt like an upended tortoise. He couldn't get them to more than kick at the air. Even as he lay there, he reached for guns that were no longer where they were supposed to be.

The masked man and the woman stood over him. The man lowered his mask. His mouth did not seem as hard as his eyes.

"We did not want this," the woman said.

Parmenter tried to answer her. He wanted to say he wasn't going to shoot her, just the men, but the words didn't come. He felt the ground around him for his guns. They had to be here somewhere.

The Mexican handed the woman his water pouch. She removed the top, knelt, and raised Parmenter's head. She trickled water into his mouth.

The Mexican man spoke.

"We will lead your horse back so your *compadres* can find you," the woman translated. "If we put you on his back, you will both be attacked by animals."

Parmenter was confused. If they put him on the horse's back, he could take himself to Rancho San Bernardino. If they helped him up, he could also breathe. For some reason, it was difficult to do that in this position.

Suddenly, the bright world beyond the faces turned russet, like the mountains at dawn. The sky and the faces grew darker as Parmenter watched, and then they were entirely swallowed by blackness.

The deputy sheriff closed his eyes knowing that he had tried to do his job. His last thought was that he wished he had done it a little better.

# 4
## TRAIL

Deputy Sheriff Love was about to have a late lunch at home when someone knocked urgently at the door of the office downstairs.

"You're as popular as a traveling doctor today," Diana remarked as she stopped ladling corn chowder into a wooden bowl.

"Wish I was as useful," Love said as he rose from the small round table. He pulled the checkered napkin from the neck of his shirt and draped it on the back of his chair. After Deputy Sheriff Parmenter had visited, Victor Eugene had come by to clear the air. He was a good man and Love knew it. Trailing ash and coal dust like a minion of the devil, the blacksmith was seeking absolution for the previous night. He explained that he had been caught between family business and conscience and had come down on the wrong side.

"The boy'll recover," Victor said. "I promise you that."

"I'm glad to hear it," Love replied. "I want you to make sure he gets to see his wife before he goes home. You owe him that."

"What if she don't wanna see him?"

"Then I'll make sure that whorin' by wives gets illegalized here and order her sent back north," Love told him. "People gotta learn that compromise is better'n open war fare."

Victor enthusiastically agreed. He assured the sheriff there would be no further trouble and left the office. The sooty smell remained, but any lingering ill will was gone. The town was too small for that. Fill it with tension and there would be no room for anything else.

Love had remained in his office after Victor's visit, looking through the mail that arrived every two weeks. There were wanted notices from other counties, letters from police departments and attorneys representing families looking for missing members, and illustrated booklets with items ranging from ammunition to clothing to office provisions. He looked through these so he would know what people back East thought people out West needed. There were square black cakes for coloring over scuffs on shoes, flat blue cakes to turn yellowed laundry white, and round green cakes of honey and sage to

191

scrub on the teeth to clean them and freshen your breath. His favorite was the glass-bottled lotion for outhouse corncobs. After they cleaned themselves, the Loves used a tub of water to rinse off the cobs. He couldn't imagine who would want their rear ends to smell like flowers.

He always saved those booklets for Diana. As much as he could never imagine anything they needed, she always found something. That was probably why they kept getting the mailings.

There was a scuffle down the road when the general store refused to accept currency from a cattleman who was visiting Rancho San Bernardino. Owner Charlotte Wyrds would have to go to Los Angeles to cash his notes from the Texas Insurance and Banking Company, which is why she dealt in silver or gold. Though the Texan agreed to give her coins, he threw a bull when she said she would accept them for their weighted value, not for what was minted on their faces. That meant the fifty dollars in coins would be worth less than ten.

Love understood that the man and his group needed supplies for the long trip home. But he did not have the authority to force Charlotte to sell him goods. The man had to delay his departure a day while he rode back to the ranch and got a note from Lugo agreeing to put the supplies on his tab. It said something about the fortitude and demeanor of the elderly Miss Wyrds that Love would rather have tangled with a small herd of enraged Texans than with her.

The deputy sheriff returned to the jail and did some repairs on the door hinges before heading up to lunch. Though the air in the region was dry, fine desert dirt got into the junctions, which caused them to pit and grow loose. He replaced the pins with new ones. The door didn't get used more than once or twice a month, usually for drunks, but he liked it to work when it did.

Diana put the soup back on the stove while he went downstairs. He took a hunk of bread with him. The jail door was heavy and moving it around had made him hungry. He forgot about the bread when he saw what was at the door.

A Chinaman from the small Asian house at the end of the street was standing there, not with laundry or homemade gunpowder, but with Deputy Sheriff Parmenter's horse. The carbine was still tucked beside the saddle and there were drops of blood on the stock. The reins were tied to the pommel. Someone had recovered the horse and sent it back to town.

"Where'd you find him?" Love asked.

"It stand by river," the young man said. "Men were going."

"Men?"

"Too far to see — but going fast."

"Did you see the rider?"

The young man shook his head.

Love lifted one of the horse's hind legs, then sent the Chinaman away with a coin. The deputy sheriff went inside and pulled his coat and hat from the rack beside the door. He didn't need the heavy outer garment now, but he would when the sun went down. He went to the stairs out back. He hurried up and stood on the landing as he called to his wife. She came away from the stove that was hissing with burning wood and bubbling with soup.

"Something's happened to Deputy Sheriff Parmenter," he told her urgently. "I'm going out to find him."

She put a hand on his chest — that meant wait in Diana-talk — and turned toward the cupboard. She put jerky and several rolls in a cloth, knotted them, and handed the satchel to her husband. She kissed him hard on the cheek.

"Come back safe," she said.

He put his lips to her forehead. "Always."

Love hurried down the steps and went to

the small stables out back. He saddled his horse and was on the plain before the touch of Diana's lips had faded from his dark cheek.

It did not take long to find the deputy sheriff. Love had followed the tracks left by Parmenter's horse. They had a distinctive curlicue cut in the center of both sides to facilitate recovery efforts like this. The only difficulty was that the horse was riderless, which caused them to cut less deep into the earth. There were times when Love lost the tracks altogether, but he knew the way to Los Angeles. He stayed true and eventually recovered Parmenter's trail.

He saw the mound of rocks from roughly a quarter mile off. They were not neat or high. He used to see piles like that on the battlefield. If a unit had to move on before the graves-soldiers could get to them, bodies were protected from carnivores and the elements in hastily assembled tombs like this.

Love had not expected that. If Parmenter were killed by the renegades he had described, they would have mutilated his body and left it — not interred him and sent his horse back. Love stopped beside the rocks and moved the top layer aside. The body was intact save for two wounds — one from a knife and one from an arrow. Obviously, there had been more than one assailant. What surprised him even more was the fact that Parmenter's guns had been placed on his chest. He checked the weapons. Neither had been discharged.

"But they ain't in the holsters," Love said. "What'd you do, boy, draw on these outlaws?"

The only thing missing was Parmenter's coat and boots. That didn't trouble Love as much as he felt it should have. They took from necessity, not greed. The deputy had been right about the guns, though. These bandits moved silently.

Love stood and looked around the grave site. There were multiple footprints from different kinds of footwear: moccasins, boots, horses. He counted at least four different people and two distinct horses, judging from the impression of the shoes made by the weight that had been on their back. He did not intend to seek them out. They were probably watching the site now, the way they must have been watching Lugo's ranch. They would be ready to run or confront him if he went after them.

Instead, the deputy sheriff moved more of the rocks and lifted the young man's body from within. He hoisted it over his shoulder and carried it to his horse. If he left now he could get home by sunset. That seemed the thing to do. He would communicate with Lugo in the morning, through someone who regularly visited the ranch. If these outlaws *were* watching, he did not want Lugo to give them easy targets to pick off. That would throw fear into the community.

These killers had some humanity. That meant they also had human weaknesses. When Love went after them he wanted to rattle *their* bones.

Love draped the body in the saddle and took the horse's reins. He would walk alongside the animal for as long as he could to ease its burden. He also wanted to keep eyes, ears, and nose open for trackers — a voice, a glint of metal, a movement half-seen, the scent of a man who had not bathed. He wanted to know where the killers were and how they worked, whether on one side or two and with how much distance between them.

The deputy sheriff did not get the answer to any of those questions. If the outlaws were trailing him, he didn't see them, hear them, or smell them. Either the bandits were very good or else they had gone away. Whichever the case, the gang would not be easy to track.

Fortunately, Deputy Sheriff Parmenter had not gone very far. Still on foot, intermittently chewing on the food Diana had provided, Love neared the northern end of the settlement minutes after the sun dropped below the western mountains. Love knew the terrain well enough to pick his way to the wide dirt road in the dark. He stayed to the middle of the deserted street. It was good to see lantern light in the windows of people's homes and businesses. When lawmen or soldiers died, their comrades liked to be reminded what they were fighting for. Not intellectually but viscerally, by seeing the works of settlers and their families. After a day in the wilderness, it was good to see the community a few brave and visionary souls had carved from it.

Though his feet were sore and hot, Love did not stop at the sheriff's office. He went directly to the undertaker. Will Christian Jr. was a second-generation undertaker, moved from the chilly north to a climate more suited to his widower mother. She was eighty-one years old and, in addition to ordering the supplies they needed from Chicago, grew all the flowers they used. When he wasn't building coffins, Will constructed beds. Most of the tools and supplies he used were the same.

Will was still in his small showroom when Love arrived. The portly undertaker hurried out when he saw what was on the deputy sheriff's horse. He was dressed in a white shirt and black string tie, with black trousers. He helped Love lower the body from the saddle and carry him inside. Parmenter's badge shined a dull gold in the glow of the hearth in the main office. There was a stand and metal rod for cooking, though nothing was on it at the moment. The Christians typically ate at the Green Grass, a restaurant not far from the Last Stop House.

They laid the man on a narrow table in the back room. Love could hear Meggie Christian moving around upstairs in their small attic living space.

Will didn't have to ask what had happened. That was evident from the bloody wounds. Nor did he have to ask where the dead man was from. The badge told him that. He simply stepped back from the table and looked at Love, his beefy face knotted with concern.

"Are you all right, Deputy?"

Love nodded. "I wasn't there when this happened. I want you to fix him up for return to Los Angeles."

"Of course," Will said.

Funerals for law officers were paid for by the county. It was one of the benefits they received for risking their lives, along with a pension for the widow or widowed mother.

Will looked down at the pale body. He touched the man's cheek. "Appears the poor fella bled out, but he still has his moisture. Where'd you find him?"

"Under rocks."

"Hidden?"

Love shook his head. "Just protected from further damage."

"Strange thing for ambushers to do."

"Yeah," Love said. He had been puzzling over that.

He left the parlor and got on his horse and rode home. He was too tired and too sore to walk home. Now that he'd stopped moving, his feet hurt even more. He dismounted carefully when he got home and removed his boots before he went inside. As he stood on the stoop, he saw a candle move from the upstairs window and down the back stairs. Bless his honey. She came around the side of the sheriff's station wearing a shawl to combat the sudden sundown chill and cast in the flickering orange light from the candle. What he saw first, however, was the look of concern in her eyes. They were not looking into his eyes but at the front of his clothes.

Diana reached him. She set the candle on the street in front of Parmenter's horse, which was still tethered to the hitching post.

"Harry, are you all right?"

He nodded.

"There's blood on your shirt," she said.

"Not mine," he assured her. Still holding her, he told her what happened.

"Why didn't you take the deputy's horse with you instead of walking back?" she asked.

"His animal was tired. I wanted to get right to him in case he was alive," Love told her.

She picked up the candle and took his arm. "Come inside and eat."

Love went with her. The strain of the long walk and the death of Parmenter caught up to him. He surrendered his stout mission-posture to that of a very tired husband who needed food, a warm soak for his feet, and his wife in his arms.

He wondered if the bandits needed the same thing after an attack, or whether they had retired to their cave or aerie to celebrate the destruction of an enemy — not just a ranch hand this time but big game, a sheriff's deputy. The more he had thought about it, the more he wondered if it wasn't a dusting of humanity that had caused them to cover the body with rocks, but the desire to protect it from wolves or bobcats, to make sure it was found.

Not that it mattered. The gang had killed a deputy sheriff. For that and their other crimes they would hang. First, though, they had to be found. With inhospitable and unfamiliar terrain to search, where anyone who encountered an enemy of the white man would be inclined to help him, that would not be an easy task.

# 5

## LEGISLATURE

It was the first time most of the men had met.

In its press for statehood, California elected a governor, Peter H. Barnett, and filled the newly formed California legislature with forty-four elected members of the state assembly and twenty members of the state senate. These individuals met in San Jose and represented the ten districts into which the sprawling territory had been divided. E. Kirby Chamberlain and Alexander W. Hope represented the combined Los Angeles–San Diego districts.

At the first state constitutional convention, the representatives voted to deny the right of indigenous peoples to vote. They wanted to make sure the white population retained control of the region. Justices of the peace were named and dispatched to help enforce uniform laws throughout the territory, though, according to the law, "in no case shall a white man be convicted of any offense upon the testimony of an Indian or Indians." The legislature also voted monies to help in the suppression of rebellious natives, Indians and Mexicans alike.

Of that money, several thousands of dollars were earmarked to pay for men and information to find the outlaw band that had murdered Deputy Sheriff Timothy Parmenter in a valley near Rancho San Bernardino. Upon the written recommendation of the Los Angeles Sheriff's Department, based upon his distinguished record of command as a field officer under General Kearny, Deputy Sheriff Love was named to head the operation that would "end the lawless activities of these renegades."

Word of the legislature's action had reached Love ten days after Parmenter's murder. It arrived by courier from Los Angeles. The rider was not a deputy but a young Negro. The Los Angeles Sheriff's office had guessed correctly that a non-white would not be accosted.

The appointment was an honor. But before he could undertake the task, Love needed a plan. He had gone back to the valley twice during the intervening period, looking for clues or a trace of the bandits. He had ventured into the foothills, found nothing. He had camped by the murder site overnight, alone, and remained awake the entire time. The outlaws did not come after him nor did he see any trace of them. Neither did anyone else. Even though the deputy foremen kept up their patrols of the ranch outlands, there were no further attacks.

Love began to wonder if the men had moved on, perhaps into Mexico. Not that it mattered. The United States had agreements with Mexico about sovereignty, but California did not. If the killers were there, he would find them. Doing so, however, would require a significant force with experienced and reliable trackers, as well as supplies to keep them in the field.

It required one thing more: an understanding wife. Not once during their relationship had Love concealed his actions from Diana, and he would not start now. She was a soldier's daughter and a peacekeeper's wife. She understood the demands of duty. From the night her husband had returned with Parmenter's body, Diana Love knew that the battle would be taken to the killers, and she knew before the legislature did who would take it there.

The same day he received the message from Los Angeles, Love had already cut in stone what had been buzzing in his ear for days: that an effective pursuit would require at least twelve mounted men and four relay riders for the supply lines. He had decided his field unit should be comprised of ranch hands as well as deputy sheriffs from along the north–south corridor. That would provide a good mix of skills and leadership. When the official sanction arrived, Love hired a Chinaman to ride to the Veehall and Lugo ranches to arrange a meeting with the owners. Love didn't want to make the trip himself in case one or both spreads were being watched. John Lao went out with a wagon load of fake laundry, and he returned two days later with responses from both men. They agreed to meet the deputy sheriff at the Last Stop House. They would play poker at Love's usual table, surrounded by noise, smoke, and familiar faces. Anyone who wasn't known to them or looked at all suspicious would be followed by ranch hands and interrogated.

On the day of the meeting, Love had dinner with his wife, then went to the saloon. The ranchers were already there, drinking California Common — a double-fermented beer invented in northern California a year before. Love had met both men several times and knew them on sight.

Love walked over and pulled a stack of white chips from his lower vest pocket. He set them in two smaller piles beside a thin wad of cash. When the chips ran out, players bought them back with currency.

"You playin' with the state's money?" Lugo asked when Love sat down. The rancher was a dark-skinned man with a barrel chest, pale gray eyes, and black hair that reached past his collar.

The deputy sheriff lit a cigarette and blew smoke. "The idea hadn't occurred to me, Mr. Lugo," he replied.

"That's 'cause you're a lawman, not a businessman," Veehall said.

"Don't businessmen follow the law?" Love asked as he took a deck of cards from another pocket.

"Sure. The law of survival," Veehall said. "You been out here long enough to know how that works."

Love shuffled the cards. "You kill the fox 'fore he can kill your chickens," the deputy sheriff said. "What can you tell me about the fox we're hunting?"

"As much as I can tell y'about the man in the moon," Veehall said. "Nobody who's seen him has lived to tell about it."

"No one on our side, you mean," Lugo said.

"Yeah. Whoever rides with him, they seen him for sure."

"Do you have any idea if these are local people?" Love asked as he dealt.

"We don't keep track of Mud Bricks and Redskins," Veehall replied sharply.

"What's it matter?" Lugo asked.

"These outlaws moved through the area without being seen," Love said. "They knew when Deputy Sheriff Parmenter came to visit. They're gettin' information somehow."

"Some Pechangas got spared a beatin' when the Brick leader put a knife in Trench's back," Veehall said.

"What was the 'beating' about?" Love asked.

"Horse thievin'," Veehall said.

"A crime that may have been committed by the bandits we're lookin' for," Love pointed out.

Veehall shrugged. "Could be. But the Injuns need a reminder every now and then about who runs things."

Love looked at his cards without seeing them. He anted without thinking. He was contemplating the breadth of assistance the Indian tribes in the region could provide to a small band of outlaws. He didn't think a tribe would be foolish enough to give them shelter. That would invite relocation at best, extermination of the warriors and leaders at worst, and hardship for the women and children they left behind. But he had seen a similar arrangement during the war when Mexicans living in California agreed to help the dragoons in exchange for concessions when war was over.

"Have you reminded them of anything since Trench died?" Love asked.

Veehall asked for two cards. "My men in the north valley were murdered by an Injun," he said. "That's what the wounds told us. We sent everyone we had to the Pechangas. Chief Ao-ti's off on a mountain prayin' and his son Kunga was missin'. They said he was at a tribal meeting, but I don't believe anything a Redskin tells me. I asked for the meetin' with Parmenter so's he and his boys could watch the northern lands."

"Why would the chief leave his people to help an outsider, one who ain't even an Injun?" Love asked. The former captain knew a great deal less about Indians than he did about Mexicans. One reason he'd landed this post was because Los Angeles County felt that the defeated, embittered Mexicans would pose a bigger threat to the region, as immigrants and insurrectionists, than the more cooperative Indian population.

"They got a weird code. Someone helps

the tribe, it means the chief's spirit is his till they help him back."

"Who runs the tribe while he's gone?" Love asked.

"His own eldest son, who just don't like white folk."

"What did your men do at the settlement?" Love asked.

Veehall showed a pair of aces and swept the small pot to him. "We took some of their striplings with us. We returned 'em a few days later but kept one — the chief's kin, his sister's son."

Love looked at the rancher with open displeasure.

"Don't give me shit, Deputy. We figured they'd get word to Ao-ti or Kunga and they'd come for him," Veehall said.

"The legislature's new laws don't make kidnapping Redskins legal," Love said tensely.

"You got a better way of findin' out if Kunga killed my boys?"

Love gathered the cards and shuffled. He noticed a Mexican walk in from the moonlit street. Mexicans were allowed to drink here, in a corner section, though Indians were not. The newcomer was wearing white peasant pants and a matching shirt with a dirty tan sarape around his shoulders. He shook off the dust as he entered and went directly to the bartender, who held out his hand. The man placed a coin in it and the bartender motioned him toward the back room.

One of the ranch hands turned to the card table and looked at Veehall.

Veehall looked at Love. "You see that?"

"They got a Negress out back for Mexicans and Injuns. He probably came to visit her."

"From where?" Veehall asked. The gray-haired man looked at Lugo. "That Brick work for you?"

The rancher turned and caught a glimpse of the man as he entered the whore parlor. "Nope."

"Me neither. So where'd he come from? Especially at night."

"They got cheap rooms for Mexicans in the Chinaman's house," Love said as he dealt a fresh hand.

"He was covered with dirt," Lugo said.

"It's windy," Love pointed out.

Veehall made a face, then nodded at the ranch hand. The big cowboy left the bar and entered the back room.

"What're you doin'?" Love asked.

"Our man Rodrigo speaks Brick. He's just gonna talk to him."

"About what?"

"Trench was killed by a Brick. Those people chatter to each other. Maybe he knows something."

Love got up. "You don't hammer everyone to try and get the right one," he said. "It leaves you weak and it ain't accordin' to law. Rodrigo!" he yelled as he moved through the crowd.

"Let him be!" Veehall called after him.

The men at the bar parted to let Love through. This wasn't the way to do an outlaw investigation or prepare for a hunt. Veehall was right about the "chatter," though. Word of brutality would spread quickly. It would strengthen rather than weaken the will of the people to resist. It would give allies to the outlaws instead of informants to the sheriff's department.

Love entered the back room a few paces behind the ranch hand. He had already stopped the young Mexican. They were talking in the narrow corridor, which was lit by a single lamp hanging from the ceiling.

"*¿Qué está haciendo aquí?*" the ranch hand was demanding.

"Leave him be," Love said as he edged around them.

The cowboy looked at the deputy sheriff. "I take instructions from Mr. Veehall," he said.

"You'll take 'em from a jail cell if you touch this boy."

"I wasn't touchin'. I was askin' what he's doin' here."

"What if he asks you the same question?"

"I'll punch 'im in the air hole."

"That's not an answer that helps us," Love said. "We're tryin' to be secret here. Go back into the saloon."

Veehall entered the corridor. "What'd he tell ya, Rigo?"

"Nothing yet, sir. We was just startin' to jaw."

"You were finished," Love said to the man. "We're all goin' back."

"Deputy, didn't you hear what I said back there?" Veehall said. "These Bricks talk to each other."

"That's why we're goin' back."

"He may know something!"

"An' if you scare him, he may make somethin' up just to get away. Worse'n that, you risk turnin' a kid who was here for fun into a telltale."

"If that happens, we turn him into a corpse and leave him like they left our men in the valley," Veehall said.

Love turned and faced the rancher. " 'They' didn't do this. We don't know who did."

"Ain't that why we're here?" Veehall asked.

"We're here to plan, not to fight. You go to battle before the generals are ready and a whole lotta folk won't be comin' home, needlessly."

"We take too long and the same thing can happen," Veehall said. "I'm losin' men out there, Deputy, and so's the sheriff's department. I came to a meeting to make decisions, not to talk."

Love moved closer. He looked squarely in the other man's eyes. "We're fielding the largest force this area's seen since the war," he said. "We don't even have our supplies organized. Now you go back and wait for me, figure out who you can spare for a couple of weeks."

Veehall shook his head. "You're settin' a bad precedent, Deputy. Whatever happens, this Brick's gonna say we were soft."

"He'll say we were fair," Love said. "When we ride out, I'd rather have goodwill at our back instead of extra guns."

Veehall sneered at the Mexican. "I'd rather have more dead Bricks."

The rancher left the corridor and Rodrigo followed him out.

Love looked down at the small, frightened man. "My Mexican's not too good." He grinned. "We always had interpreters. *Usted haga lo que vino aquí a hacer.* Do what you came here for. Scoot. *Vaya a su mujer.* Go and see your woman."

The young man smiled and backed toward a door at the far end of the hallway. He knocked and entered and shut the door — all of it while still facing Love. The deputy sheriff felt bad that the young man had been so frightened.

Love went back to the saloon, oblivious to the grunts and cries coming from the rooms to either side. He knew he had done the right thing sparing the man a beating or worse, but he wasn't sure he had done the best thing. Veehall was right about one thing. During the war, Mexican soldiers and their Indian allies respected strength. They took advantage of apparent weakness. The key was to make sure it was only "apparent" and not "real."

Veehall and Lugo were still at the table, though Rodrigo was nowhere to be seen. The deputy did not ask about him. As long as the ranch hand didn't do anything stupid, Love didn't care where he was. He would watch the bar himself, as he did most nights. As he watched, he played cards and talked to the ranchers about manpower and horses, about what supplies they could provide. He intended to move his posse to the west, simultaneously pushing up through the valley and through the mountains to a point outside Los Angeles that was already being patrolled by deputy sheriffs up there. The idea was to catch the bandits between them.

The ranchers were mostly silent until the three-hour meeting was nearly ended. That was when Veehall pocketed his winnings — Luge had broken even, Love had lost again — and looked at the sheriff.

"I don't hang with what you're doing," the rancher said. "Deputy Sheriff Parmenter agreed that the best way to deal with these vermin is to crush 'em all, Brick and Injun alike. Whether they did anything or not, they're always gonna side with those who are against us."

Love couldn't dispute that. But he also couldn't prove it. And in the America for which he had just fought a bloody war, that mattered.

"Whatever the outlaws do, we will not become like them," Love said. "Not while I'm deputy sheriff and leading this posse." He leaned on the table and glared at both men. "And gentlemen — if you're gonna try and have me replaced, don't go round my back to do it. Tell me to my face."

Lugo shook his head. "It's your war,

Deputy. I just want it over."

Love looked at Veehall. "Sir?"

"I'm with Lugo. We'll provide our share of the manpower. As long as this thing goes our way, you're leadin' the team."

Love rose. "Thank you. I appreciate your input and your honesty."

"But Deputy?" Veehall said. "It's been quiet since the deputy's murder. If I lose more men, we're gonna have to have ourselves a new talk."

"If you lose more men, Mr. Veehall, just make sure it's not 'cause of something they did."

The deputy sheriff excused himself and stepped outside. A strong wind was coming from the west. Facing east, he rolled another cigarette and lit it. He stepped into the alley and smoked in windless shadow, the smoke curling away behind him. White moonlight turned the street the color of ash. He preferred blackness; somehow it didn't look quite so dead.

As he smoked, he watched Veehall and Lugo leave to go to the rooming house down the road. There was probably enough light to ride home, but they were probably tired — and concerned about the outlaws. They walked together, rivals in business but united by a common enemy. Love wasn't sure he could trust them to leave the up-coming track-down in his hands. But there was also nothing he could do about that, other than to perform his duties as best as he could.

When he finished the smoke, Love returned to the saloon. There was a different world just over the horizon — literally, to the north, in Sacramento — with new laws and more people who wouldn't like them for one reason or another. He was sworn to enforce those laws. That job came with the pension and free burial.

Love stepped to the bar. He was looking forward to talking with the men, possibly breaking up a brawl or dragging a drunk to jail.

The kind of simple, one-man operation he had ironically left the dragoons to find.

# 6
## ALLIANCES

Joaquin listened at the door until he was sure the men were gone. Polly Bailey sat on the edge of the thin, sagging bed and watched him by the dull light of a single candle. He had never met the runaway daughter of a slave before tonight. All of their communications had been through Mexican members of his growing band.

"I think that was Mr. Veehall out there," she whispered in broken Spanish.

"I'm sure it was," Joaquin replied. "The deputy spoke differently to him than he spoke to the other man. And the Pechanga said the ranch chiefs would have to hold a powwow sometime."

Joaquin walked toward the bed. He saw fear but hope in her round face. It was encouraging to know that so much had happened without his participation. There were the tribesmen who watched the ranches and used runners and mirrors to inform Kunga of the whereabouts of the cowhands. There were the Mexican immigrants they escorted through the valley who told them of a woman recently bought from a barkeep in Missouri and forced to work here. Joaquin had learned there was enormous strength in a union of the oppressed. Their ears were invisible and their eyes far-reaching. Every soul that was rescued added to what Joaquin and his band could hear and see.

Polly's room did not have a window. When he was sure the corridor was clear, he took her by the hand and led her to the window in the back. She was wearing everything she owned: her clothes, a locket her mother had given her, and a small purse tied about her waist with a silk ribbon. It contained the few coins the saloon owner allowed her to keep. She was expected to use them to buy perfumes and powders to make her more appealing to her clients.

Joaquin climbed through the window, then helped her out. Beyond them was a field that had been trimmed of grasses to prevent wildfires from coming up to the structure. Moon glow glinted from the broken bottles and empty casks that had been tossed there by the owner. Just a few steps to the west, mice moved through a compost pile that smelled of white man: fat and bones from beef mixed with discarded tobacco. In Joaquin's band, fat was mixed with meat and placed in sun-dried sinew to form *salchicha,* a long-lasting sausage.

They moved low and silently along the backs of the structures. The buildings cast shadows that helped to hide their movements. Polly's hand in his, Joaquin led her toward the Chinaman's house. Though these people were looked down upon by the whites, they had not taken up Joaquin's cause. They were content to live separately and look after their own, yet they were also happy to provide services for those who could pay. Though they were an overwhelming minority here, with strange clothes and a stranger tongue, they insisted that they were a golden race with more members than all the other races combined. Joaquin didn't know if this were so, but it gave the Chinamen pride and confidence he found inspiring.

Kunga had instructed his tribesmen to pay the house owner, Hong Woo, for the use of a room that would remain unoccupied for much of the day. Joaquin had decided to make the rescue himself. He had not been to this town and wanted to see what the people were like, in particular the deputy sheriff. He had watched him during the day and followed him into the saloon. Harry Love seemed both rational and cautious. That made him a dangerous adversary. Unlike the ranchers, he would not be goaded into careless maneuvers. Not that the cowboys had been active lately. Their patrols were quick and they posted sentries at their campsites. Fires burned all night. They were afraid. They had also been so preoccupied with their safety that they had stopped bothering the small parties of immigrants who moved through the land.

Yet Joaquin did not imagine that anything would change if he and his band moved on. In time the cowboys would forget the danger, or their lust and violence would overcome their judgment. For that reason he must continue to grow his group of spies and warriors. If the rumors he heard from travelers were true, law was coming to California. Hopefully, that would embrace all men who dwelt here.

Joaquin went to his room at the Chinaman's house. He had left his whip and knife there. He also had a change of clothes for Polly, something Donato San Julian had bought earlier. The girl had been wearing a simple floral pattern dress when he had seen her. She had on torn undergarments; they had been ripped by an eager client weeks before. Only Joaquin's arm and a blanket she took from the room had protected her from the cold night wind.

Joaquin had left Libertad hidden in a grove outside of town. No one who saw the horse, who might recognize it as once having belonged to a Veehall hand, would connect it to Joaquin. They would go to Libertad in the small hours of the night, when even the drunks were asleep.

Joaquin felt nothing about being alone in the room with this woman until she asked if he would hold her the way he did when they were walking in the cold darkness behind the buildings. He sat himself beside her, his arm around her slender shoulders. Polly smelled different than Juanita had. She felt different too. Bonier, with a way of gently shifting her shoulder up and down that was both hungry and giving. Then her cheek was against his.

"No man has ever done for me what you did," she said softly, struggling to express herself in Spanish.

"I hope no man has to do so again," he replied.

"I have never been held this way either, except by my mama," she added. "It's nice."

Joaquin held her a little closer. He had not thought about women since Juanita's death, and this was not the time or place to act on what he was thinking now. But it felt nice to be close, to be appreciated. They sat that way for a while. At one point Polly's breathing became so slow Joaquin wondered if she were asleep. He didn't move for fear of disturbing her.

Finally, with the young woman rested and welcome silence from the streets, it was time to go. Joaquin had paid the barkeep in Pechanga silver for a full night with the woman so they wouldn't miss her until the morning. With his whip and knife tucked in a canvas bag, and Polly wearing a shawl over her head, Joaquin walked her from the first-floor room to the street. On the way out, the small, middle-aged Hong Woo stopped the man.

"I believe you are the man the whites speak of, the Devil. Only he would have the courage to do this," the Chinaman said in perfect Spanish.

"Thank you for your hospitality," Joaquin replied.

"Your selfless acts bring honor upon us all," Hong Woo told him, bowing his head and putting his fist in his open hand.

Joaquin thanked him again and led Polly outside.

It was quiet and very windy. The sinking

moon threw a long, long shadow across the dirt road as they made their way into the valley. As soon as they were outside, he slid the knife sheath onto his belt but left the whip in the canvas bag. He threw it over his shoulder.

Three shadows joined their own. Joaquin noticed them at once, though he didn't know whether they were following the couple or not. It was only when one of them called out that he knew he and Polly would not get away as easily as he had hoped.

"I recognized your outfit from the Pechanga tribe, you bastard," a voice said. The speaker had to shout to be heard over the wind.

Joaquin leaned toward Polly. "What did he say?"

She told him.

The young Mexican continued walking with his arm around the woman. "My horse is tethered in a grove a half mile outside of —"

"You killed Trench, you son of a bitch. Turn around or I'll shoot you in the back!" the man yelled.

Polly translated, then added, "I have seen that man at the bar. He is a pig."

"Go into the valley," Joaquin said to her.

"They'll catch me and take me back. I'd

rather be with you."

Joaquin did not have time to argue. He faced the men, his back to the whore who wanted to be free. Three burly silhouettes were framed against the moonlight. All of them held guns.

"Get the rope from my horse. We'll hang this killer, then hang the Chink who let him stay at his house," the man said to one of his companions. "Then we'll take the nigress back to her boss and let him buy us a few rounds for puttin' the bitch back on her back."

One of the men ran back down the street to where a row of horses were tethered to a post. Joaquin looked around. He was angry that he hadn't noticed the animals. There were probably Veehall markings on the saddle. He should have allowed for the possibility that the man in the saloon had been at the Pechanga settlement the day he saved the life of the chief.

The man's partner returned with a rope. The man spoke again. When he was finished Polly translated.

"They say you must go with them or they will shoot us *both*," Polly told him. "What do we do?"

"Listen to me. I'm going to run to the left and take cover in the blacksmith's shop,"

Joaquin said. "There is an alley to your right. Go there and stay in the shadows. Don't stop until you are deep in the valley. You know where my horse is."

"We will never make it," she said anxiously.

"Do you want to go back?" Joaquin asked.

"No."

The man held the rope high. "Come over here, Brick, and do yer penance for murder!"

A new shadow appeared on the street, behind the men. "There better be a reason I'm woken up, Rodrigo," Deputy Sheriff Love said.

The ranch hands on the end turned. The man in the middle continued to look ahead.

"That Brick from the saloon is the one who kilt Trench," Rodrigo told him. "We gonna let him air-dance fer that and fer tryin' to steal Polly from her rightful place of indentures."

"The man who killed Trench was wearing a mask," the deputy said. "How do you know this is the same man?"

"I seed his eyes back there," the ranch hand said. "I just placed 'em."

"I'm guessin' the whiskey you drunk tonight makes li'l Polly look like Queen Victoria too," Love said.

"You a nigress lover too now, Love?" Rodrigo demanded.

"Not that it's yer business, but I don't love any but my wife," the deputy replied. "Far as the rest of you, all I care is that you keep the peace. You want to accuse this boy of somethin' I'll hear ya. But you rememberin' his eyes ain't gonna put him in jail for murder."

"It's more'n that," Rodrigo said. "He's standin' a certain way. I know how my people walk. He's got fire in him."

Lights were being lit in the windows surrounding the encounter. Polly told Joaquin what was happening. He was glad, at least, that he had left Rawth's whip in the canvas sack.

"None o' that's proof, Rodrigo," Love said.

"I don't need proof. I'm tellin' ya, Deputy, this is the *maldito* killer you're lookin' fer!"

"Put the guns away," Love repeated.

"You are makin' a mistake. And yer lettin' him get off with that bitch — an' the Chinks are involved, too."

"You are wrong!" Polly shouted. "He is staying at the Chinaman's house. We were just taking a walk."

"Who is he and where did he get money to stay at the Chinese place?" Love asked.

Polly translated. Joaquin told her, "Tell him I won at cards in the north and had some money to spend. Tell him I am on my way home to Mexico."

The woman repeated what he had said.

"Polly, why don't you get yerself to the saloon and tell this man to go back to his room," Love said.

She hesitated. "He needs someone to tell him what you say," she said.

"Excuse me!" The owner of the Chinese house had come out into the street. He walked over to Love. "Deputy Love, this boy is speaking the truth," Hong Woo told him. "He came to rest and has stayed to the end of his purse. That is why he went to whore, to rest longer."

Polly told Joaquin what the Chinaman had said. The young man quietly blessed this good man for involving himself, for finding a reason to send him out into the safety of the night.

"Deputy, you can't believe this Chink!" Rodrigo shouted.

"If it's true, it don't matter who said it," Love replied.

"Nobody goes to a whore's room to *sleep!*"

"People got different ways about them," Love said. "Hong Woo, had you ever seen

229

this man before today?"

"Never before this morning, sir, when he came to rest with us," the Chinaman assured him.

The sheriff nodded once, but seemed reluctant to let Joaquin go. "What have you got in the bag?"

"My belongings," Joaquin replied through Polly. "I was going to spend the night in the valley."

"It's late. Yer welcome to spend it in our jail cell," Love said. "I won't lock the door unless you want it so."

Joaquin looked at the ranchers. "So I can die from a gunshot or in a fire? Thank you, sir, but I will take my chances under the skies." He waited a moment, then added, "Unless you are insisting. I do not wish to disobey the law."

"I respect that and you've broken none that I can see." Love looked at Polly and cocked his head toward the saloon. "Go now."

The woman looked at Joaquin. The lights that had come on in the windows enabled him to see the young woman clearly. There was gratitude in her eyes and relief that she wasn't going to be shot to death. But there was also sadness. The young woman had been just a short walk from freedom.

*"El excusado de afuera,"* Joaquin said in a loud whisper. *"Esté allí al amancer."*

The pretty young woman smiled bravely at Joaquin, then looked away. She strode slowly back down the street, past the ranchers. The three cowboys looked at her ominously.

"Sheriff, yer makin' a tragic *mistake,*" Rodrigo insisted as he looked back at Joaquin. "This bloody devil is the man we want."

"You got the proof, I got the eyes."

"I'll whup a confession outta him."

"I personally frown on that and the law forbids it. Now put yer gun away or you'll be the one occupyin' a cell tonight," Love said. When Rodrigo failed to move, the deputy sheriff cocked his gun and added. "Or ya can face me and take yer chances. Yer choice, Rodrigo."

The two other men on the side holstered their firearms and stepped aside. Rodrigo continued to point his gun at the young Mexican.

"Do what the deputy says, Rigo!" a voice yelled from down the street. "We're not lawbreakers."

The ranch hand looked back as Veehall walked toward him. "Mr. Veehall, I got a feelin' about this."

"It's not your battle!" the rancher shouted.

"I say it is. The souls o' my dead brothers say it is. I know cowards and this man ain't one. I can smell it."

"Bunk down and let this be or you're fired, all of you."

"Dead is bad, Rigo, but we don't want to be run out like Bricks," one of the other ranch hands urged.

Rodrigo stuffed his gun in its well-worn holster. He glared at Joaquin. "This will be my battle."

The Veehall cowboys left. Joaquin found it strange to hear them so silent. Usually men like these three arrived loudly with vows to drink and departed with a celebration of how drunk they were. Their boss reached Love's side as Polly passed them going the other way. It hurt Joaquin to see her go. Had he died on the mountainside those many weeks ago, and his wife survived, this girl could have been his Juanita. Since Donato San Julian had first heard of her a week before, since he had first made contact with her by pretending to be a customer, the men had worked to get her out. She told them when she was usually free, they had waited for a full moon, and the Pechanga had provided the silver to get Joaquin into the room.

All of it for nothing.

Love left the others and walked closer. He stopped a few paces from Joaquin. His weapon was still drawn. "You said you was goin'," the deputy sheriff told him. He made a brushing motion with his hand. "Adios."

The moon had nearly set and the men stood facing one another in the darkness. Veehall went back to the hotel and Polly was nearly at the saloon.

Joaquin looked at the deputy's impassive expression for a moment longer. This man was not like the poor soul they had killed in the valley. He was not reckless. If the man had fear, it did not express itself as aggression.

The young Mexican turned and started to walk away.

"Wait," Love said suddenly.

Joaquin stopped as the deputy walked over. He looked back but didn't turn. Love's gun was still drawn as he reached for the young man's knife. He drew it from the sheath and inspected the hilt.

"Beads," he said. "You didn't take that off no ranch hand."

Joaquin had no idea what the deputy had just said. But his tone was not threatening.

Love slipped the knife back into the sheath. He looked at the canvas bag. "You don't own very much, do ya?"

Joaquin shrugged and shook his head, indicating that he didn't understand. But the meeting was not about understanding with words. It gave Love a chance to look into the man's eyes up close. Joaquin could see the deputy studying him the way a farmer eyed a cow before buying it. The body could be firm, but the eyes told you whether or not it was healthy.

"I wonder," the deputy said thoughtfully. "You look fearful but you don't *seem* like y'are."

Joaquin smiled weakly at whatever the deputy had just said. He was trying to be respectful, an immigrant just passing through the region. A man who just wanted to be allowed to go on his way.

"Well, son, I can't put people in jail on a drunk man's say-so," the deputy said. "I just hope I don't see you again." Holstering his own gun, Love went back to the sheriff's office.

Joaquin didn't linger. He headed out to the valley as he said he would. He moved quickly in the deepening darkness of the night. He was absorbed by his thoughts and feelings as he walked from the encounter. His heart was filled with pride over the courage of Hong Woo, who had given weight to Joaquin's story. It was heavy with disappointment for Polly, and he hoped she would not give up hope. But mostly it was aflame with rage at how aggressively his own countryman Rodrigo had turned on him. Joaquin also found himself wondering what it was that had convinced Rodrigo he was the outlaw they sought. The deputy was correct: Rodrigo had seen him when he was masked. Was Rodrigo just a chained dog barking for attention or was there a quality about Joaquin that a man could sense? If so, Joaquin had to be careful. He had been in the field for many weeks. It was important to be able to make contact with good and self-sacrificing souls, to forge bonds and draw inspiration from them. But not if he somehow revealed himself to the enemy.

There were howls from the valley floor and the crunch of brittle roots and dead grasses. Surrounded by far more enemies than by friends, Joaquin Murrieta felt very much alone.

He also felt beaten — and cheated. He had been chased from a region his people had inhabited long before the whites knew where it was. He had been driven away from a woman who wanted to be with him.

This was a region that hoped to be a state of the American Union?

His brain joined his gut in resenting what

had just occurred. It wasn't right.
They had to learn that.

# 7
# DAWN

Polly was tired and emotionally frayed when she returned to her room. She had only just met that man and had given all her trust to him. She did not blame him for what had happened, but it was a devastating blow.

And yet — for a few minutes, at least, she felt like a bird soaring where she wanted, when she wanted. She hadn't been listening for the dreaded knock on the door of her small room that meant a new customer had come, someone who hadn't bathed in weeks and reeked of tobacco and liquor. She didn't have to fight with a man to put on the rubber skin that kept her from having children, or take him in her mouth to make sure the encounter didn't get that far. Many of them were so drunk they could never finish what they started anyway, and settled for being held and stroked until their time was up. She felt less violated when the traveling doctor visited each Monday morning to make sure none of the girls had acquired bugs or warts or anything else that could put the back room out of business. Now and then he used long, sharp instruments to terminate babies that had taken root in one or more of the girls.

For a few precious moments on a night filled with hope, those thoughts had been far, far away.

Polly lit a candle and lay facedown on her bed and cried, but not for long. She barely heard the shuffling of boots in the hallway, but nearly cried out when she heard the hard knuckle-rap of a customer.

She said she would be right there in Spanish and English. She looked at herself in the mirror. She quickly dragged a brush through her hair and sprayed perfume on her neck. With smiling eyes, she wondered if it might be her savior returned. Perhaps the deputy sheriff had told the barkeep, Mr. Haveles, that the young man should stay with her until it were light enough to travel.

She opened the door and her eyes immediately lost their luster. Rodrigo and his two companions were standing outside her room.

"We paid for the rest of the night," Rodrigo said.

"Hope it's better'n lyin' on dirt," one of

the others said.

The men moved in, filling the small room with their large frames and eager smiles. They surrounded Polly, who tried not to be intimidated and asked which of the men wanted to go first.

The man standing to her left was playing with a kerchief. The man behind her was running his hands along her bare upper arms. Rodrigo stood in front of her, his arms crossed. He reached out and began unbuttoning the front of her dress. His thick fingers had no trouble undoing the buttons. The holes were so large they slid out easily. He unbuttoned it to her waist, revealing a white chemise. He dropped the top of the dress from her shoulders and unlaced the single drawstring at the top of the undergarment. He tugged it down. The room was cold and her skin tightened with goose flesh. Foul as most of her customers were, they were warm and held her close. The ranch hand looked at her breasts in the candlelight. He bent and rubbed his stubbled left cheek against her left nipple. She winced but did not recoil. He moved to the other breast and rubbed it hard before stepping back.

"Did ya like what I just did?" he asked.

"I — I do not enjoy pain," she replied. "I

know one of the girls who —"

"Hush," he said. He rested his hands on her bare shoulders. She was shivering as much from fear now as from cold. He leaned close to her ear.

"Sweetheart, you're gonna have a lotta pain unless you tell us who you was with out there," Rodrigo whispered. "Tell us what ya know and we'll leave."

Polly was trembling openly. The man behind her walked closer. He put his arms around her chest and placed his rough hands over her breasts. He hugged her tightly to him, her arms pinned. The woman started to sob. She shook her head.

"I don't know him, I swear," she said.

Rodrigo stepped back. He sneered and undid the rest of the buttons on Polly's poor dress. It dropped to the floor. He gave the chemise a tug and it fell as well. She was standing naked, save for the lace boots buried beneath her clothes. The ranch hand put the palm of his right hand to her cheek, then along her jaw, then clutched her throat and squeezed hard. She opened her mouth to suck down air. When she did the man on the left pushed his kerchief in her mouth. At the same time the ranch hand behind Polly put her in a bear hug. Breathing was difficult with her chest constricted. The woman didn't waste air by screaming.

Rodrigo released her. "Who was he?"

The woman shook her head quickly. Rodrigo punched her hard in her small, slender belly. Polly doubled over as the man behind relaxed his grip and she coughed into the gag.

"Who was he?" Rodrigo demanded.

Still bent over, Polly shook her head again. The man on the left grabbed her hair and pulled her erect. Rodrigo snarled and punched her again. She screamed into the kerchief; her cry was no different from the groans coming from the adjoining rooms. The man was still holding her hair. Her eyes were big and tears streamed from the corners. She tasted the meal she had eaten earlier that afternoon.

Rodrigo punched her a third time. The food came up and the rancher on the left removed the kerchief so she could vomit. She managed to reach the chamber pot at her bedside. When she was finished she fell to her knees. The men picked her up and crammed the kerchief back in her mouth.

"Who is he?" Rodrigo asked as they turned her toward his leering eyes.

She meant to shake her head, but it just sat there. She was too weak. If the man weren't holding her, she would fall.

"We paid two bits each," Rodrigo said. "We got you for three hours, whore. You can use those hours to sleep or you can use 'em to get beat up where it don't show. It's your choice, nigger."

Polly put her tongue behind the kerchief and tried to push the gag out. It clung to the side of her mouth, but she was able to draw a short breath and say, "I don't . . . know him."

Rodrigo pushed the kerchief back into her mouth and stepped away. "Hold her on the bed," he said.

The men dragged her backward. Polly was too weak to fight them. She was too drained to cry out. She hoped that they were going to use her and leave. That, at least, was a pain she knew.

The men pulled her down, on her back.

"Flip 'er over," Rodrigo said.

Polly was flopped onto her belly. She had been in this place too. She would survive. A moment later she felt something cold and hard enter her. Her brain told her what it must be, though she didn't want to believe it. She winced as a metal piece raked along her insides.

Rodrigo leaned over her back as the other men laughed.

"We ain't gonna ruin your business end,

but we are gonna make it hell for you ta work," he said. She heard a click. "Unless the gun happens ta go off. In that case, you gonna pop like nobody ever popped before. All ya gotta do is tell us who that son of a bitch was an' I'll stop."

Polly didn't know if the gun was loaded. She couldn't even think about that: The raised gunsight at the front of the barrel cut her soft flesh and continued to dig at it. The awful burning grew quickly. She tried to close her legs, to shut the barrel out, but the men wouldn't allow it.

"Gimme what I want and this is over," Rodrigo said. He turned the gun around so the sight was on the bottom now. There was a moment of relief, and then fresh agony as he resumed his motion.

Polly thought of the man who had saved her, his angry eyes but his careful, gentle hands. If she told Rodrigo what he wanted to know, they would get the sheriff, track him, and hang him. Not only would he die, but the despair of others like herself would go unheard. She cried into the kerchief. This searing anguish caused her to writhe like a hare in the teeth of a fox. But it would be far worse to live with the pain of betraying Joaquin and those he might help.

Then she felt blood running freely down

her legs. One of the men pulled her chemise back up her leg to wipe it from her thighs. After a time Rodrigo removed the gun and the garment was pushed into her body. The men flipped her over. The single sheet was soaked with her perspiration. Rodrigo pulled the kerchief from her mouth and looked down at her. She cried despite her efforts to control herself.

"You got anything to say?" he asked. "We got a lot more time an' I'm bettin' you have a lot more tears."

Polly lay there. She looked past him. Her buttocks hurt from just the pressure of her body resting upon them. The cloth they used to stop the bleeding irritated the wound the man had inflicted.

Rodrigo snickered and shoved the barrel in her mouth. She gagged, but there was nothing left to vomit.

"Clean it," he ordered.

Polly did as she was told. The men continued to laugh. When the barrel was clean, Rodrigo slipped it back in the holster.

"We know yer mouth is workin'," he said to the woman. "Let's see if it got any smarter. Who was that man?"

"A . . . customer," she replied, spitting weakly from the side of her mouth.

Rodrigo nodded. "Take off her boots and

hold her legs," he instructed.

The men moved quickly. Polly was too weak to resist. When they were set, Rodrigo took the candle from the wall-mounted holder. He brought it close to the bottom of her left foot. The heat gave her strength, but she was unable to wrest her leg from under the weight of the man holding it.

"Can't sit . . . can't walk," Rodrigo said. "What good will you be?"

He moved the open flame closer to her toes. She screamed into the cloth as the fire scorched her flesh.

"You gonna talk or burn?" the ranch hand asked.

Polly screamed until her mind had become the fire and there was nothing else, not even her ravaged insides. She screamed until her throat was bloody, her leg weak as the cloth beneath it.

Rodrigo backed away, but the pain continued.

"That was just the heat." He laughed. "No bubblin' flesh. We don't want the sheriff thinkin' we hurt ya. But I *will* have the name of that murderer you was with. His name and where he was gonna take you."

"To freedom," said a voice from behind.

The men had been too busy laughing at the muffled cries of their victim to hear the door being opened. A masked man was standing there. Polly knew him at once, not from his clothes and posture, but from the eyes she saw above the bloody mask. He no longer held a canvas bag, only a whip. He stood motionless, but just for a moment. The lash snaked out and hit the candle, knocking it to the bed. The thin blanket caught fire as the masked man charged into the room. Rodrigo had started to rise. The newcomer hit the cowboy's chin with the flat of his palm, snapping his head back and knocking him onto the burning bed. The masked man hit another ranch hand with the bottom of the whip handle while at the same time he yanked the flaming cover away from the bed and threw it over the third man.

The three men were shouting. The masked man moved quickly.

He ducked his shoulder under the arm of the wounded girl while he coiled his whip and hung it from his sash. "Be strong," he said in Spanish.

Polly was able to pull herself up with the masked man's help. He drew his bead-handled knife and backed toward the door, half-carrying her as he watched the men. One of the ranchers was on fire and the others were too busy trying to swat out the blaze to worry about the masked man. Reaching the door of the tiny room, he scooped the woman in his arms and ran toward the window at the far end of the corridor. He had obviously come in that way and had left it open. She was just beginning to hear voices coming toward them from the main area of the saloon.

The masked man passed Polly through the window. She leaned against the outside wall, but her burned foot and weakened legs couldn't support her and she dropped to the mud. Her savior swung out and lifted her up. The pain was still everywhere in her body, but the cool air felt good.

A horse was standing on ground that had gone solid in the long, cool night. The man drew a blanket from the back of the animal and wrapped it around the naked woman. She held it to her. The brisk night invigorated her slightly, enough so that she was able to stand on her own while the masked man jumped onto the animal's back. He pulled her up behind him. It hurt to straddle the horse's back. The chemise had fallen from between her legs and Polly was bleeding again. The ride was going to be very difficult. But she pressed her lips together so she wouldn't cry out and held tightly to the man's waist to keep from falling off.

To their left, down the corridor, Polly could see the shadow from the dancing orange glow of the flames. As the masked man turned the horse around, she heard voices moving toward the whores' rooms. There were shouts when people reached her room. She heard women screaming as they ran from the blaze. Men were yelling for water from the saloon. The rooms were made of thin, dry wood, but the fire had been small. Polly hoped it would be extinguished quickly. She didn't want to see the girls put out of work. The other whores had always been kind to her. In nineteen years on this earth she had never experienced prejudice among the lowborn.

Polly cried into the masked man's back, partly from pain and partly from relief. She clutched him tightly as he guided the animal through the backyards they had negotiated not long before. The horse breathed heavily and its hooves clopped hard on the sections of solid earth where the masked man led it. Though it was dark, the rider had obviously walked this area before and knew how to get to the main street. Once there, he swung the horse about and thundered toward the valley where she had last seen him, bent and defeated.

Or so she had imagined.

Before he left he had told her to meet him at the outhouse at dawn. She did not know what had driven him to take this risk now. Perhaps he feared she would be subjected to the very sort of humiliation and interrogation she had endured. That would not surprise her. He seemed to know what was basest in men.

She looked back and saw the smallest orange glow in the windows of the Last Stop House. A bucket brigade was bringing water from a well in front of the blacksmith's shop. It looked as though the fire would be extinguished.

Polly also saw a light go on in the sheriff's office. Deputy Love ran out. In the faint firelight she saw him look from the burning building toward the valley. She couldn't tell whether he saw them or not. It probably didn't matter. The men would report what had happened and the deputy would pursue them — with a posse composed of very willing ranch hands and other citizens. Except for the fear of wildfires, she could imagine them setting out at once, by torchlight.

That didn't happen. Nothing pursued them but the wind. The fire in the village quickly became a pale smudge on the horizon, like a setting sun. As it vanished behind the foothills, the masked man slowed to give his horse a rest. He stayed on what seemed to be a straight course until the first light of dawn began to brighten the sky behind the eastern slopes. Then he turned the animal to the north and galloped toward the nearby foothills. He dismounted when they reached the grassy lower peaks and helped Polly slide forward and hold the horse's mane. Then he led the animal up a narrow pass. The climb was steep but the rocks did not retain hoofprints. The man obviously knew where he was going.

For the first time in years, since strange rough men started coming into her bedroom, Polly felt safe. Now that her thoughts were her own, not shared with pain, she felt pride in not having given those men what they demanded. She was surprised at how quickly their own cries of fear had erased the laughs and the evil, confident whisper of Rodrigo as they tortured her.

She leaned forward as far as she could to reduce the thumping of the horse's back against her own. As the minutes passed Polly began to feel faint, both from the ruthless abuse she had suffered and the loss of blood. She remembered looking out at the valley as sunlight fell on the ground nearest her first, the golden sheen growing as the sun shortened the shadows of the mountains. She saw a family of deer around a dawn-ruddied pool of water, the fawns drinking and the mother sipping but watchful. Polly smiled as they finished and jumped toward the foothills in odd, lopsided bounds.

*Perhaps all of life is like that,* she thought. Even her own. A stop here, a sidewards leap there, and then a new direction revealed itself.

She was wondering about her own new direction as the world swirled black and her eyes shut.

# 8
## PLANS

Deputy Sheriff Love watched the rider vanish into the darkness, then ran to the Last Stop House. He slid inside the doorway and stood there with his neckerchief over his mouth. The fire had been extinguished, but a tester of pale gray smoke crawled from the backroom corridor. It mixed with the already dusty air to produce a thick chalky cloud that reached from floor to ceiling.

Owner Pete Haveles — a humorless Boston transplant — was busy yelling at his girls to get back into their rooms and out of the way while trying to keep the departing fire bucket brigade away from the bar. Swinging pails and frightened patrons had already broken several bottles that had been sitting on the counter. One table had been overturned in the panic, the leg snapped. Love didn't feel bad for the Boston transplant. Haveles made plenty of profit from the vices of the locals. Besides, Love did not have time to concern himself with the mousy little mound of greed. His attention was full of a renegade in the field and angry locals.

Edison Veehall had also returned to the saloon. He arrived shortly before Love, and stood near the exit as his men emerged from the smoky corridor. They staggered outside, followed by their employer and the deputy sheriff.

"What happened?" Love demanded. He shook out his neckerchief. Particles of ash drifted away.

"Witch tried to scorch us," Rodrigo coughed. "We paid for her — she didn't want to be with us and lit the fire."

"What about the rider?" Veehall pressed.

"He was waitin'," Rodrigo said.

"Where?" Love asked.

"Inside, in the hall." Rodrigo glared at the deputy. "Same bastard I told ya about, the one you let walk outta here. Only now he had his mask back."

"Then how do you know it was the same man?"

"Jesus, Deputy. He was wearin' the same clothes, had that cut-yer-heart-out look in his eyes."

"What clothes was he wearin'?" Love asked.

Rodrigo stared at him. "Deputy, it was

dark and then there was the fire. He was wearin' the clothes that migrants wear."

"So — it could've been anyone."

Veehall shifted impatiently. "We don't need to talk about this. We need to organize the men and ride after the damn killer."

"That's not how we're gonna do this," Love said.

"He hasn't got much of a jump on us —"

"But he does *have* one," Love said. "He could be on his way up the mountainside by now. Wherever he is, we don't know whether he's got men out there watchin' his flank."

"His arse be damned, I want him!" Veehall shouted.

"So do I," Love replied. "But we don't chase him, we track him. That's how you keep from gettin' picked off."

"That's yellow talkin', Deputy," Veehall snarled. He instructed one of the men to ride back to the ranch for reinforcements. He told Rodrigo and the other man to saddle up. He regarded Love. "You let that kid walk away once. We're not lettin' that happen again."

"Mr. Veehall, you ain't been deputized. And you still don't know it's the same kid."

*"What?"*

"Deputy, all I know is that's the man what

kidnapped my nigger," Pete Haveles said. The saloon owner had been standing in the doorway since the last of the fire brigade left. He hurried over. "I want her back to stand trial for fire-startin' and work off the damage. If you can't get her, you need to step aside."

"I'll get them both for questioning," Love said. "But we don't run off without supplies or proper arms."

"I'll have all the supplies and arms I need to catch that Brick, but only if we leave now," Veehall said. "Don't worry, Deputy. I'll bring him back alive if I can so you can try him and hang him."

Veehall turned to go. Love grabbed his shoulder.

The rancher spun angrily on the deputy. "You crazy, Harry?"

"I'm warnin' you not to do this," Love said.

"You're boring me, Deputy." Veehall wrenched his arm away.

"I'm tryin' to educate ya, Mr. Veehall," Love said evenly. "Ya got two perils. One is ambush. The kidnapper probably knows that terrain better'n us and he may have allies."

"I got guns. I ain't worried. What's the second 'peril'?"

"Me," Love told him. "You pick off the wrong man, maybe someone who's just out there helpin' the nigress or givin' her water, someone who had nothin' to do with this, an' I'll come after you."

"You try an' I'll have your badge on my trophy wall," Veehall warned, poking the sheriff hard in the chest. "Nobody who helps that nigger or her Brick-nigger bandit is innocent."

"That's what I'm talkin' about, Mr. Veehall. Anger's runnin' this chase, not good sense. You leave it to me and we'll get 'im."

"I leave it to you an' the masked man will be in fuckin' Texas before you enter the valley," the rancher said.

Veehall was finished arguing. Rodrigo and the other ranch hand rode up with their boss's horse. The street was beginning to fill with dogs and stable boys and early risers like the blacksmith and barber. The deputy caught the eye of young Will Eugene, son of the blacksmith. He was an enterprising kid who maintained the best-kept stables in town, behind his father's shop. Will nodded and ran off.

Love didn't know whether Polly had slowed the escape and whether the kidnapper was in danger. He did know that three men were riding into danger. The deputy was tired from a long, sleepless night. But he knew what he had to do to help protect them and to safeguard whoever they might find. He grabbed the reins to Veehall's horse as the rancher mounted.

"You're pushin' me, Deputy," Veehall warned.

"I'm comin' with ya," Love said.

That seemed to take the rancher by surprise. "You just finished tellin' me that's crazy —"

"It is. But you may need an extra gun."

"To join the fight or stop it?" Veehall asked.

"To uphold the law," Love replied. "You ain't got a problem with the law, have you?"

"I ain't got a problem with what's right," Veehall said. "If yer comin', you know where to find us."

Love released the reins and the men rode past in a line, pounding hooves and dust rolling into the westerly wind. The deputy turned and walked to the sheriff's station. He grabbed the saddlebags he kept on hand for unexpected rides. There was jerky, water, and dry socks in the bags along with extra ammunition, maps, pencils, and lined paper for making notes or sending messages back with riders. He didn't bother to wake Diana. The saddlebags sat beside his desk at all times. When his wife came down and saw them gone, she would know that he was too. With the double bags slung over his shoulder, Love walked briskly toward the Eugene Stables. Young Will was just walking his horse around. The deputy kept the stallion in his own modest shed most days. Once or twice a week, though, he left him with the boy for a good grooming. Patronizing the well-liked and ambitious lad also helped to spread good will through the town.

The boy had already saddled the horse and was leading him over. "Here you are, Deputy, sir."

Love gave him two bits. "Thanks."

"You're welcome, sir. And sir?"

Love looked at him as he climbed into the saddle.

"I heard my dad say Miss Polly went a little round the bend last night," the kid said.

"So it's told."

"Dad'd whup me for sayin' this, but she was always nice to me whenever I'd see her at the creek, washin'. She ain't bad. I know it."

"I believe that," the deputy assured him. He smiled. "And I won't tell yer dad we spoke of her."

The deputy spurred the horse gently and rode off after the small tawny cloud, all that was left of the Veehall trio.

Love did not catch up to them immediately. They were riding their animals hard and they would tire quickly. Love did not want to do that. He had learned, chasing Mexicans and their native allies during the war, that many of the tribesmen would run their horses to exhaustion and light a fire under their bellies to get them on their feet. Then they would ride the animals until they died. That was usually enough to put them out of the reach of dragoons who needed their animals for a return trip.

It was early afternoon, when Veehall and his two men stopped by a lake, that Love reached them. Until their rider caught up to them with supplies and more men — probably not until tomorrow — they would have to live off the land.

Love offered them some of his jerky. Rodrigo and the other cowhand accepted. Veehall did not. He used a vine and his shirt to rig a sling. He lowered it into the lake and, on top, scattered a paste made by crushing together insects and the skin from berries. It took him just a few minutes to snag a small bass. He skinned it with a folding knife he carried in his pocket.

"A gift from my wife, for all the nights I used to spend in the field," Veehall told Love as he skinned and gutted the fish on a flat rock. When he was finished, he ate the meat raw, cutting it into tiny slices and stabbing them with his blade. He squatted by the rock as he ate. Veehall's men were sprawled beside the lake. "You stand, I don't sit," Veehall said as he looked up at Love. "We both like to be ready."

"I don't 'like' it," Love said. "It's just good sense."

"You make as good a target lyin' as standin'."

"For a rifle maybe."

"Right. These boys just use primitive weapons," Veehall said.

"If it is that gang, yeah," Love said. "Right now I ain't got enemies I know of who'd be shootin' at me with long guns."

"Deputy, I can't believe yer still takin' the side of the Brick and nigger," Veehall said.

"I ain't the one takin' sides, Mr. Veehall."

"Sure y'are. You want order and statehood as much as any of us, yet you're lookin' after the Brick and his nigress. Either you're for us or against us —"

"That's not the law. That's war," Love said. "Without order nobody got rights, nobody's safe."

Veehall spit out bones. "Well, I felt safe enough till now. But I'm actually glad yer here, Deputy. You know well as I do those two ain't gonna let themselves get took. You'll be a witness to whatever we're forced to do."

Love squinted to the west as something appeared in the foothills. It glowed white in the noonday sun and moved slowly, tentatively. A moment later the two ranch hands saw it. They called to Veehall, whose back was to that side of the valley. He was immediately on his feet with his gun drawn. The figure was only a few hundred yards up the green slope of the foothills.

Leading his horse, Deputy Love went over to meet whoever it was. Veehall followed, his handgun hip-high and pointed ahead. The two ranch hands followed, one with a revolver, the other with his carbine. General Kearny used to warn his men to keep their hands off their guns unless they were going into battle. Otherwise, they might find themselves in one. The more weapons that were in hand, the more likely it was that someone would use one.

After a few moments, Love could tell that the person approaching was a Spanish woman. He held his hands up so she could see they were empty, save for the reins. She too was unarmed.

"Put the gun away," Love told Veehall.

"She may be a distraction. There could be people watching us."

"That's exactly why," Love said.

Veehall continued to hold his weapon. His expression was taut, his posture bent, as though a puma were approaching them and not a woman in a white blouse and matching dress. She wasn't very surefooted among the rocks and used her hands to steady herself as she neared.

"*Señores,* welcome," she said.

"A Brick," Veehall said to Love. "At least she's not an Injun."

"Why?"

"You wouldn't find one out here lest she was up to no good." He still didn't put his gun away.

Love was more interested in why she had said "welcome," as though this were her valley and they were intruders. There was no work here for migrants. All of that was in San Diego, on the Veehall or Lugo spreads, or in Los Angeles.

The woman reached the floor of the valley and approached. She was young, though her clothes were dirty, as though she'd been out here for a while. There were dark brown spots on her dress — mud or blood, Love couldn't be sure.

"Do you speak English?" Love asked.

"I do."

"Who are you?"

"Beatrisa San Julian," she replied.

"I'm Deputy Sheriff Harry Love. What are you doing out here?"

"I care for my cousin Esteban," she said. "Our family was moving through the valley and he was hurt in a fall."

"How many of you are there?"

"Four," she said.

"Why did you come down?" Love asked.

"I came for water," she said. She reached their side and showed them a pouch she was wearing from a sash about her waist.

"Take us to them," Veehall said.

"But why, *señor*?"

" 'Cause we're lookin' for someone an' I want ta make sure yer not hidin' him," Veehall replied.

"I am hiding no one," she said.

The woman seemed a little nervous, which was to be expected. But she was also bold to be approaching four armed men like this, even if one of them was wearing a badge. He couldn't imagine a young woman doing that unless she was very innocent or very sure of herself.

"All right," Love said. "Get your water and go back."

She thanked him and started to go around

the men. Veehall grabbed her arm.

"Deputy, this is horseshit. You believe what she just told you?"

"What I believe is that you should let her go."

"Why?"

*"Do it!"* Love snapped.

Veehall pushed her away. She continued to the lake.

"If she came fer water, she would've waited till we was gone," Love said.

"For once we agree, Deputy. She came to find out what we wanted. Now she knows."

"She already knew that," Love said. "People don't leave town without water or supplies and camp under a hot sun. If she's part of the people you came for, they know they're bein' chased. She's the net to bring you to 'em, but not on your terms."

"You sayin' we should run? We got fire-arms."

"If they're here, they got position," Love said. "Look up at the foothills. Rocks and ledges startin' fifty-some feet above you. The range of a good Injun arrow is more'n triple that. They can pick you off before you know where they are."

"Except that we got a hostage," Veehall pointed out.

"If this is the man from the whorehouse,

he's bettin' I don't let you hold her," Love said.

"Would he be right?"

Love said nothing.

Veehall snickered. "Three guns to one, Deputy. If I want a hostage, I got a hostage."

"One gun can still do a lot of hurt," Love pointed out.

"You were the one who didn't want us out here because it was too dangerous," Veehall said. "Now ya want to deny us an edge."

"A human shield ain't an edge. It's a big banner that says, 'I'm afraid of you.' You got three guns," Love said. He nodded toward the hills. "If the outlaws are up there, they got knives and bows. Take 'em on man-to-man."

"I ain't out here to prove I'm a man but to stop a lawless gang."

"By becomin' one," Love said. He shook his head. "I won't stop ya from goin' into the hills. But I *will* stop ya from doin' what you accuse the masked man of doin', namely, kidnappin' a lady."

"Now Bricks an' nigresses is ladies," Veehall said with disgust.

"If you can chase 'em for settin' fires, I can protect the ones who don't," Love replied.

Veehall shook his head slowly. "Brother

Love, you are on the wrong side of the fence."

"Mr. Veehall, any side of a fence is 'wrong' as far as I'm concerned," Love told him. "Look around. Do you see fences?"

"Not yet, but they'll be here soon enough out of necessity," Veehall said. "What do you think is gonna keep order here? Laws? I've met soldiers like you, Captain. Men who fought for ideas. I always thought more of the men who fought for pay and to impress pretty girls with their uniforms. Those soldiers had a clear vision of things. You idealists — ya killed, but then you didn't go home like sensible men. Ya stayed to atone for what ya did."

"I have nothing to atone for," Love said. "In doing what was right, we gave you a place to build yer nice little empire."

"And a town grew up around what me and Lugo cut from the valleys with our backs and sweat, and that settlement gave you a job and a sweet spot to bring your missus," Veehall said. "That's how countries are built. Without men like me, men like you would have nothin' to do. Now you're standin' there tellin' me I'm off my hog tryin' to keep things peaceful?"

The Mexican woman started back toward the foothills. She flashed a small, grateful smile at Love and he nodded back. Beatrisa was far enough away, and the wind was sufficiently gusty, that Love didn't think she had heard what they were discussing. If there were bandits in the valley, the deputy didn't want them to know that the small scouting party was divided. Veehall's two ranch hands stood there with startled expressions. They didn't seem to understand why they were letting her go.

"With respect, Mr. Veehall, I would never say you was crazy or mean-natured," Love said. "Just too touchy about what's 'yours' and what's 'everybody's.' The way to keep the peace is not to crush people's hopes."

"You forget, sir. They attacked us."

"I didn't forget," Love said. "But don't *you* forget I fought these people for two years. They're not ornery by nature. They're like those soldiers you talked about, the ones who just want to work, get paid, and go home."

"What're you sayin'?"

"These fellas are fast-tempered and territorial as dogs," Love said, glancing at Rodrigo and his companion. They were also out of earshot. "I wouldn't put it past them or hands like them to provoke a showdown — sorta like now. You go ahead with this encounter, Mr. Veehall, and it may end the same way the others did, with dead ranch hands on the valley floor."

"You see somethin' up there we haven't?" Veehall asked suspiciously. "You know somethin' we don't?"

"Only that little people count on bigger folk to underestimate them . . . and to overestimate themselves."

Veehall stood stone-still in the brisk wind. He seemed oblivious to his fluttering coat-tails and the hair blowing along his cheeks. He looked from Love to the hillside as the girl retreated. "I never got anything in life by bein' cautious."

"You ever have a gunfight at night, lit by gunfire?" Love asked. "I have. You shoot wild, kill yer own, and nobody wins. I prefer the daytime when I can get it."

"I've faced enemies I couldn't see, hidden in tall brush or up in hills like this," Veehall said.

"Sir, did you ever do that when you had a *better* choice?"

"There are always better choices, *safer* choices," Veehall replied, but he was obviously thinking about what Love had said.

"Boss?" Rodrigo called out. "We gonna follow 'er?"

Veehall did not reply. He continued to

stare ahead. "I don't like runnin', Deputy Love."

"That's not what we're doin'," Love said.

"Smells like it. Feels like it."

"Mr. Veehall, we know where these people are. This scoutin' party was a success. We need to come back with a larger posse, better equipped."

"That'll give 'em two days or more head start."

"You know that won't matter when we have extra horses to close the gap," Love said. He moved closer. "We'll follow them. We'll find them. Nobody leaves a place without droppin' tracks of some kind. And if these aren't the killers, we'll find the ones who was."

Veehall hesitated. "I don't like this." He regarded Love. "I don't like turnin' over my safekeeping to this thing you call 'the law.' "

"With humility, Mr. Veehall, I helped win you the territory. I believe I can secure this valley."

"But for who, Deputy?" The rancher returned his gun to his holster and glared at the former soldier. "Fuck me and I'll have more than your badge." Veehall turned and stalked back to his men. He motioned them back in the saddle and the three headed back to town.

Love walked slowly to his own mount, which was tied to a cactus near the lake. He looked up at the foothills.

"The law is all we have," Love muttered.

Even the strongest dogs and wildcats were cowards who attacked only when they were hungry or their young were threatened. Men were more complex. They fought for those things as well as for greed or sport and ideas. Wherever they gathered, conflict was inevitable. Without rules and the tolerance that followed, there would be no peace, no statehood, no union.

For men like Harry Love, it also meant there would be no rest. He would leave the valley no better than he had found it and in his logbook that was a loss.

# 9
## ARMIES

Kunga rose as Beatrisa approached around a bend. He had been crouched behind a large pyramid-shaped boulder on the edge of a low cliff, watching the valley. There was an arrow in his simple bow. The Pechangan relaxed the string and lowered the weapon.

"They didn't threaten you?" he asked.

"I did not feel in danger," she replied.

Kunga watched as the deputy rode after the other men. He did not seem in a hurry to catch them.

The Pechangan followed Beatrisa back to the camp, which was located on the other side of a large arête. The rocky ridge protected a long flat ledge that was accessible only from the east. It faced the remainder of the high mountain range. It was here the rest of the party had waited for Joaquin with their horses. They had lit their campfires in small caves so neither the glow nor the smoke would be seen. The band's two horses, belonging to Joaquin and Kunga, were grazing on a small field of low, amber grasses just below. Two members of the San Julian family were with them — Beatrisa's father Donato and his younger brother Rodolfo.

Beatrisa brought the water to Joaquin, who was with Polly. She was lying deep in the shadows below one of the ledges. This section of the cliff side was never in the sunlight and was the coolest spot on the mountainside. Polly was still unconscious. She was still bleeding slightly from her mouth and between her legs. While Joaquin used what was left of their own water to clean and refresh her as best as possible, Beatrisa used the water she had obtained to make a paste of snowberries and wintergreen leaves she had gathered on the slope. She mixed them using a piece of bark as a bowl and a rock as a pestle. The poultice was for Polly's foot, which had been badly burned.

When the water pouches were empty, Kunga slipped his bow over one shoulder, the three empty pouches over another, and went back down the hillside to the lake. Although the band had picked up several stragglers over the past few days, their skins were unreliable and they carried few supplies of their own. Two of them were young Mexican soldiers who had deserted from the army of General Santa Anna and did not know that the war was over. Unused to living off the land, they were thin and weak when the band came upon them in these shallow caves. The men were slowly regaining their strength.

The other two who had joined them were a white trapper and his wife who until recently had lived in a very small log shack. The man, Richard Siegel, had originally been a hunter employed by the Veehall spread. He bagged deer and rabbits, which his wife helped prepare for the cook. When Richard complained to Veehall that the ranch hands were getting "sassy" with his wife, the owner told him that men were men and she had to expect that. Richard said that where he came from — San Francisco, where he'd worked as a fisherman until he could no longer stand the smell of the sea and the stink of the streets — men knew how to treat a lady. The Siegels had decided to try and settle in the mountains, though they were less successful as builders than they were as hunters. Two weeks ago a driving rain had washed a wall of mud against their home, crushing it. They had not yet found a spot to rebuild when Kunga found them. They decided to join the small band and see where it ended up.

Joaquin himself had no idea where they were going. When he had heard about Polly Bailey, he had resolved to stay in the area until he could rescue her. She was the same age as his late wife. The idea that she was being forced to work as a whore had upset him deeply. But as this afternoon's sortie by the deputy and Veehall had proved, they were not safe here. The men would be back in force, and soon.

Beatrisa knelt beside Joaquin as she mixed the poultice. "There were men in the valley," she said.

Joaquin looked up. "What kind of men?" He had expected pursuit but not so quickly.

"There was a deputy, a man named Veehall, and two ranch hands," she said.

"You're sure there were only two ranchers?"

Beatrisa nodded.

"The third was either injured by the fire or went for help," Joaquin said.

"They're gone now, though."

"But they saw you."

The young woman nodded. "I'm sorry. Polly needed the water and the salve and I didn't know how long they'd be there. I was afraid they'd seen me already anyway and I didn't want to run."

"It's all right," Joaquin said. There was no urgency in his voice or manner, but he felt it inside. He had seen what the ranchers carried when they camped. It would not take them long to assemble supplies and return. "Look after," he said with an encouraging smile.

"Joaquin, I'm sorry."

"I told you it's all right," he said. "I didn't think they would come after us directly. It's my mistake."

The woman nodded glumly as Joaquin went to the edge of the ledge. He called down to Richard and to Manuel and Félix, two *soldados de primera*. The privates were accustomed to following orders. They also carried flintlock muskets that the Mexican government had bought from Britain. The old, surplus weapons didn't have great range, but they were quick to load and easy to use. Joaquin hoped they would prove useful. His band hadn't taken any weapons from the dead men, and the ranchers might not expect to be fired upon.

Joaquin put the men to work constructing a stretcher for Polly. They uprooted a pair of saplings and the soldiers used their blue and red jackets for a sling. They didn't wear them during the day and reasoned they wouldn't be traveling during the cold nights.

Joaquin got on Libertad's back. He told the men to follow him into the valley when they were ready.

"We must cover as much ground on open land as possible," Joaquin told them. "We have only a day or two before we must go back into the mountains."

Manuel spoke English and translated. From Joaquin's haste they understood that someone must be after them.

"I can rely on you?" Joaquin said to Manuel before he rode off. He knew little of these men save that they were deserters with guns.

"We ran from a tyrant, not a leader," the former soldier told him. "You can count on us."

Joaquin nodded in gratitude, then went round the arête and down the slope. He saw Kunga at the base of the foothills walking toward the lake. He looked off in the distance, hoping to catch a glimpse of the retreating horsemen — perhaps a glint of silver or a cloud of dust.

What he saw alarmed him. He did indeed see the retreating riders to the southwest. But he also saw a cloud of dust, and it belonged to a horseman who was coming toward them. He was moving along the eastern wall of the valley, invisible to the others because of a row of low hills between them. His route suggested that he had come from the Lugo ranch. Perhaps he had a message for the others? Word of additional riders or supplies, perhaps a rendezvous point.

Thoughts, fears, and options blew threw Joaquin's mind like a dust storm. He was not kicking up a cloud, so the rider would probably not notice him. But he might see Kunga, who was exposed on the valley floor. With his back to the south, the Pechangan might not notice him. Nor was there anywhere to hide if he did. In the open, his bow would not be a match for a handgun.

Moreover, Joaquin wondered why Veehall and the deputy had left. They had come this far. They had to know Beatrisa would not be out here on her own. Why didn't they investigate further? Perhaps they believed Joaquin's numbers were greater than they were, or his weapons and fortifications stronger. He didn't want to destroy that illusion while they were still here. If this rider shot at Kunga, the gunfire might bring the ranchers and Deputy Love back.

Joaquin reached the valley floor without any options. The rest of the small, wounded band would be down here soon. He couldn't afford to let this man see them. The rider would undoubtedly inform the others.

Turning his steed, Joaquin raced due south. He could see the tracks the deputy's party had made. When he saw Joaquin or Kunga, the rider might try to intercept the deputy. Joaquin's only hope lay in cutting him off.

Joaquin used his heels to drive Libertad to a gallop. The young man didn't have a clear view of the onrushing horse and couldn't tell what kind of weapons the man might be carrying. The animal appeared to be laden with bundles and saddlebags. That would slow it down.

Joaquin rode low and hard. Because he was well to the west, riding along the foothills, the other man did not notice him at first. The rider had obviously been watching Kunga. As soon as he spotted the other horseman, the rider did what Joaquin had expected him to do. He cut west across the valley. The rider knew the others had not turned back toward the ranch or they would have passed him. They had to have been stopped ahead or they had turned back toward town.

The cowboy reined hard. Perhaps he was deciding what to do. The man hesitated, then surprised Joaquin. Instead of riding for help, the man rode toward him. Joaquin realized, then, that a hand at the Veehall ranch would certainly recognize the horse. Perhaps he imagined himself becoming a hero by bringing Joaquin in single-handedly. The men were roughly a half mile apart. As the young Mexican continued his own charge, he saw a flash of metal on one side of the horse and then the other, the ranch hand cutting away the extra weight he was carrying. Joaquin thought he saw a carbine sheathed on the now-exposed right shoulder of the horse. To use a firearm accurately, however, the rider would have to stop and dismount. Unlike the cowboy, that would give Joaquin a stationary target — provided he was close enough to take advantage of it. Joaquin would have to ride directly at the man wherever and whenever the rider stopped. Joaquin did not want to give him more than a straight-on profile of the horse at which to fire.

Libertad was breathing heavily as Joaquin tore across the flat valley floor. The young man hugged the horse's powerful, bucking neck with his left arm and stroked him firmly with the right. Spittle flew from the horse's mouth. The sun cooked sweat from Joaquin's own forehead and upper lip. The drops flew from him like hot summer rain. It was strange to feel the strong wind on his cheeks and mouth, to be pecked at by windblown sand. It had been a long time since Joaquin had galloped this hard without his mask.

The other rider was in an equally furious charge, not sparing his spurs, and whipped the horse relentlessly with the looped end of his reins. The ranch hand had obviously decided to close the distance between them as quickly as possible. He did not want to give Joaquin time to think better of a confrontation, to call it off and vanish into the neighboring hills.

The two low, tawny walls of dust closed on one another. One rider was in white, the other in sun-bleached brown. One rode low and the other tall, both driven by a different vision of the future that did not have the other man in it. Though the spoils were different, and the size of the opposing forces was as small as could be, it was a territorial war as old as time and as big as the world.

With just moments until they reached one another, the ranch hand suddenly reined and swung from the saddle. In the same move he pulled his carbine from the low-hanging sheath. He knelt and put it to his shoulder.

He was aiming for the horse.

Joaquin uncoiled his whip. He was some

thirty yards distant. He did not have very many options. He could not turn and retreat in time to get out of range. He could stop and dismount, but there were no high grasses, no boulders, no gullies in which to hide. That would leave the young man a target in the wide-open field. He could continue his charge and risk having the animal shot from under him, which would leave him in the same position.

Or he could try to distract the gunman.

Joaquin began spinning the whip hard at his side, like a riata. He lowered it to the ground where the flayed end kicked up loose earth. Small stones flew forward, landing on and around the gunman and his horse like angry hornets. The animal bucked and complained and the ranch hand had to lower his carbine to protect his face. He fired once, the shot going well wide of Libertad. He did not try to fire again, but scrambled to the other side of his own horse, opposite Joaquin's fusillade. That was all the time Joaquin needed to close the breach.

The young man swept across the ranch hand's line of fire. The whip was still swirling as the ranch hand turned to fire from the waist. Joaquin caught him across the forearm, causing the gun to discharge into the ground. The man screamed and dropped the weapon. Libertad charged past the other horse so quickly that the animal reared and fled. These animals were trained to be around cattle and stampeding herds, but only when there was a man in the saddle. Without a rider, they gave in to their natural instincts. Joaquin spun his own mount around and came back at the ranch hand, who was shaking out his arm and reaching for the carbine.

Joaquin was too far away to hit him again. He had no choice but to charge the fallen cowhand. The rancher saw him coming and jumped away before Libertad could trample him. But it wasn't the Veehall hand Joaquin was aiming for. It was the carbine. The horse crushed the stock as he galloped by, rendering the weapon useless. Joaquin slowed the steed, turned it round, and slipped from its back. The ranch hand was still on the ground, on his side. Joaquin snapped his whip just above the man's head to keep him there. The young man's bloodied forearm was raised defensively, but there was a handgun in a holster and it was within his reach.

"Do you speak Spanish?" Joaquin asked.

The man shrugged and shook his head. The ranch hand was wearing a dark, uncooperative expression.

Joaquin switched the whip to his left hand and shook it out so he'd be ready to strike. His right hand rested on the beaded hilt of his knife. He indicated for the man to rise with his hands raised. The man started to get up. Joaquin watched his eyes. That was where he would see the first signs of possible resistance.

The man got to his knees. His arms were raised halfway, crooked at the elbow. Joaquin stepped in front of him as he rose. The cowboy was facing the sun and had to squint to see. The Mexican youth used the whip to point at the man's gun belt. He gestured for the ranch hand to drop it. Joaquin intended to leave him here and take his horse. The man could keep his water pouch and fill it at the lake. It would take two to three days to reach the town. If the gunman rationed his water, he would survive dehydration. He would have to take his chance with predators. A big stick would keep most of them away. The man's shin-high boots would get awfully hot, but they'd protect him from most of the rattlesnakes or scorpions he happened to step near.

The man undid the buckle with his left hand, as Joaquin instructed through terse pantomime. His right hand remained above his shoulder. The holster was on the right side. The cowboy loosened the belt. As he did, the rancher dipped his forehead slightly to lower the brim of his hat. That protected his eyes just a little from the direct sunlight. At the same time he crossed his waist with his left hand and reached for the gun.

The ranch hand must have figured that he could outdraw the whip or survive a snap. He hadn't counted on the knife. Joaquin drew it and flung it in a clean underhanded toss from the palm. The blade flew straight into the man's gut. It landed with a hard pop with sufficient force to knock him backward several steps.

"You bloody butcher!" Joaquin yelled. "I would have let you go!"

Still trying to draw, the man dropped the gun back into the holster and lowered both hands to the wound. He remained standing, but like a reed in a marsh moving from side to side without conviction. A moment later he was back on his knees, leaking blood from around his palms. The cowboy winced, the blade jarring the wound as he landed. He looked down at the knife as though seeing it for the first time and withdrew it, moaning as the exit sliced his flesh anew and released more blood. He dropped the knife from his bloodied fingers.

Joaquin went to him. He removed the gun from the holster and tossed it aside. Then he bent beside the man and helped him lie on his back. He fixed the man's hat so that it sat mostly on his forehead, protecting his eyes. Touching his shoulder gently, Joaquin rose and went to Libertad. He had not brought water with him and went to collect the other horse, which had stopped and was grazing a few hundred yards away. Joaquin took the reins and led him back to where his owner lay dying. He unhooked the calf-skin water pouch from the saddle and gave the man a drink.

"I knew we was right . . . about you. You woulda made me . . . a hero," the cowboy whimpered after he had taken a few swallows.

Joaquin had no idea what the man said. It didn't matter. He wasn't thanking him for anything he had done. The young Mexican made the sign of the cross over the forehead of the dying man.

The man chuckled weekly. "A Brick . . . guts me like a steer . . . then gives me absolution. What a fuckin' world."

The ranch hand's skin was the color of the dust when he exhaled weakly but with finality. Joaquin had stayed there, standing over him until the end. He did not feel sad for the man who had done this to himself. He felt sick about the twisted passions that had caused the showdown.

Joaquin recovered the man's gun and put it on his chest. He wanted those who found him to know that the small band was not arming for combat nor looking for a war. All they wanted was what God Himself and the American Founding Fathers had promised: freedom and equality for those who inhabited the land. He didn't know if the ranchers would care, but he hoped that the deputy would. Joaquin had never been the aggressor. Anyone who had seen what the cowboys had done over the past day would understand that.

There were no large rocks out here, so Joaquin covered the body with several large branches from a nearby camellia shrub. The showy red flowers secreted an oil that many animals found objectionable. Joaquin and Carlos used to line the corners of the house with them to keep mice away. It wasn't foolproof, but it was the best Joaquin could do for the dead man. When he was finished, the young man rode back the way the cowboy had come. He gathered up the supplies the man had dropped. There were bandages, new "friction matches," and other non-food items his band could use. Joaquin reattached those to the dead man's horse, took the reins, and rode to the north. He encountered Kunga, who had evidently seen Joaquin hurry to the south and had run after him. The Pechangan had more stamina than anyone in their little band.

The native mounted the saddle horse. He didn't have to ask what had happened. There was the horse and there was Joaquin's knife, which he had also recovered. There were spots of blood on the beaded hilt.

The men rode quickly to rejoin their group and to put as much distance as possible between themselves and the inevitable pursuit.

■ ■ ■ ■

# PART THREE:
# AUGUST 1849

■ ■ ■ ■

# 1
## POSSE

Deputy Love's posse never went out as planned.

When Veehall's rider did not show up in town or back at the ranch, Rodrigo and a half dozen other cowboys decided not to wait. Love had not yet pulled enough deputies from the ranks of townsmen, or supplies, to field a posse when Veehall led his men back into the valley. Two riders returned shortly before sundown with the body of the gut-stabbed ranch hand. They picked up supplies and rejoined their boss in the field. With the ranks of available riders further depleted, Love was unable to mount a pursuit. He refused to join Veehall on his. The ranchers were too angry to listen to reason; if they found the band, there would be nothing Love could do to stop them. Instead, he waited until morning, said a long good-bye to his wife, and rode out for Los Angeles. It was a three-day ride, which he took along the western wall of the valley. That was where they had seen the Mexican girl and Rodrigo had found his friend's body.

After two days, Love overtook the hard-riding Veehall party at the end of the valley. He had divided his party into two groups, one of which he had sent into the mountains. They stayed in contact using mirrors. Neither group found the outlaw band. Love was not surprised. The mountain range was vast. Only luck would reward blind pursuit. Veehall was still angry at Love for letting the Mexican girl go. Love didn't care. If the rancher had waited as Love had suggested, his cowhand wouldn't have died and the outlaws would not have had a reason to make such haste. After abducting Polly, they would have put some distance between themselves and any pursuers, then probably slowed. That was when Love would have chased them.

Love had made this journey five or six times. Each time it was different, depending upon the season and the weather. Closer to Los Angeles the weather remained more constant than it did in the high desert: hot during the day and slightly less hot at night. It was never as cold as it was at home.

The valley and the surrounding mountains

looked more or less the same as Love pressed through. Sometimes the terrain opened to endless fields that ran to new and distant ranges. Shacks owned by miners who prospected the hills and rivers, and a stagecoach stop, told him when he was just a few hours from the township. On the way, he encountered two military men with tripod-mounted instruments. He recognized the gear from his days with the dragoons. The young men were Lieutenant Edward O.C. Ord and his assistant, William Rich Hutton. The "detachment of two," as they called themselves, was surveying the *pueblo* of Los Angeles for the legislature.

"Gold rush hit and prices went way up," Ord told the deputy. "Our pay wasn't holding us so our commander let us do a little outside work."

"*I* was ordered," Hutton said.

"By his uncle the paymaster," Ord said as he made notations on a large map he had drawn. "It makes his rolls look better having two less soldiers to feed."

Love wished the surveyors well and rode on. He passed a mission, a large spread of sheepherders, and then a settlement of Cupeño natives who aggressively tried to sell him pouches of clean water, leather boots, and other necessities. Shortly thereafter, marked by a hovering cloud of gray smoke, was the township itself.

Los Angeles was far different from the street-long settlement of Rancho San Bernardino. The spire of the Plaza Church dominated the city, whose streets were arranged in blocks that opened to other streets nearly as far as the deputy could see. The roads were busier and noisier than anywhere in the East, and the buildings were taller. The structures were all wood, many of them reaching three stories tall. Love arrived at lunchtime, and smoke from cooking fires came from many of the structures. Without the constant winds of the high desert, the smoke and odors hovered in the streets. So did the smell of the horses, their waste, and the outhouses. There were houses in the hills overlooking the heart of the town. The first time he was here Love had decided it would be worth the ride to live up there rather than down in the din of the growing city.

The station manned by Sheriff Hyde Drumseller and his deputy was located in a wide, one-story building just off Sunset Street. It was the only brick building in the area, with two desks and a poorly constructed cagelike cell in the back. The brick building served as a temporary town hall while a more permanent facility was being built on the northwest corner of Spring and Jail Streets. When completed, the new structure would have a modern jail cell along with the new sheriff's office.

Unlike the desert sun, the heat here was milder. It had something to do with their proximity to the ocean. Love had never been to the ocean himself. He'd never had the time. He hoped to take Diana one day. The deputy tied his horse to the post outside the office. Only the sheriff was at his desk. A small fire burned in the hearth behind him. There were wanted posters on the wall to his left and an empty, uncluttered desk in front of him. The sheriff was not expecting him, but Drumseller was usually at his post. He was what they called "a tent-commander" in the best sense of the word, a holdover from his own days in the military as a colonel in the Regiment of Mounted Rifles stationed in St. Louis. The short, stocky blond-haired sheriff started as a quartermaster and stayed in the supply corps for most of his military career. During the war, he helped keep thousands of men armed and fed across hundreds of miles of plains, mountains, and deserts. His appointment showed the determination of California's legislature to settle the territory with organization as well as lead.

His family really were drumsellers, two generations ago in England.

Hyde Drumseller was not an outgoing man and he was not surprised to see Deputy Love. He rose from behind his small desk, shook the newcomer's hand, then sat back down.

"When one of my patrols encountered some of Veehall's men, I thought you might be along," the sheriff said. "Can I offer you anything?"

"I could do with coffee," he said.

"Help yourself," the sheriff said, pointing toward the pot.

There was a tin cup hanging from a nail on a board beside the hearth. Love took it down, picked up a cloth to hold the tin pot, and poured himself a cup.

"I was damn sorry about Tim Parmenter," Love said.

"Hard worker. Family has a law firm back East. He knew how to handle the landowners."

"Your people haven't seen anything of this bandit?" Love asked.

Drumseller shook his head. "You know those hills. Band splits up, moves carefully, doesn't send up much smoke — you won't see them."

"I told that to Veehall."

"From what I'm told, he doesn't hear too well," Drumseller said. "But I'm glad you came, Harry. I was gonna send for you anyway. Gold fever is making things crazy up north. We got more people passing through here from Mexico and South America than we got tumbleweeds. My patrols in the valley haven't heard a chirp, except from Veehall. I'm half-thinking these boys we want may have cut west to the coast, joined the migration San Francisco ways, and slipped by."

"Is there any suggestion they did that?" Love asked.

Drumseller pointed to a chair in the corner, but Love shook his head. It felt good to stand after the ride. The sheriff pulled a pouch of tobacco and paper from his desk and began rolling a cigarette.

"Just the fact that we caught two wanted holdup men that way," the sheriff said. "We got two harbormasters watching for us. Fares are high. Anybody that's got the money to pay over that rate for immediate passage gets checked out."

"As far as we know, these people never took weapons or money," the deputy informed him.

"Which is how they may have slipped by,"

Drumseller remarked. "They may have paid normal fare and waited. Lots of folks doing that, throwing up tents along the shore. We don't have enough reliable eyes and ears in the hotels and on the street to watch them."

"What *have* your patrols seen?" Love asked.

"Besides the bottom of a bottle?" Drumseller asked. He was not being flippant. "They've spotted a few campfires, investigated, found migrants who had nothing but the clothes on their back and the rabbit on the spit, or else nothing."

"Nothing?"

"Nothing but dying embers," Drumseller said. "People must've heard the clodhoppers coming and gotten spooked, ran into the night."

"Or else used the campfires to lure your guards there," Love said.

Drumseller looked at him, "Why would the renegades do that and not try to jump my deputies? Wouldn't they want supplies, weapons?"

"These people and their leader aren't war parties the way we usually think of them," Love said. "That's one reason I needed to see you. Chasin' them down like this ain't gonna work."

"Like what?"

"With force of arms, the way we did against Mexico. They got to be hunted, carefully."

Drumseller used the lantern on his desk to light his cigarette. He blew out a thick cloud of smoke. He studied Love. "Well, this gets to why I was going to send for you. The legislature wants them caught. They gave the job to me and I gave it to you. I don't much care how it's done, but it needs to happen soon. Though I'll confess, Harry, I'd prefer that this thing be done in a big, visible way."

"Why?"

"We've got a freshwater reservoir being built, new construction on the ground and in the hills, agriculture of all kinds, transportation growth, and people coming with gold fever and deciding to stay. We've tripled our population since last year. Then there's statehood on the horizon. I need something to show folks that we have civilization here. Besides, Veehall has a big mouth to go with that deaf ear. I don't want him squawking up Sacramento way that this department can't do its job."

Love sipped coffee, then put the cup on the desk and leaned forward. "Sheriff, I don't know about such things. You want the outlaws caught, I can do that. I can make some noise if that suits ya. But I need a posse I can count on. Not drunks, not ranchers, but good men."

"What do you propose?"

He reached into the side pocket of his short duster. "I got a letter from my father-in-law sayin' that they've formed something called the Home Department in D.C." Love put the envelope on the desk. "They're supposed to look after matters that affect settlers. They've got a military detachment camped along the Mormon Route east of here, helping people not to die."

The Mormon Route was the name that had recently been given to the only southwesterly segment of the nine-year-old Oregon–California Trail. That ten-fingered roadway led from the three principal jumping-off points for settlers: Independence, St. Joseph, and Council Bluffs. The Mormon Route passed through Salt Lake City and continued through the lower tip of the territory of Nevada into Southern California. Because the routes were established, outlaws knew where to prey on emigrants. Because of highwaymen and disease — primarily cholera — three of every ten people who traveled the Oregon–California Trail did not survive. That number was higher along the southwestern route where the heat and lack of water took an added toll.

"I knew the soldiers were there," Sheriff Drumseller said as he read the letter. "I didn't think we could just up and borrow them."

"Blood has its privileges," Love remarked. "So does my former rank. I'm going to ride out to Point Burgess. There are twenty men garrisoned there. I'd like to pull some of them from the outpost, and see if we can't find our quarry."

"Would you consider linking up with Vee-hall, just to keep him quiet?"

Love nodded. "I'll pick up his trail and take a few of his most reliable men, send the rest home. That'll stop him from kicking up dust. Then we head northwest through the mountains."

"You really think your bandit's still out there?"

"I don't think our bandit'd go out in the open on a boat or wagon caravan," Love said. "He got himself a mixed party o' reds, blacks, and browns. I don't think he'd split 'em and that kind o' group calls attention to itself. If he's out in the field, he prefers rough terrain, an' I don't blame him. Gives him places to keep his people and his campfires well hid."

Drumseller folded the letter away and returned it to Love. The cigarette was hanging from his mouth and he sucked out a long drag. "I hear what you're saying, Harry. I still think our boy would be a fool to stay out there with people looking for him. But we've had no luck with anything else. Besides, a foray like this will reassure the legislature and the public that their protectors are on the job."

"That assumes they think the fellas we're chasin' are bad," Love said.

"What do you mean?"

"Fella like this masked man, saving nigress whores and helping Injuns — there's a piece o' the population that'll think that's a good thing."

"Murder isn't a good thing no matter how it's done."

Love shrugged and sipped more coffee. "We murdered lots o' Mexicans a few years back. Lots more don't think that was right."

"Lots more Mexicans," Drumseller pointed out.

"Yeah, but they're here too."

The sheriff took a long drag. "You plan on staying in town tonight?"

"I thought I'd get a start while it's still light, see if I can reach your outpost before dark," Love said. "Figured to stable the horse for a few hours, catch some food and a nap myself."

"I'll see to your horse. I've got a cot in the storeroom you can have. I'll have the saloon send over a steak."

"Thanks."

The sheriff rose, pulling again on his cigarette. "We got a broadsheet here, the *Star*. I'm going to talk to the editor, Dave Peel — a good man from Chicago. We need to get the word out about this mission, show everyone that this department won't tolerate lawlessness."

"Use the news to burnish our stars," Love said. "Good thinking."

The deputy finished his coffee, then excused himself. He filled the washbasin from a pitcher and cleaned his face and hands. The small room was stuffy, so he opened the back door to let in air. The sunlight revealed ammunition, shotguns, and rifles, as well as manacles and a ball and chain. There were also ropes and filing drawers, which, like his own, probably contained wanted posters and communiqués from other sheriff's departments. There was a silhouette of a woman with an inscription, "To My Beloved Drum, Millie."

Millie was the sheriff's late wife. She had died of cholera over a year before when the disease had moved through Los Angeles and other southern settlements. Rancho San Bernardino had been spared. Some residents believed that even disease and the devil did not much enjoy the desert.

The steak arrived quickly, brought by a Negro girl of about thirteen or fourteen who arrived at the back door and left with a curtsy. She made Love think of Polly. The deputy wondered if the whore found life on the run a hardship, or whether it was better than bedding with men for pay. For all he knew, she was still a whore for the Brick and his partners. He didn't envy the woman her life, and imagined that having a roof and regular meals was better than running.

The meal was perfect, and after another cup of coffee and a visit to the privy, the deputy took a much-needed nap. But there was something about the serving girl he couldn't get from his mind: whether two or three years from now she would still be a waitress or whether she'd be a whore.

He had fought a war to free a population from the whims of dictators. As he thought of this pretty little member of the population, he found himself wondering whether she would have any more choice than the steer did about becoming Love's lunch.

Love shut the door to darken the room

and lay back on the cot. The thought nagged at him as he slipped into a deep, restful sleep.

# 2
## PARTNERS

Love was awakened by a hard rap on the inner door. It took him a few moments to remember where he was. He had been in a deep, dreamless sleep.

The deputy rose and opened the door. Sheriff Drumseller was there. Someone else was standing behind him.

"How long have I been asleep?" Love asked.

"I left here three hours ago," the sheriff replied. "Got your horse settled, then went to see Mr. Peel here. You've got about four hours of sun left. You probably won't reach our outpost, but you can put a good dent in the trip. Think your mount can do that leg today?"

"Yeah." Love looked past the sheriff. He nodded at the tall, salt-and-pepper-bearded gentleman standing behind him. The man nodded back. Love guessed him to be about fifty or fifty-five years old. He was dressed

in a red cotton shirt and chaps that resembled a batwing, tight near the waist but
hanging loose below. That allowed air to
circulate. Mr. Peel evidently intended to do
some riding. "Are me and my horse the only
ones going?"

"Mr. Peel feels a story about the pursuit
of this outlaw is newsworthy," the sheriff
said. "The *Star* is a weekly, so he's going to
spend four or five days at your side collect-
ing information. His son will run things
while he's away."

"You wear a gun, Mr. Peel?" Love asked.

"I do. You won't have to nursemaid me,
Deputy."

"Wasn't plannin' to. That's why I asked."

Mr. Peel nodded again and the sheriff led
him to the desk, where he gave the publisher
an order for another hundred wanted posters. On the six days when newspapers
weren't being printed, the *Star* offices hired
out their printing press. From what Love
overheard, they had a contract with the
sheriff's office, which struck him as a
conflict in the making: If their income was
partly derived from a state office, how could
they report fairly on state doings?

Love didn't like that, and he didn't like
the idea of turning the posse into players in
a serial drama. He understood what Drum-

seller was doing, but it put a funny taste on the back of his tongue, like bad cheese.

The deputy went out the back door to see about his horse. He followed the alley to Sunset and walked to the stable. The building occupied roughly a half acre, with red walls and a flat roof that sloped inward. There were tin pipes to catch whatever rain or moisture gathered there. The pipes fed the troughs, which sat in each of the twenty-five stalls. Though only a few of them were occupied at any time, Love learned from the owner that he expected them all to be filled within the year.

"A lot o' tho' gold-diggers who went no' — dey gonna come 'way poor an' lookin' for a place to start over," the bent, lanky older man said as he took Love to his horse. The man had no teeth, which made his speech difficult to follow. "You ever bin no', Dep'ty?"

"No, sir."

"Cold dere. Dirty. No' like heah."

The deputy smiled. He reached for his horse's bridle, but the man motioned him off. This was his place. He brought the animal to the big front door, not its owner. When they reached the street, Love tipped him a penny for his efforts. The man thanked him warmly and wished him well.

"You huntin' de mask' outlaw?" the stable man asked.

Love nodded. "How did you know?"

"Din't. Guessed. People talk 'bout 'im. Figgered new gun heah, it's to bring 'im in."

"What people talk?" Love asked.

"Muckers. Coloreds. Mexicanos." He pointed to a rocking chair beside the door. "Ah sit heah, smoke, lissen. He's like a prophet t'dese folk."

"How will they feel when he's hanged?" Love asked.

The man raised, then lowered his bony shoulders.

It wasn't a helpful answer, but it was an honest one. Love walked his horse back to the front of the sheriff's station, where Peel was waiting beside his own white horse. The sheriff was just saying good-bye to him. The editor had strapped on a gun belt with a pair of ivory-handled Colts.

"Where'd ya learn to shoot those?" Love asked as he mounted his own horse.

"Eleven years ago, before I left Chicago," Peel replied. "A reporter makes just as many enemies as a lawman. He's got to know how to defend himself."

"May I?" Love asked, holding out a hand.

Peel handed him one of the .31-caliber

percussion pistols. The brass trigger guard was dark on the inside. The man had fired the gun often enough. Love returned the weapon.

"You didn't check the sight," Peel noted. "Looking for notches?"

"Something like that," Love replied.

He mounted his horse and Drumseller handed him an envelope. "This letter tells the patrol they're to take orders from you as pertains the disposition and pursuit of the outlaw," the sheriff said. "Take as many as you need, but send one back to let me know what you're doing and where you're going."

"Soon as we got that figured out I'll send word," Love promised.

"Keep safe," Drumseller said.

Love turned his horse toward the east. Peel followed. The men rode side by side onto Sunset.

"Sheriff gave me some of your background," Peel said. "You've had a lot of experience tracking."

"Goodly amount, though it's different when someone's draggin' a cannon or a cart fulla wounded. These fellas are smart and they're different."

"Different how?"

"They don't want what bandits usually

want," he said. "They kill but they don't rob."

"The sheriff said they take horses."

"But they don't take weapons or money."

"Horses are stealing —"

"Horses are survival," the deputy interrupted. "That's what confuses me about these people. Ya murder a man, it don't seem like much if ya take his gun too. But they don't."

"Any idea why?"

The deputy shook his head slowly. "In the dragoons we took all the weapons we found, even if we didn't have the shells to feed 'em. Way we saw it, that was one less weapon in the hands o' the enemy. These boys — and ladies too — leave fully loaded weapons behind."

"Do you think they're trying to tell you something?"

"Mebbe. I don't know if this is their message, but they obviously don't need 'em. They're killin' just fine with arrows and knives. But I don't think that's it. They seem to have this line they won't cross."

"A bid for clemency of some kind?"

"I don't know about that either," Love said. "What troubles me is it shows that they're thinkin'. If an enemy is thinkin' an' you can't figure out how or why, they got the jump on ya."

"So without cannon to leave tracks or a strategy you understand, what makes you think you can track these outlaws?" Peel asked.

"Even the carefulest animal leaves a trail," Love said. "Campfires can be buried, but small animals dig up bones for the juice inside. Folks and horses shit and flies find it. A woman does what she always does, picks a flower for her hair, you can see the stem or smell the aroma where it don't belong. No water around, people get ripe. Women bleed. There's lots o' ways to find people, Mr. Peel. All ya gotta notice is what ain't normal to a place."

"Impressive," the editor remarked.

Love shrugged. "Ya wanna know the truth, Mr. Peel? The one's got it tough is the fella tryin' to escape. He doesn't get to rest — not really. One ear is always listenin', his decisions're always a compromise between what's right and what's safe. He has to avoid groups o' people 'cause one'll always point him out for gold. And all the while we close the gap and cut off his retreat."

"I still say that kind of thinking is impressive," Peel said. "And my readers will think so too. It will make them feel safe, like

God's angels are on the job looking out for them."

"That's a heavy overpraisin', Mr. Peel," Love remarked. "We're men, no more, no less, tryin' to make the wilderness safe for more than tarantulas and eagles."

"You're trying to make hell habitable by chasing devils who cut the throats and open the chests of their victims," Peel said as though he were dictating the first line of a story. "That makes you angels."

The deputy snickered. "Leave it to you boys to dress up a posse like one of those Crusades."

"What do you think this is?" Peel asked. "There are infidels out there, killing and mutilating and fighting the advance of civilization. You are *no* different than the Knights of Malta trying to recover the Holy Land from such as they."

"Well, I'm different," Love said.

"How so?"

"I'm not interested in wipin' anyone from the face of God's earth. I'm more like a poker player tryin' to shuffle the deck, makin' sure all the cards are lined up and facin' in the same direction."

"You're too modest," Peel said.

"No, sir. Just realistic. God took a personal interest in Jerusalem. I think He made this place, all beautiful and hard at the same time, like a society girl, then got busy with somethin' else. Truth is, folks this clever — I'd rather have 'em on my side than be huntin' 'em. Nobody can conquer this place and nobody can hope to survive here alone."

"People don't want to read that," Peel said dismissively. "They'd much rather hear they're on the side of the angels."

"Even if it ain't true? Even if their people are bein' gutted an' stuck under piles o' rocks?"

"Especially then," Peel replied.

Love just shook his head as the men rode from the city in silence.

# 3
## EXODUS

It was the scale of the mountains that had always made them seem so empty from the valley floor. They were not, as Joaquin had learned. There were many people in caves and tents and simple log cabins. They were here for relief from the heat, for water that ran with regularity from the snowy peaks, for the game. They had come to California from the south or east, or from the plains they once called their own. They had gone as far as they could and scraped out a secret, hidden existence that could hardly be called a life. Then someone with a horse and a vision came along, talking about a community and land, showed them a band of mixed souls, and they trusted him without question — not just because he had a dark skin like their own, whether that color was red or black, but because he and everyone with him was an outcast. The group that once consisted of Joaquin Murrieta and his rage was now made up of twenty-seven souls. Seventeen of those were adult men, three were children, the rest were women.

By moving in small groups — often after the sun was down in the valley, but not on the higher slopes — the band had stayed ahead of Veehall and his clumsy pursuers. The ranchers did not move with cunning, just speed and force. They watched for campfires and looked for the prints of feet and hooves. But the band walked on stone or in water, or along bare ground that caught the desert winds and erased any hint of their passing. They lit campfires, then left, knowing that the men would be drawn to them. Sometimes the band waited nearby and followed the men out, moving behind them so there was no trail for the ranchers to follow.

Yet with all of that, Joaquin found himself growing removed from the group. He had come to California to build a home for his family. He had been turned toward vengeance with no plan beyond that. Now he was a shepherd heading north as he had originally dreamed, but more to escape capture than to make himself a home. That was not what Joaquin wanted. More importantly, he would not make the land safe for others by running.

The band was well ahead of the ranchers when they stopped in a long, steep dale that ran between two green-grass hills. There was running water and fruit growing from the trees. The air was cool due to the shade of the bordering slopes. This was the kind of paradise he would have wanted above a settlement.

Joaquin sat away from the group with Kunga and Beatrisa. In just a few weeks the young woman had grown into quite a leader. She was tough when she had to be, quickly and quietly mobilizing the group if Joaquin or Kunga thought there was danger. She also made sure they had sufficient supplies. Whenever water, jerky, or fruit was low, she made sure there were scouts looking out for fresh stores. Polly was also an enormous help, taking a personal interest in everyone, making sure that new members had someone to look out for them. It was inspiring the way everyone had pulled together. It was the kind of harmonious community Joaquin had always dreamed of, though not as nomads. It was difficult to stay healthy in climates that changed from sweltering to freezing, wet to dry, depending on how high they were forced to travel. It was difficult to raise and feed families, to educate the young, to rest without listening for the approach of men and beasts.

"I want you to move on without me," Joaquin told the others.

Beatrisa was surprised. "What are you going to do?"

"It is honorable to migrate but we can no longer run," he said. "I plan to stop the ranchers from following us."

"We go together," the Pechangan told him.

"No. I need someone who can protect the group," Joaquin told him.

"It isn't fair that you make this decision for all of us," Beatrisa said. "There are men *and* women who will want to fight with you."

"Leadership is not about what is fair. It is about what is necessary," Joaquin replied.

"It is necessary that we have you lead us, even if that is into battle," Beatrisa told him. "I speak with the people more than you do. Polly talks to them. We all share your vision of a place where we can settle without being hunted. We have not come together because we want life to be easy. We want it to be worth something — even if that means sacrifice."

"You have sacrificed enough without surrendering your lives," Joaquin said. "Some of you have become fugitives —"

"By choice," Beatrisa repeated. "Many of us would be dead had we not joined you."

"Many more may die if you stay with me," Joaquin said.

"That too is our choice," Kunga told him.

"I do not agree. Both of you, listen. These men must be stopped. We cannot continue running like this. I can move more easily on my own, then catch up with you later."

"You can watch more sides with the help of others," Kunga said. He added definitively, "I am going."

"As am I," Beatrisa said. "I protected our group from ranchers once. I can do it again."

Joaquin was touched by their devotion but he was also angry. He did not like being pushed. He had always been an independent soul who set his own horizons. What good was being a leader if people did not obey?

He looked away from the others. The sweet air of the flower-filled glen filled his nostrils and softened his indignation. Joaquin was about two hundred feet above the bottom of the hills. Deep ravines, created by runoff, led to the valley. No one could easily ascend here. He saw plumed quails in the trees below. If anyone tried to approach, the birds would flap away with their deep, distinctive flutter. He felt safe and allowed himself to enjoy those smells, the cool grass and dry, delicate breeze. He imagined Juanita beside him and wished that life could be like this moment, fragrant and perfect. Perhaps one day it would be that.

First, though, their home had to be secured, wherever it was. As a leader, his job was to make that happen. But did that mean as quickly as possible or as safely as possible? For the moment, they were ahead of the ranchers. What if more men joined them? What if the little group were struck by illness, or someone was hurt, and they were forced to slow or stick to shallower inclines? It was difficult carrying Polly along some of the steeper slopes. What would he do if, further ahead, there were two Pollys and sharper crags to negotiate? And how could he lead a woman into battle?

"Joaquin, what are you thinking of doing?" Beatrisa asked tentatively.

The young man looked back at the others. The woman did not look like his Juanita. The eyes were harder, the sharp mouth more like leaf than flower. She had larger shoulders and stronger arms. Her voice was deeper, less melodious. Perhaps he was wrong to think of all women as delicate, just as it was wrong of white men to think of everyone else as lazy or ignorant or uncivilized. And Kunga — he came of his own will, heroically fighting alongside

Joaquin not because he had anything to gain, but because it was the right thing to do. Joaquin had no right to tell these people what to do.

"Do you mean to lead them in another direction or to fight them?" the Mexican woman asked.

"If we are to be three against the ranchers, we must gather as many weapons as possible," Kunga said.

"You are both very good people," Joaquin said. "Have I said how much I owe you both?"

They looked at him.

"We owe you a great deal as well," Beatrisa said. "But we do this not just for ourselves and our group."

"I know that," Joaquin said. "I understand."

The question was what to do. As Kunga had suggested, they would need to arm themselves regardless. Attempting to mislead the white men could be even more dangerous than confronting them. That would allow the enemy to remain at full force, and there was always the chance that Joaquin or the others might stumble or be outflanked or outsmarted. Nor would the men hesitate to shoot at them. From the ranchers' perspective, pursuit and attack were the same.

Yet something Beatrisa had said stuck in Joaquin's head. He asked the others to leave him for a few minutes, and he sat alone on the slope. The Mexican woman and the Pechangan walked up the hill together. That alone was remarkable, he thought. That two people he had only recently met, and from far different backgrounds, were willing to risk their lives for an idea. Small, proud tears ran from the sides of his eyes. He took his bloody mask from his pants pocket. He always carried it with him as a token of remembrance. He ran it between his fingers.

"We have to attack," Joaquin thought aloud. It was a strange thought to have as he looked out on such tranquility. Yet there was no denying the necessity for it. Until now their actions had been dictated by the need to provide what the government was not giving them: justice and human rights. But it had been a defensive war, cautious and designed to protect rather than provoke. Despite that, the ranchers still pursued them. Joaquin found himself wishing he had taken some of the guns. He had not wanted anyone to be tempted to use them, since the noise would draw attention to their location. That did not seem so important any longer. "I haven't wanted to kill anyone, *mi mariposa*," he said to the image of Juanita in his head. "I had to punish the men who took you and Carlos from me — the rest have never left us a choice. Now I'm afraid we must stop them before they can hurt us." He folded his hands around the mask and shut his eyes. "I hope you understand. And if you see Our Lord, please tell Him I am sorry. I must do this to help those who cannot help themselves."

Joaquin made the sign of the cross and rose. He tucked the mask back in his pocket and looked down at the foothills. What Beatrisa had said gave him an idea. As dangerous as it was, it would end the pursuit. The question he needed to ask — and answer — was whether it would make the region safer for immigrants or more dangerous? Would they be gunned down out of hand by frightened white men, or would they be allowed to pass unmolested?

*How much worse could it be than it is now?* Joaquin wondered. They were being raped and murdered. How many victims like Juanita and Carlos had there been that they knew nothing about?

Mexicans, natives, and Negroes would not get justice through the legal system. The only way to stay safe was to stand up for themselves, to make the battle costly for the oppressors. The only way to do that was to take the battle to those oppressors — not when they were on the hunt but when they were unprepared.

The young man turned back to the campsite. He explained to Beatrisa and Kunga what he had in mind. They went back to organize the rest of the group. Though tired from the long chase and poorly equipped, they all collected themselves quickly and were gone from the dale within the hour.

The band moved as they normally did, with economy and care. The women were on horseback and most of the men were on foot. This time, however, instead of Kunga remaining in the rear with Joaquin at point, both men stayed in the back of the line. They were joined there by Beatrisa. While they walked, Joaquin and Kunga collected what they would need to move against the ranchers.

The group moved north along the western foothills. The last they had seen of the ranchers' campfire put the pursuers at the base of the eastern side of the slopes. Joaquin had watched the men who were constantly searching the hills, looking for signs of dust or reflected light or smoke. The band was careful to keep those to a minimum and to use the intervening peaks as a barrier as much as possible.

As nightfall neared, Joaquin and the others dropped farther and farther back. Then, with light still striking the tops of the hills, they set off on foot while the others made camp.

# 4
## SIEGE

Supplies from the ranch arrived shortly before sunset. Veehall was glad the rider had made it. They were running low on whiskey and coffee. More than food, more than clean blankets, more than progress itself, the men needed their drink at night and hot coffee in the morning.

Edison Veehall himself wanted to see progress. His supply rider had heard that the Los Angeles Sheriff had organized a posse and would be picking up their trail. The rancher was glad to hear it. Veehall didn't want to lose the outlaws. Now and then they saw tracks, heard noises, caught glimpses of colorful fabric, and knew they were closing in. But every time they tried to nab the Brick and his people, the band managed to hunker down out of sight.

Still, they couldn't hide forever. As soon as the rancher had the posse to send against the killers, alongside his men, the bandits would be found and they would be executed.

The rider also brought updates from Willa Veehall. The rancher's wife was running the spread in his absence and kept him abreast of any news. He made notes on her letters and sent them back with the rider. She was doing a confident job as he knew she would. Without having to chase him, his cigars, and his muddy boots from the house, she had a lot more time to do what was important.

Maybe that was how he kept her from taking over. Veehall smiled. By distracting her with small things.

The men were busy making a campfire and tending to the horses while their boss read the letter and made his notations in pencil. When he was finished, he joined the other men for dinner: chicken from the ranch, butchered just three days before and carried here in a pouch of salt water to keep it fresh. The strips were placed in a skillet and roasted over the fire. One of the men skewered a loaf of bread over a steaming pot of water to restore some of the freshness. Then he cut thin slices and passed them out. The rider had brought more bread, but they ate the older supplies first. At least the loaves didn't get moldy in the dry desert heat.

"That chicken smells like home," one of the younger men said. There was longing in his voice.

"You'll get to go there soon enough," Veehall promised.

"Yes, sir. I wasn't complainin', sir."

The men sat silently as the meat sizzled. Coyotes howled in the distance as they did every night.

"Ya think them coyotes'd eat cooked meat?" another man asked.

"I think they'd eat anything that came from a bone, live or dead, cooked or raw," another replied.

As the men spoke, Veehall saw a light in the distance. Because there was no moon, it shone unusually bright as it moved toward them. He hushed the men and they followed his gaze to the northwest.

Rodrigo rose. He had been silent, as he was most of the time. So did the man standing beside him. Both men drew handguns.

"Do not shoot!" said whoever was approaching the camp.

"That's a lady," said one of the men.

"A Brick," said another.

"Entertainment for t'night," another man said.

"Be quiet and watch her," Veehall said. "She's gotta be one o' them devils. There ain't nobody else out here."

"Why don't we just cut her down?" Rodrigo asked. He was uneasy, his fingers wriggling around the walnut grip.

"Careful with that torch, woman!" someone yelled. "She's kickin' off sparks! You'll start a fire!"

"I am very sorry," she said. The woman lowered it slowly to a patch of bare sand and rubbed the flame out. Her orange-hued figure vanished into the blackness of the night.

"Come forward slowly," Veehall ordered.

"Yes, sir," she replied.

The woman rematerialized on the fringes of the camp. She drifted toward them like a ghost in the darkness and the circle of men parted to admit her. They remained standing in a horseshoe shape at the edges of the light. She was dressed in a white blouse and black dress, which was tattered around the hem as though she had traveled through bramble. She carried a large water pouch around one shoulder, but did not appear to have any weapons.

"Stop and turn round," Veehall said as she reached the campfire.

The woman did so. There was no weapon tied to the back of her waist.

"Raise your dress," the man said. There

was nothing licentious in his tone. He knew that many dance-hall girls wore small pistols and knives strapped to their ankles or thighs.

The woman did not hesitate. She lifted the garment to mid-thigh. There was nothing but leg there. She had obviously expected that. After a moment, she let the dress drop and stepped forward. The gunmen remained alert with their weapons pointed toward the newcomer.

"Why're you here?" Veehall asked.

"I am tired of running," she said. "I want to go back to Mexico."

"We would love to have you go back to Mexico and we'll give you safe passage as far as my ranch," Veehall said. "But we want something in exchange."

"What would that be?" the woman asked. She took a step closer, to the edge of the fire.

"I think you know," Veehall said. "We want you to show us where the outlaws are hid up."

She hesitated.

"Otherwise, you can turn yourself around and head back into the darkness," the rancher added.

The woman considered their offer. "May I warm myself for a moment?"

Veehall nodded.

Rodrigo was between the woman and the stone barrier that protected the fire. He stepped aside. The woman removed the pouch from her arm and held it close as she moved nearer.

Suddenly, she pulled a knife from a sheath behind the pouch, plunged it into the bottom of the bulging sack, and cut laterally. Water gushed from the deerskin, drowning the fire in the quick deluge. The men could hear the hiss of the steam from the kindling and the skillet. Those standing nearest the cloud were scalded and their cries joined those of the distant coyotes.

"Get her!" Veehall shouted into the impenetrable night.

He heard men moving, but he did not know whether they were the men who had been burned or the hands trying to find and restrain the woman. He could not imagine that she had come here without planning to leave immediately after dousing the flame. That did not concern him as much as whatever else might have been planned. Darkness could not have been the end of the girl's plan.

Veehall heard the low whoosh of arrows, one and then another. There was the sickening thud of their contact and renewed cries of his men. The rancher wanted to tell them to get down, but he had no idea how close the enemy was and he did not want to reveal his own position. He dropped to the ground, facedown, and wormed his way from the fire site. He heard the frantic movement of feet, shouts, screams, bodies hitting the ground. It was apparent that the bandits had been watching from somewhere nearby and had noted where their targets were. The girl must have left the circle at once so she would not be harmed. In the distance, he heard the neighs of his horses. The animals were frightened, a reaction to the noise from the camp. The sounds were coming from one place. The interlopers were not stealing them in the dark.

Not yet.

Well wide of the campsite, Veehall turned toward the animals. If he could reach them, he could cautiously ride off on one — slowly, putting enough distance between himself and the attackers and hiding until daybreak. The rocks and midget cacti cut his shirtsleeves as he made his way to the north. He resisted the urge to rise and run lest an incoming arrow strike him by mistake.

The shouts grew fewer and distant. Veehall wasn't sure how far he'd gone or how many men had been wounded or killed. He only knew that he wanted to get away, to put as much distance between himself and the campsite as possible. He heard sounds like branches cracking amidst the dying chaos, though he knew there were no trees in the vicinity of the camp.

The site fell silent, save for the occasional crunch of feet on the ground and moans from fallen ranchers. Suddenly a light flared ahead of him. It was so brilliant in the deep black night that he had to look away. When he looked back, he saw the girl approaching with the lighted torch in her right hand. There was a box of matches in her left hand. He remembered now that she had placed the torch down carefully and walked toward the campfire with measured steps. She had been marking the spot so she could find it again in the dark.

"You look like you belong there, on your belly," Beatrisa said.

Now that he was lit by the torch, Veehall saw no reason to stay on the ground. He rose and looked around. The light did not reach far enough for him to see the campsite. He turned back to the girl, snarling.

"You're all gonna hang for what ya did here," he said.

"For defending ourselves from murderers and rapists?" she said.

There were footsteps behind Veehall. Two men approached. One held a bow and arrow, the other wore a bloody mask and carried a whip and a knife. Veehall turned to face them. He did not draw his gun.

"Your men raped the wife of our leader and cut apart his brother's body," the girl said. "*You* have caused this to happen."

"You're all trespassers, intruders," Veehall said. "You use my land as though you have a right to it!"

"We do," said the native. "Your fences have been raised on *our* land."

The man stepped closer into the circle of light from the woman's torch. It took Edison Veehall a moment to recognize the man as Kunga of the Pechanga. The rancher wasn't surprised. The young brave had always been critical of the natives' peace with his ranchers.

"You don't own what you couldn't defend," Veehall told him. He looked at the masked Mexican. "Either of you." His eyes moved back to Kunga. "What did you ever do but strip away the animals and vegetation and move on? I came here and replenished the land, the livestock. I brought people who buy your goods. I earned the right to put up fences!"

"Fences that keep us *in!*" Kunga shouted.

"You have cattle on one side and my people on the other while you move where you wish and do what you wish. *You* tell us where we may live and hunt and grow. You say this is a right you have earned, but I say it is a right you enforce with death and fear." The Pechangan extended an arm toward the camp. "Now we have done as you do. Now we have earned the right to be where we wish."

"You shot my men in the back, in the dark."

"You killed this man's family in the light, facing them," Kunga said. "This must make you braver than we are."

Veehall looked from one man to the other. He didn't know if they were going to let him leave here. But if he didn't make a move to apprehend them, to punish them, he would have no credibility as a leader. Not to the settlers of the region or to himself. His hand shot toward his gun. It never got there.

The rancher screamed as Beatrisa pushed the torch against the base of his skull. Veehall felt his backbone and legs give out as terrible heat engulfed his head and neck. He dropped the gun, landed on his knees, and sprawled forward. Though Beatrisa had stepped away, he continued to cry out as his flesh held onto the pain of the flames. He reflexively reached for the wound and felt the brittle flesh, the blistered blood. It sizzled anew under his touch and he pulled his hand away. He tried to push off the ground, but his body did not cooperate. He fell back to his heaving chest.

He heard footsteps go around him, then walk away. His left cheek was in the dirt. He tried to raise it. A soft-soled moccasin pushed it back down. The foot remained on his face, pressing it into the pebbled earth.

"We are letting you live," Kunga informed him. "You may keep your gun for protection from animals, but we are taking your horses. You will have to bury your men yourself."

"I . . . will . . . find you," Veehall swore through his distorted mouth.

"Perhaps," Kunga said. "But by then we will be far from here and our numbers will have grown as plentiful as the grasses. You will never be able to cut us down, Veehall."

"I'll burn you down —"

"Fire moves in all directions," Kunga said. "Without justice, without peace that embraces everyone, you will burn as well."

The native left, following the light provided by Beatrisa's torch. Veehall was alone in the blackness. To his left, the moaning had stopped. He heard the horses whinnying as they were taken away. He reached for his gun and was surprised to find his hand trembling. He used an elbow to pull himself around. The rancher had it in mind to aim at the torchlight. Through the tears in his eyes, squeezed from him by the searing agony in his neck, he saw the girl's flame. But the figures below it were hidden by the horses, which were crowded tightly together. They were all moving away, like a will-o'-the-wisp over marshes in the north. After a moment only the hot, throbbing pain in his lower scalp and along his shoulders seemed real. That and the hard ground below him and the fact that he needed to get up and find a place of safety until daylight, a large rock to protect his back or a gully. It wouldn't be long before the coyotes smelled death. Without the light, without the presence of other living creatures, the carnivores would come for the remains of his men. He had no intention of trying to shoot them in the dark. He didn't know where the matches were, where the other guns had fallen. He might need the bullets he had to defend himself.

Veehall began to shuffle along, feeling his way with his feet. He held his gun tightly at his side in case he stumbled. He did not want to holster it in case he needed it to fight off a predator.

As he picked his way toward a wall of rock he had remembered seeing on the lower western slopes, Veehall seethed. They had let him live to humiliate him. To send him back with a warning not to pursue them and not to harm the people who lived off his land even though they had no right to do so.

The rancher's body ached where he had been cut and burned. But that was nothing compared to the fierce rage in his chest. He wanted to shoot those murdering, horse-thieving dogs in the head, one after the other after the other. This savage little war was not over. At sunrise, the rancher would gather bullets and another gun and head south. He would shoulder whatever other supplies he could carry — water and some jerky. Whether it took hours or days, he would listen for the drumming hoofbeats of the posse that was coming his way. He would fire a shot so they would find him. Then he would join with them and murder every member of the band that had attacked them, whether Harry Love approved or not.

But Veehall thought the deputy sheriff would go along with that. They would never know how many of those cowards fired from the darkness to kill his men. And the rancher wouldn't let them spare any women who were with them. It was a woman who had started this deadly attack.

Perhaps Veehall would burn her like civilized folk used to do with witches. Perhaps he would save her till second to last to give the head Brick something to think about.

Right before they sent him to hell.

# 5
## POSSE

The day dawned hot with a strong, dry wind creating a thick dust storm as the line of riders made its way across the valley floor. The peace officers rode one after the other so that the man in front could make sure the path was free of ruts, sudden drop-offs, and rocks. That point man was Deputy Love, who wanted not only to check the path, but to set the pace. The other men had spent the last few weeks sitting in valleys and on hillsides drinking and occasionally patrolling. They had forgotten, if they ever knew, how to maintain a steady march. The men moved steadily but slowly through the choking cloud, since a lamed horse would cost them two riders: the one without the mount and the one who had to take him back to Los Angeles.

The dust stung the men's sun-bronzed faces and made it difficult to see. They all wore masks up to their eyes and squinted into the onrushing pale brown mist. But there was no protection against the howling of the wind, which made it difficult to think let alone to hear.

The posse would have missed Edison Veehall in the murky daylight, save for the fact that they were looking down to avoid the oncoming wind and he was crawling. The high grass here afforded the rancher some protection from the gritty attack. Love raised a right arm and shouted for the line to stop. Veehall was practically upon Love's horse before he looked up. The rancher just stayed there on all fours. Love did not imagine that Veehall had good news for the posse.

The deputy dismounted and went to the rancher. He squatted with his back to the wind. That also helped to shield Veehall.

"What happened?" Love asked.

"Ambush."

"When?"

"Day before yesterday . . . I think."

Love checked Veehall's water pouch. It was empty. The deputy shouted for one of the men to bring food and drink.

"It was nighttime — they fired arrows into the camp," Veehall said. "My men were killed where they sat."

"Not you."

"They spared me. Dared me to chase them. Dared me to avenge my men."

"Who dared you?"

"Their masked leader and Kunga of the Pechanga," Veehall said. "And some Brick woman. They said the land is theirs and they'll kill anyone who tries to stop them from goin' where they please."

"We'll find them and we'll stop them," Love told him.

The junior deputy arrived with beef jerky and water and helped protect Veehall from the wind while he took a few bites and a long drink. Love took the man to his own horse and helped him into the saddle. He just now noticed the wound on the rancher's neck.

"You get burned?" Love asked.

"The Brick girl did that," Veehall said. "Stuck a torch to me so I'd crawl at the feet of the Injun."

"I'll get somethin' for it."

"No need," Veehall said. "It helped me stay awake. I'm used to it now."

"All right," Love said. He took Veehall's weapons.

"What're you doin'? I want to keep those," the rancher objected.

"An' I want this damn storm to stop in its tracks, but that ain't gonna happen," Love replied. He handed the guns to the next man in the line. "You'll get 'em if we need 'em," he told Veehall.

"If?" Veehall grabbed Love's arm. "I hope you're not thinkin' o' sparin' those killers, Deputy."

"I'm thinkin' of nothin' but findin' them," Love said. He took the reins of his own horse and, walking beside it, started the line moving with a wave of his arm. The deputy pulled his hat low to help protect him from the biting sands. "How many are there now?" he asked.

"I don't know," Veehall said.

"Still movin' north?"

"Yeah, through the mountains."

"I expect they'll move to the valley for speed, now that you're not on their tail," Love said.

"They'll run, all right. They're cowards, striking in the dark." Veehall shook his head. "And you let their leader go."

"You said he was wearing his mask."

"There's no mistaking the hate in those eyes. It was like poor Rodrigo said. The Brick in town was their leader. And you set him free."

"You had no proof who he was."

"We had enough reason to keep him," Veehall said.

"Not as far as the law matters."

"I told those killers about the law and they spit on it. They don't deserve its protection. What're you gonna do when they attack us in the dark? Talk to 'em about our rights, their rights, the rights of all men?"

"That's a different thing," Love said. "A kid in a bordello ain't a masked man shootin' at my deputies."

"An' this ain't Philadelphia where a bunch of gentlemen farmers and New England lawyers decide what's good for a frontier more unfriendly than a kind God would have created. This ain't the marble halls of a legislature. This is an anvil, Deputy, and you're either the hammer or the shoe."

Love didn't want to keep shouting through his neckerchief, especially to debate something with which he did not agree. Every man and woman in this territory was born with the right to choose what he would be. Veehall had rights by law. So did the ranchers who had been slain. But so did the men and women who might stand accused of having slain them.

The dust storm lasted most of the day. It finally settled when winds from the northwest beat the southerly winds back. The men lowered their face coverings, but Love tasted dust for the rest of the day. It had penetrated everything and emerged in puffs as they walked.

As they walked, Love tried to decide what they should do. Veehall had no idea how large the outlaw band might be. The rancher told the deputy that as far as he could tell, the attackers had not taken any guns and were apparently still just using more primitive weapons. The posse would have that advantage, at least. But the ranchers had had the same advantage and it hadn't helped them.

Still, Love decided not to turn back. The bandits' — the *killers'* — trail was not exactly hot. But it would only grow colder in time.

The storm had prevented editor Dave Peel from asking questions or doing more than observe the recovery of Edison Veehall. After it had subsided, he rode up alongside the rancher. Peel introduced himself and asked how the rancher was. Veehall, somewhat recovered from his ordeal, said he was all right and agreed to talk to the man. Slumped forward on the deputy's steed, he answered Peel's questions about the attack. Then Veehall was asked how lawlessness among natives would affect California.

"It won't stop people from comin' here and it won't slow the drive for statehood,"

Veehall said. "We're too big and the country is too rich to leave California just lyin' around out here. But the kind o' people you want out here, families and schoolteachers, railroads and stagecoaches, industry and banks — they won't come till ya show ya can bust up the wolf packs and hunt down the members."

"Deputy, I understand that you were here under Mexican rule," Peel said to the rancher.

"Just durin' the war."

"Did General Santa Anna have the same kinds of problems?"

"We never talked about it," Love said.

"I didn't mean —"

"I know what ya meant," Love interrupted. Since they'd left Los Angeles, he'd noticed the reporter took everything exactly as it was said. That was probably a good thing for a newspaperman to do, but the deputy enjoyed tweaking him about it. "It was different. There were fewer folks out here but more of 'em was Mexican an' they didn't fight so much one against the other."

"Why was that?"

"They didn't have nothin' to fight over," Love said.

"That's why we have to be very aggressive an' protect what we have," Veehall insisted.

"The law," Love said. "That's what we need to protect is the law. If we do that, the rest will follow."

Peel made notes as the men spoke, then thanked them and dropped back. Love walked alongside in silence. There was nothing else to say.

It was noon of the next day when they reached the site of the massacre. The riders saw the location long before they reached it. Vultures and crows were circling the devastated campsite, calling their fellows to the feast of flesh. The wind from the north carried the tart smell of the bodies that had spent several days rotting in the sun. Love did not see any of the ranchers' horses nearby.

Veehall seemed angry, then disgusted, then ashamed as they approached. He looked away as they neared the remains of the men. He was obviously unhappy that he had not stayed to bury the men. Love didn't know if he blamed Veehall for moving out quickly, but the results of that decision were miserably clear. There were bloody footprints from coyotes and wolves. Many of the men were missing limbs and there were more organs than flesh on the gore-soaked ground. The feeding birds flew off as the riders arrived. The pale gray ash of the doused campfire had blown here and there adding a fine coat of deathly stillness to the scene.

There were arrows sticking from the backs and limbs of some of the men. What looked like knife wounds could be seen on the bones of others and on what was left of the flesh of several chests. Love wondered if these had been the initial wounds or the "finishing cuts" to make sure they were dead.

"Stinking cowards did this," one of the junior deputies barked. "These poor boys got cut down where they stood."

"All of them," Veehall said. That was all he said.

Love didn't want to discuss the ambush and he didn't want to linger. However much he disagreed with the rancher and his tactics, no one deserved to be killed in the dark and left as carrion. Except for the clothes he had been wearing, the deputy couldn't even tell which of these men had been Rodrigo.

"We'll say words over 'em on the way back," the deputy said, then assigned two men to burial detail. He had the other men collect the weapons and whatever supplies they might be able to use.

Love and Veehall waited at the far end of

the campsite. The deputy scanned the horizon looking for any sign of movement ahead. He saw none.

"We're going to kick up the pace to a forced march, close the gap some," Love decided.

"This change your mind about those bastards?"

"I don't want them running across any of the homesteaders further north," Love said.

"You see that they're monsters."

"What I see is that they aren't afraid anymore," Love said. "I don't want them attacking other white folk who get in their way, but there's somethin' else."

"What?"

"Civilized landowners don't like what they're doin', but a lot of hard-up people might." Love looked at Veehall. "That's somethin' ain't changed since the days o' General Washington. Discontent follows a leader. I don't want these people swellin' their ranks."

" 'People'? *People* didn't do that," Veehall said, throwing a thumb over his shoulder. "They're animals. A pack of them, ruthless and bloodthirsty."

"Animals attack when they're hungry or frightened," Love pointed out. "These people may have some o' that, but mostly they're rational. They make plans and carry them out."

"Christ, you're soundin' like you admire them!"

"I respect them as enemies."

"Respect? The *pigs* that kilt my men? You're gettin' soft on me, Deputy."

"That's enough, Mr. Veehall."

"No, Cap'n. You forget who you work for. I've listened to all your endless blow about laws. You forget that your number-one job is to keep the taxpayers of this territory safe."

Love looked up at the mounted rancher. "Get down."

"What?"

"Get off my horse."

Veehall did as he was told. Love looked at him eye to eye, then swung into the saddle. "Go back to the campsite and wait. You ain't learned a damn thing about a damn thing."

"Are you stupid?"

"Must be, 'cause I let ya come this far when I shoulda sent you home crawlin', like I found ya. It's time for me to do what I just said, work up a sweat and find these outlaws. Tell Junior Deputy Strongman to leave you with guns and supplies and stay here till we get back. There's runnin' water in the foothills. You can see the sparklin' from here. You burn the fire at night and you'll be safe enough."

"You *are* stupid! I'm comin' with you!" Veehall insisted.

"Unless you can run real fast that's not gonna be practical," Love said. He stood in the saddle and whistled. He motioned for the rest of the men to follow. Then he looked down at Veehall. " 'Less you know how to make a spark, I'd catch Strongman before he rides out. He's the boy with the extra matches."

Love rode out and the remaining deputies fell into line behind him. Veehall called to Strongman and angrily passed on Love's instructions.

Harry Love indicated for the men to form a lateral line, well apart, so they could watch for horse apples or signs of human passage through the valley. He knew that if he succeeded in stopping the outlaws, Veehall's anger wouldn't matter. David Peel wrote his newspaper for common folk, and those people would rather read about how a former dragoon captured a bandit gang — which people were calling "The Devil's Rangers" — than about how he got a wealthy landowner all spleened up.

The key, of course, was stopping the

outlaws. And it was to that alone the deputy turned his attention.

# 6
## MISSION

It was an odd little building in the middle of a narrow pass. And it was home to a padre, a crazy man, the crazy man's sister, and the husband of the crazy man's sister, a curious fellow with eight fingers. The crazy man's name was Jack. The husband's name was also Jack. Because five of his fingers were on the same hand, the rest on another, his wife referred to him as Three-Fingered Jack. His wife just called her brother Jack, not Crazy Jack.

The band, now thirty-two strong — having picked up Mexican immigrants heading north for gold — had passed a small native encampment before being directed to the mission. They were told that they would be welcome and, more importantly, protected in the sanctuary of the church. Joaquin liked the idea of getting off the road for a time until he could determine whether they were being followed.

The elderly padre — Father Santiago, who was born in Madrid and came here to convert heathens — explained about the two Jacks to Joaquin. The young Mexican felt worse for the sane Jack than he did for the crazy Jack. He asked the missionary how Jack had lost his two fingers.

"Fighting off a large wolf that Crazy Jack was trying to pet," the bald padre replied.

The band was given shelter in the barn and sanctuary. Santiago enjoyed having people around, especially people with whom he could speak, people with news of events to the south.

Joaquin did not tell him of the killings. Not immediately. He waited until they had eaten and slept in a warm place, until his mind was sharper than it was when they had arrived. The morning after they arrived, Joaquin asked for confession. The padre was happy to provide it.

"Bless me, Father, for I have sinned," Joaquin said. "It has been several years since my last confession."

"Our Blessed Savior understands the demands of our lives and forgives your lapses and He will forgive your sins."

"I have sought vengeance," Joaquin said. "I have killed those who raped and murdered my wife and castrated and murdered my brother."

The padre was very silent for a long moment. "Go on," he said.

"I don't know what to say," Joaquin replied. "I — I have never wished to harm anyone. But I have killed others. I don't even know how many." He began to sob. "Five? Six? I'm not even sure. After I took Polly from the whorehouse, they chased us. Ranchers. They would have killed us. We had to stop them."

"For taking the woman?"

"For being 'Bricks,' as they call us. For being 'niggers.' For being less than they are."

"All are equal in the sight of God."

"God forgot to tell that to them," Joaquin said. He drew a dirty, ragged sleeve across his eyes, then folded his hands. The small confessional booth was hot and the young man was perspiring. He felt as though his body were trying to clean itself, as his soul was trying to do. He didn't know how successful either of those attempts would be. Pain burned inside him, not just for what he had done, but for the burden he had carried these past weeks. All of that was built on the loss he had suffered to put him on this difficult and unhappy road.

"God forgets nothing," the padre said. "Sometimes men fail to hear."

"He should make them hear," Joaquin said. "That way I would not have had to do it. I would not bear this pain."

"Christ on His cross bore pain He did not wish to bear," the holy man replied. "If you earnestly repent your grave sins and return to the light of God, you may yet know peace."

"I *want* peace," Joaquin said. "Dear Father, I want it. But I also want my wife and brother returned to me. Some things cannot be."

"This can," the padre urged. " 'I have not come to invite the self-righteous to a change of heart, but the sinners.' "

Joaquin leaned the side of his head against the lattice that separated him from the clergyman. "If I stop what I have begun, if I turn myself over to the sheriff, I will be tried and hanged along with Kunga and Beatrisa."

"Take their sins upon yourself and let them go forth, offending God no more."

"Is that permitted?" Joaquin asked.

"It is written in Job that the misled and the misleaders can be healed if the bonds imposed by the ruler are loosened," Father Santiago told him. "Each individual must make his own peace. You must turn yourself over to God in this world so you can be with

Him in the next."

"The others cannot be protected."

"Not by you, my boy."

"And what becomes of the other people I have brought with me, people who left their homes to find a new one?"

"What will become of them should you remain in their midst?" the padre asked. "Will they not always fear the arrival of those who pursue you — and who may yet come for them?"

"They were afraid of that before they met me," Joaquin said. "They will fear it if I am gone. Now, at least, they have each other."

"I have seen leaders among your band," the padre said. "God will provide."

"He did not protect them before. He did not help the whore or the boy who was being burned alive. He did not help my Juanita."

"Your bride is with Him now. If you wish to be with her in Glory, then you must repent your sins and accept the judgment of God."

"I wish there to be no more angels like her, taken violently before their time," Joaquin said.

"That may be beyond your control."

Joaquin was silent. He didn't know why he was sitting here. He was angry at God for having abandoned him and so many others. And though his deeds weighed on him, Joaquin would not have done anything differently. He could not. He had been pushed too far. Honor and justice demanded no less than what he had done.

"Thank you for listening, Father. I was wrong to come here." Joaquin stood and opened the door of the booth.

The padre called him back. "Feeling guilt and remorse are not the same as embracing repentance."

Joaquin hesitated.

"Your life is at risk, but so is your immortal soul," Father Santiago told him. "I implore you to reconsider. You have done well to confess your vengeful acts, to seek the forgiveness of God. Perhaps you cannot repent at present, but at the very least you must refrain from compounding your sins."

"Father, what I have done is a terrible burden to me, one from which I will never be free," Joaquin said. "But there is so much that is wrong with this land. What will happen to our people when other settlers arrive from the east and the south? Sin or not, I don't see how I can turn back. I came here looking for an answer and I fear I have found one."

"The followers of Christ chose peace over war. They perished for their beliefs and by the grace of God a great faith has taken root. Those who embraced it, who sacrificed for it, are by His side."

The padre emerged from the booth and confronted Joaquin. His brown robe and simple wooden cross were powerful reminders of the churchmen Joaquin had seen in his youth.

"At least stay with me a few days more," the padre implored. "Accept the food and sanctuary of the church. Let your people work in our modest fields. Perhaps we can talk again."

Joaquin placed his hands on the padre's shoulders. "All right. You are a kind and gentle soul. Would that all men were like you."

"Then I should have nothing to do here." He smiled.

The priest left the small chapel. Joaquin stood there a moment. He looked at the pale adobe walls, which were decorated with scenes from the Passion of the Christ. There was a single window on the southern side of the structure. As the sun passed overhead, it fell on each of the paintings in turn. Right now the sun was upon the scourging of the Holy Son.

"It's like God is watchin' us, wouldn'tcha say?"

Joaquin turned. Three-Fingered Jack had entered and was walking toward him. Joaquin had learned that the man was nearly fifty years old. He surely looked it, with long gray hair falling down the sides of his head but none in the center, his bony hands scarred and his back bent. He was dressed in ragged, loose-fitting clothes and was barefoot. Joaquin had also learned that the man's real name was Manuel Garcia. He was called Jack because he had grown up poor near a rich section of Mexico City, where men of little means were known as "Jakke fools." He survived working odd jobs until nearly twenty years before, when he decided that he could combine hard work and hate for the rich into a successful career as a robber and killer. In one case he spared a landowner but took his daughter named Maria, who was still his wife. Her brother came along since she never went anywhere without him. The brother's name really was Jack.

"Is He watching over us or judging us?" Joaquin asked.

Jack shrugged as he neared. "He's God. Who knows?"

"I don't think He is watching over us,"

Joaquin said as he watched the sun crawl across the image.

"Yeah, we'd probably be doin' better if He was. So. How long you intend on staying here?"

"A few days, no more."

"I've been here a couple of weeks," Jack said.

"I know."

"We ran into a string o' hard breaks. Horses died, boom, boom. One tripped in a ditch, the other choked to death on I dunno what. We had nowhere to go and nothin' to do."

"How long will you stay?" Joaquin asked.

"Till I get the guilts. I been tellin' Father Santiago that I repent for what I done, but I don't. It's a stinkin' world and if ya got nothin' in yer pocket but yer hand, ya gotta stink to survive."

"You feel guilty about lying but not about killing?"

"Lyin' to a padre is worse than killin' a noble. That's what I feel." The short man had reached Joaquin's side. "But I wonder — where you people goin' when you leave hereabouts?"

"North."

"That's where we was makin' to go before the horses left us. Hear there's nice country up there." He moved closer. "I got money. I want to buy a place where they don't call us Bricks."

"If there are people coming after us, it might not be safe."

"Injuns sent you here?"

Joaquin nodded.

"Injuns send everybody here. If there's people comin' after you, *here* won't be safe." Jack held up his finger-reduced hand. "I'm known. My face has been drawn and printed. I'm famous an' wanted in these parts."

"I'm sorry about that —"

"My wife says it had to happen one day."

"But I don't know how I feel about this. About the way you live."

Jack seemed surprised. "I hear you done a little killin'."

"To survive, not for profit."

"You think I cut men up for the fun of it, boy?"

"Do you?" Joaquin asked.

Jack looked at him, then grinned like a boy who'd been caught slicing a piñata to drop the smaller treats. "A few," he admitted. "Rich men kill us in the fields, on their farms and plantations, and just 'cause they got up with an itch to do so. I don't see what's wrong doin' the same."

"That's why I don't feel comfortable having you along," Joaquin said.

"You only take in people who agree with your way o' doin' things?" Jack asked indignantly.

"So far."

Jack scowled. "You want to form a religion, you can pick the god ya want to worship. You want to form a community, you can make laws about all kinds o' stuff. But ya want to form a caravan goin' hundreds o' miles, ya better have a way of protectin' yourself from whatever might beset it. People in a fight for their lives don't have to agree on a whole lot, only that they want to come out of it breathin'."

Joaquin didn't like the man's attitude, but Jack was right about one thing. It didn't matter why they were fighting on the same side.

"I'll take yer orders for as long as we're with ya," Jack said. "Just let us travel in your company."

"All right," Joaquin said. "What kind of weapons do you have?"

"We got two shotguns, ammunition, and a couple o' knives between us. Plus an Army saber we took from someone's grave. He wasn't gonna be needin' it."

*Grave-robbing too,* Joaquin thought. If he

wasn't doomed before to the inferno, he was now.

"We haven't used guns until now," Joaquin said. "We were afraid they would give away our position."

"Then we'll save the ammunition unless we absolutely need it," Jack said. "I hope it doesn't come to that. It'll mean more people than we can hand-fight."

"We've sent someone back to scout for signs of pursuit," Joaquin said. "When he returns, I will let you know what we're planning."

"Thank you," Jack said graciously with a near-toothless smile.

The older man made the sign of the cross as he looked at the sun passing from the Christ. Then, still smiling, he left the little chapel.

"Jack!" Joaquin called out.

The man turned in the doorway.

"Repent to the padre. In earnest."

"I'm a killer, not a liar," he said and departed.

Joaquin watched as the door closed and the chapel was once again dark, save for the pure light on the mural. "What would you have done?" he asked Jesus, his voice plaintive. Realizing that he was standing, Joaquin fell to his knees on the hardwood floor beside the booth. He folded his hands. "I'm sorry, My Lord. I did not mean to be rude. I am humble in Your sight but I am confused. You lost Your temper in the temple, Lord. You threw out the money changers. What they were doing — that was not as bad as what the ranchers did to my family or to the others, was it? I would like to think You understand my actions and forgive them. I also hope that my wife and brother are not cross with me. You know, if I had been the one to die, I think I would have told my brother to go home. Isn't that strange?"

Joaquin didn't expect an answer. He remained a moment longer to pray for the souls of the departed and the members of his party. Then he rose and left the chapel. He felt a little less burdened than when he had entered. Whether or not God would ever forgive him, Joaquin was a little surer that he had made the only choices that were right for himself.

He emerged in the noonday sun, surprised to find Beatrisa and Richard Siegel, the trapper, waiting for him.

"We didn't want to interrupt your devotions," the woman said.

"What's wrong?" Joaquin asked. He looked at Richard, whom he had sent to scout for signs of pursuit. The man was covered with the dust of the plains. His face and neck were damp with the sweat of a hard ride. He had only just left the previous afternoon, when they had arrived.

"They're comin' this way," Siegel said. Beatrisa translated for Joaquin. "Deputies. Steady pace, like an army. I counted seven of 'em. Looked like they was well-stocked and well-armed. Way they was set up, they had a man just behind point watchin' the ground for a trail. Checkin' scat, trampled grass, cactuses where blood from a horse coulda been."

"Were you able to make out the men's faces?"

"They was too far," Siegel said. "But I also heard a gunshot behind them, direction o' the Indian camp. Those Kawaiisus ain't got gunpowder. So there could be more law comin'."

This was probably the deputy sheriff from Rancho San Bernardino. He had proud shoulders and a good lawman's persistence. He would not be made a fool of for freeing Joaquin.

"I don't know if they suspect we're here, but they'll surely see us when they pass through," Siegel said. "If they decide to camp, they'll be here tomorrow."

Joaquin did not have to ask, "If not?" He saw the answer in Richard's troubled eyes. That was the danger with traveling along valley floors and plains instead of the mountains. You couldn't help but leave a trail.

The young man thanked the trapper and hurried to gather his people.

# 7
## REPENTANCE

The number of prints in the dirt — both hoof and foot — told Harry Love that he was no longer facing a band but a small army. As he crossed a plain that led to the valley beyond, he didn't know where exactly he would meet the bandits. He did know when, though: soon. The prints were fresher than any they had seen. They were deeper and more clearly defined, which meant the winds had had less time to disturb them. He reckoned they were less than a day old. What he didn't know was whether the entire outlaw band would be riding together, whether they would stay in the basin, or whether they would place spotters in the hills of the next valley. Love did not want to be ambushed the way Edison Veehall and his men were.

He did know that the enemy had put someone in the higher elevations to the west. The group had changed direction regularly and went where there were lakes or rivers. Someone had to be pointing those out and signaling them, probably with mirrors. The tracks had helped Love's posse keep up, since they were able to replenish their supplies as well.

Now the tracks took them through native settlements where Love and his men were greeted with hostile looks. He wondered if that was because they were strangers or because they were pursuing "one of their own kind," a non-white. David Peel tried to communicate with a few of them using crude sign language, but they did not want to talk to him. Love didn't bother. He wanted to keep up their steady pace and overtake the enemy as soon as possible.

As they entered the heart of a third settlement, inhabited by the basket-making Kawaiisu, there was a stir. Several young braves on horseback formed a line in front of the posse. They did not seem inclined to let the men pass.

Love approached them alone. "You speak my language?" he asked.

The man in the center of the line, a handsome older brave, shook his head once. He touched a fist to his bare chest, opened his hand palm-down, and swept his long arm in front of him. Then he pointed at Love and shook his head.

"This is yours. We don't belong here," Love said. He pointed to the ground, then to his own eyes. Then he made a crawling-ahead motion with his fingers. "We were following men."

The brave shook his head again and pointed to the north. He wanted the posse to leave their grounds.

Love pointed to the south and nodded, then motioned the braves aside. "We'll go. Just move out of the way."

The brave was adamant. Love walked his horse forward until the animals were nearly head-to-head. Both horses shied slightly. The men did not. Love wondered if maybe the animals were smarter than their riders.

A large, rough circle had formed well away from the intruders. There were children and their mothers among them.

"Nobody draws unless we are fired upon!" Love shouted without turning. "Everyone acknowledge."

There was a muttered volley of "Sir" and "Yessir."

Love regarded the brave. The deputy put his open palm to his chest — softly, so as not to suggest aggression — then pointed ahead with one finger. Then he backed away and returned to his line. "We are going to go around this line to the west," he said. "On my signal, move left in position."

Love was hoping the Indians would understand this as a show of deference. He didn't know whether these men were protecting the outlaws' flight or their own sovereignty. In either case, though he did not intend to provoke a confrontation, he refused to turn around. That would slow the chase and demonstrate weakness to a posse that didn't know him very well. If they were going to war against a much larger force, he could not afford to have them question his courage.

"Slow walk — *left!*"

The posse turned. These men weren't military and it wasn't a pretty maneuver, but it put the posse in motion. The circle of onlookers parted to that side. The next move was up to the braves.

"On my signal, walk right!" Love said. If the braves didn't move, he intended to go around them.

The brave who had been facing Love backed from his fellow warriors. He barked something at the others and rode toward the western end of the line. He drew a knife from a leather sheath he wore on his belt. He swung his horse a quarter turn and stopped at the end of the line. He was waiting for the posse. Or more specifically, for Deputy Love.

"He's calling you out," Peel observed.

"He's not the enemy," Love replied.

"He's makin' himself one," a junior deputy remarked.

That was true. The brave was looking to shame the trespasser in front of his men. Either he had to accept the challenge to fight, or go around. Only a coward would go around.

Love turned around and spoke to the man behind him. Ransome Battle was a mostly reliable man, the head of the field force the sheriff had sent out. "Deputy Battle, I want you to take the posse ahead. If I don't catch up, you know the mission. Capture if possible, destroy if necessary."

"Yes, sir."

"You're going to fight this Indian?" Peel asked. He seemed surprised and impressed.

"I'm gonna make sure he doesn't get in our way, whatever that requires," Love said.

"Why don'tcha just shoot him, sir?" Battle asked.

" 'Cause that's not how I do things," Love replied.

Love stopped and faced the brave while the posse rode around him. The other braves did not make a move to stop them.

The deputy did not have a knife. He pointed to it, faced another brave, and held out his open hand. The brave facing him grunted to one of his fellows, who dismounted and presented the deputy with a knife. Love had been in two hand-to-hand engagements in the war and had rudimentary knife-fighting skills from his basic training. He did not know how he would fare, but part of him was curious to find out. The part that was a soldier, not a husband. Unfortunately, the Indian hadn't given him a choice as to which he wanted to be.

There was a commotion behind the deputy. He turned and saw the Indians parting and jumping aside. He saw a bobbing head in the middle of the crowd and a familiar figure below it. The face was unshaved and the clothes were even tattier than before, but there was no mistaking the man who owned them both.

Edison Veehall.

He rode beside Deputy Love and stopped. "They missed one o' my horses," he said. "Where're the others?"

"They went on," Love said. "You go and join them if you must."

Veehall saw the drawn knives. "What is this, a blood-brother ceremony?"

"Move on," Love told him.

"Deputy, we need all the men we can muster on the trail o' the murderers. I've ridden hard to get here —"

"Ride *on!*" Love ordered.

"You're gonna fight him," Veehall said. "That could put us one man down. I won't have that." He drew his gun.

Veehall fired at the brave before Love could stop him. The man's chest opened in a spray of red. He was knocked backward and slipped awkwardly over the right rump of his horse. The remaining steeds bucked and reared and it was all their riders could do to control them. The villagers fled.

"You bloody bastard!" Love screamed as the two men spurred their horses forward. They had no choice now but to run.

Veehall stopped, turned, and aimed at the Indians, who were beginning to rally and mount a pursuit. Love reined hard and put himself between the rancher and the Indians. The deputy turned circles to keep himself in the line of fire. He never took his eyes off the rancher.

"Don't make me draw on you!" the deputy warned.

"I'd cut you down!"

"And they'd have my revolver and my carbine," Love said. "And they will come after you."

Veehall hesitated, a murderous look in his eyes. Love looked back without emotion but with a bottomless well of resolve. With a snarl and a shout, Veehall galloped ahead.

Love faced the braves. They had remounted and were talking and gesturing among themselves, apparently organizing for a pursuit. Two men had stayed behind to look after their fallen tribesman. They were carrying his bloody corpse on a wicker mat. A woman came over and covered his body with a blanket to keep the flies away. Love still had the knife the brave had given him. When the Indians finally looked over, he turned the hilt toward them, threw it to the ground, and raised his empty hand. He did not want a fight. However, he did not move. To capture Veehall, the braves would have to come past him. Leaving him alive among the squaws or killing him unarmed would both be dishonorable. The braves remained where they were.

Love pointed to himself. He pointed to Veehall. Then he made a fist and squeezed it tightly. He touched the star pinned to his chest.

"I will bring him to justice," the deputy promised.

Love waited a moment longer, then turned and followed Veehall. The rancher was already pushing up a heavy cloud of dust. The Indians did not follow.

The deputy didn't know how he would make Veehall pay for what he had done. It was not a crime to kill Indians. The brave did have a knife and was threatening a deputy in the midst of a criminal pursuit.

The law didn't always allow for moral or practical truth, as Veehall had said back in town. But it was still better than the "justice" the rancher was doling out.

Love couldn't help the slain Indian. But as he rode from the wounded tribe, he vowed that there *would* be a reckoning with Veehall.

# 8
## Pursuit

Beatrisa and Kunga organized the group for travel. They assembled everyone beyond the large vegetable garden as Siegel and the others brought over the horses and supplies. The padre had been generous in provisioning the travelers. Several people worked at filling the pouches from the well.

While they worked, Joaquin considered his options and the risks to the group. The worst thing he could do was to ride with them. If there was a posse in pursuit, they might shoot and hit innocent people. Joaquin hoped that if he were not among them, the others would be allowed to go on.

The question was whether he should ride ahead of the group or fall back and try to intercept the riders. That would surely result in his capture and execution. But it would spare the group being stopped and questioned, perhaps savagely, for information they did not possess about his deeds and whereabouts. Joaquin also considered staying here. The padre once again had offered him the sanctuary of the chapel. But Joaquin did not want anyone here to be hurt in a siege or assault.

When the group was ready, Joaquin went to talk to Kunga and Beatrisa. Three-Fingered Jack was nearby loading apples into a canvas sack with the help of Richard Siegel.

"I am going to ride back, into the mountains," Joaquin said. "I'll let the posse know I'm there and try to draw them away."

"We don't want you to face them alone," Beatrisa said.

"It's how I started," he replied. "I'll be all right."

"No — you'll be hunted. And when they can't find you, you know they will come after us." The woman moved closer. "I know you, Joaquin. You'll give yourself up to prevent that from happening. That is not what we want."

"I told you, I'll be fine. The important thing is to get the group to safety. I'll find you when I'm able."

The young woman looked at him. "You can't go alone."

"He ain't." Three-Fingered Jack walked

over eating an apple. "I'm coming with him."

Joaquin looked at him. "Why?"

"So's my wife and her crazy brother can get away," he said. His big smile suggested that he was lying. He was also fingering the bandolier he wore. It was stocked with ammunition for his shotgun. He was looking for a fight.

"We don't engage unless we have to," Joaquin said.

The man held up his wolf-mangled hand. "Three-Fingered Jack here — *not* Crazy Jack," he said.

Joaquin looked at Beatrisa. "I'll take Jack and we'll go —"

"And Richard," the hunter said. "I've got a gun too. And a friend I want to see survive."

Joaquin smiled tightly as Beatrisa translated. The words snagged in his throat as he tried to speak. He coughed and said, "Very well. I will take Jack and Richard and we'll go." He looked at Kunga. "I need you to stay with the people, to protect them. To *lead* them."

"Only until you return," Kunga said.

"Until then."

The Pechangan nodded. Kunga was a realist. He had been with Joaquin since the beginning, yet he did not argue that he should go with him. The Pechangan knew that with Jack and Richard gone, he was the only seasoned warrior with the group. If there was further pursuit from ranchers or members of a posse, only he would know how to deal with it.

Joaquin embraced Beatrisa and Kunga. He felt content as he walked toward the tree where his horse had been tethered, eating grass. Either he would see them again or he would be with his wife and brother.

The young Mexican pulled himself onto the back of Libertad. He rode with just a blanket and a leather rein. He leaned forward and whispered into the horse's ear, "No rest yet, my friend. We must do this one more time."

Tugging on the thin leather straps that one of the group members had made for Libertad, Joaquin rode off. Once again, his knife and his whip were at his side as he went into battle. He was followed by Jack and Richard. He saw the padre emerge as they galloped past the front of the mission. Joaquin thanked him with a wave. He did not wish to talk to Father Santiago. The padre would only try to talk him out of doing what must be done. Joaquin would refuse and that would only waste time, allowing the enemy to draw closer.

Which was already closer than Joaquin had expected.

The three men left the mission grounds and rode south. They moved quickly, hoping to stop the men as far as possible from the retreating Kunga and his group. The dust cloud of one rider, obviously a scout, rolled toward them from the horizon. They could try and intercept him, keep him from reporting back. Their horses were surely fresher than his. He was pushing hard.

Then Joaquin noticed the larger cloud beyond the scout. His gut burned: The man wasn't a scout but a guide. He must have spotted them earlier and was leading the posse to them.

"We have to go back," Joaquin said.

"I was just thinkin' that," Richard said gravely. "They evidently got our room number."

"Hell, we can hold 'em," Jack said. He pointed to groups of rocks between them and the men. They were large, rust-colored rocks dropped here and there on the floor of the plain. "We take up positions down there, they can't go through or around. Anyway, why would they bother? You let 'em know you're down there, they got no reason to go further."

"How long you 'spect to hold 'em?" Richard asked. "We got two days' wortha water."

Jack thought. "Two days," he said. "Gives our group a good jump on 'em."

"But not good enough," Joaquin said.

" 'Specially if we're kickin' up daisies," Richard added.

"I wanted to keep them busy for a week or more, maybe pick them all off," Joaquin said. "They know three men aren't out here alone. If we want our group to get away clean, we have to make sure none of these boys gets back and tells where we've been. Making a stand here isn't going to do that." He watched the approaching band closely. "With the scout, it looks like they've got a total of nine riders. If we had Kunga and a few of the others, we could stop them all."

"These boys got guns," Jack said, nodding toward the horizon. "Doin' that could cost us some innocent blood."

"I know," Joaquin said. "Not doing it could cost more."

"We do this an' it'll lead the riders right to our respective kinfolk an' friends," Jack added.

"They've followed the trail this far," Joaquin said. "They'll be able to follow it further. We go back."

With his belly no longer on fire but his

heart beating like thunder, the young Mexican swung Libertad back in the direction of the mission.

# 9
## SHOWDOWN

They were obviously very close.

Harry Love saw the horses ahead of Edison Veehall. He saw them come over the flat horizon at a canter, stop, then run back at a gallop. Someone from the enemy camp must have come out to look for water or game or signs of pursuit and had found at least one of them.

Veehall had refused to join the others. He was powered by some kind of madness that Love simply didn't understand. Even during the war, when he had come upon a family of white homesteaders who had been massacred by retreating Mexican soldiers, he did not let his outrage hurry him. A horse will only go so far, so fast, and then it'll lay down. You get farther by pacing it.

Veehall obviously didn't care what happened to his horse. He wanted to get where he was going. He probably figured he'd take back one of the steeds the Bricks had stolen.

Maybe he would. But at this blind level of rage, the rancher was just as likely to ride into an ambush or a fusillade. Especially now that they'd been spotted. Love cared, but not enough to try and stop him. The deputy had his mission and saving the rancher from himself wasn't a priority.

David Peel had pulled up alongside Deputy Love when he noticed the riders ahead.

"Do you think they're members of the gang?" Peel asked.

"There's a very good possibility o' that," Love said.

"How do you feel right now?"

"Busy," Love replied. "How about you rejoin the rear and do somethin' else, like observe?"

"Busy and what else?" Peel asked, undeterred. The man's natural brass, plus having the sheriff's blessings, would account for that. "What are you feeling right now, before we confront the enemy?"

"Cautious," Love said, saying the first thing that came into his head. Then he added, "But determined. You do not have to respect your opponent, but ya gotta respect what his abilities might be."

"You have a lot of guns, they have none," Peel said. "That should make it a pretty quick fight."

"We don't know that they have none, only that they ain't used any so far," Love replied.

"You think they could be luring you into a trap?"

"I don't know. But you don't survive expecting a 'quick fight.'"

The journalist wrote in his notebook, then fell back behind the deputies. He was inquisitive. And like Love, he wasn't foolish.

Love's heart began to beat faster. He had the sense any good and seasoned officer did about impending confrontations. He felt one coming on. He watched as Veehall slowed. Obviously, his horse was beginning to tire. However, the rancher did not turn back. He drew his gun as he continued to press on. He had obviously seen the other riders as well. Love began to wonder if the loss of so many men and horses had torn something loose inside the man's head. He wasn't thinking straight. Even his survival instinct was gusting here and there like a tumbleweed. The deputy didn't intend to waste manpower looking after him, however. Not unless he got in the way.

The riders crossed the position where the three men had been sighted. The tracks led through damp grasses that were still crushed where the riders had passed. They entered a lush valley. Though the valley floor was relatively narrow, the hills were too far for anyone to mount a successful ambush. There were boulders men could hide behind, but Love didn't see broken grass or footprints around them. There were three sets of hooves and they all moved north.

There was a mission on a small rise in the distance. Veehall was heading toward the stone wall out front. Love told his posse to split up and go around the building in two directions. If either group was attacked from inside, the other would ride to its assistance. He had one man stay behind to cover any attack that might come from the rear. Missions often had stone aqueducts to carry water from nearby sources. Men could hide in those.

Not unexpectedly, a priest emerged to meet them. Veehall reared to a stop in front of him, sending dirt in all directions. The rancher dismounted. Love broke from his group, which had gone around the mission to the north. He rode over. The deputy would not let Veehall get rough with a holy man.

"Mr. Veehall!" Love shouted as the rancher strode toward the priest.

Even as he said that, Love realized it was the wrong thing to have done. Veehall was standing with his right side facing the open door. A shot cracked from inside, dropping the man with a wound to the leg. He gripped the knee-high wound, screaming as he writhed on the ground.

"Wait!" the padre cried, looking to the door and then out toward the deputy. "In the name of God Almighty stop this!"

Love had dropped to the ground, chest down, arms at his side. He was looking ahead at the mission. "Padre, get out of the way!" the deputy yelled.

The clergyman had knelt beside Veehall. "This man needs help!" Father Santiago sprinkled dirt on the blood and brushed it away. He looked down at the wound. "I need someone to get water!"

The deputies on both sides of the mission had stopped but they remained mounted, revolvers and shotguns in hand. The riders could now see entirely around the structure, yet no man was close enough to another to allow a gunman to shoot one and quickly turn on another. Anyone inside the mission would have to aim. That would give the other deputies time to spot him and fire.

"Padre, leave or you may be hurt!" Love yelled. It looked as though Veehall had been felled by a small-caliber weapon. Most of his leg was still intact. Realizing that he was probably out of range of whatever the weapon was, the deputy rose slowly, drawing his handgun as he did. He peered through the bright afternoon daylight into the darkness beyond the door. "Whoever's inside, the mission is surrounded. Come out or we *will* come in."

"I implore you to stop this!" the padre said. "Let me talk to the two men. Perhaps they will see you."

*Two?* Then the third man was somewhere else. Perhaps behind them, but more likely ahead. The bandit leader might have left two men here to stall the law officers while he hurried to get the rest of his band.

"Padre, I don't have time to argue about this," Love said. He approached cautiously, his hat pulled low to block the sun. His eyes never left the door and he cocked the hammer of his gun. "Clear away."

"This is my church! I will not leave it!"

"At least get down or step aside —"

"I am going to help your man inside!"

"No, Padre! They'll kill him!"

"I will not let them!" Father Santiago turned and yelled into the church. "No one needs to die!"

"I'm not here to kill no one," the deputy replied. "We need to have words with the men inside. All we want's their leader, though we also got an issue with whoever just shot one of our people."

"Veehall's a killer!" someone yelled from inside. "His men rape and murder! They killed the wife and brother of our friend Joaquin!"

"An' yer friend Joaquin kilt 'em back," Love said. He still approached, moving cautiously across the dry golden dirt and scrub. The perimeter wall was about thirty feet away, the mission itself a hundred or so feet beyond that. "Like the padre said, it's time for the killin' to stop."

"Then leave and let us be on our way!" the man yelled.

"I can't do that," Love insisted. "Yer friend has to answer for what he done. There ain't no need for the rest of ya to be drug into it, though. He comes with me, I promise he'll get a fair hearing."

"Nobody's leavin' with nobody!" the man yelled.

Love reached the wall. The nearest deputy on either side of the house was still visible to him. The gate was opened. He did not yet step through. Veehall was still lying on his side, rocking back and forth. Love could hear him whimpering now. He didn't feel too bad for him, though.

"Padre, I don't wanna shoot up your

church," Love said. "But I got a writ from the legislature and I intend to serve it. Either you get the men out or *you* clear out, 'cause we're goin' in." Love shouted, "An' whoever's inside — if you had the courage, you'd come out an' spare the padre this grief!"

"Yer the ones threatenin' violence," the man said. "Turn back an' we'll all be fine."

"Joaquin — are you in there?" Love asked. "Do you understand me?"

"Go to hell," the same man said.

"He's the one we want."

"Go. To. The. Devil," the man repeated.

Love didn't bother to say anything else. He wished he knew where the leader was. Then it wouldn't be necessary to attack the mission. But he didn't know, and so he held up a hand to the men on the right and the men on the left. They signaled with an okay sign that all the doors and windows were covered. With just two men inside, it shouldn't be difficult to move in.

"Padre, is there anyone else inside?" Love asked.

"I sent them all to the fields," the priest said. He was weeping. "I implore you, sirs —"

Gunfire barked from inside the mission. The deputies returned fire. No one had shot

391

from the front door. Releasing the hammer of his gun, Love ran forward. He leaped over Veehall and pushed the padre down against the adobe wall, out of the way. Love stopped to the left of the doorway. Whoever had shot Veehall had been behind the open door itself. The sound of the shouting had come from there as well. Now there was the sound of gunfire as the outlaw fired from a window on the west side of the mission. The door was made of oak planks, too heavy to shoot through. Love took a breath and held it so his arm would be steady. Then he stepped into the doorway and kicked back the door. He saw the man behind it turn. He was crouching near the window, his back to Love. The man had long gray hair pulled into a pair of tails on either side. The deputy let him see that he had a gun. He did not want to have to use it.

A bullet came through the window. It entered the back of the man's head and popped a red hole through the forehead. His eyes rolled in odd ways and he fell forward, his gun discharging when he hit the wood floor. The bullet went wide of where Deputy Love was standing. The gun remained in the man's hand. His other hand was empty. It had just three fingers. The deputy immediately turned to his right, to the direction from which other gunfire had been coming. It had stopped before he entered the mission. A man lay on his back by the window. He looked almost ethereal in the square of white daylight that came through the window. He was an older man dressed in muddy buckskins. He was also white.

The leader, Joaquin, was not here.

Deputy Love slid his gun into his holster and walked back outside. The padre was huddled against the wall. He was not cowering, but crying. Love put strong hands on his shoulders. Behind the deputy, his men moved toward them. He cocked his head, indicating that they should go in and collect the bodies. He signaled for one of them to see to Veehall.

Suddenly, there was a lumbering sound from the other side of the mission, like a log being dragged across cobbles. Love walked to his left, around the western side. Beyond the chapel, past the agricultural fields, a crowd of men and women was racing toward the mission. The group was still a quarter mile past the mission. Some of the people came on horseback, others ran behind them. All moved with an unerring sense of purpose.

"Damn this," Love muttered.

The deputy saw at least a dozen or more women in the group. He didn't want them involved in any gunplay and he cursed the cowardice of a man who would use them this way.

Three other deputies had come around the structure.

"Cook's doctorin' Mr. Veehall with holy water," the young man said as he looked across the plain. "Moore took the padre inside and'll join us."

Love nodded. "Get them. Set up a cross fire along both sides of the mission. Nobody fires unless I give the order. Tell Cook to leave Veehall inside."

"Yes, sir."

The men left to rally the others. Love continued watching the horde to the north. He thought he saw Polly walking at the eastern end of the mob. And in front of them all, ahead by just a few paces, was a man in a mask, the man Love had released back in Rancho San Bernardino. He held the horse's mane in his left hand and a coiled black whip in his right. He sat hunched forward, as though he had a place to go and a reason to get there.

A woman rode slightly behind him on one side, an Indian on the other. As they reached the far end of the field the group stopped.

The leader and his two companions rode forward.

"Where are our friends?" the woman shouted.

Love considered telling her they were inside, which was partly true. He felt it might give him something to barter with — the return of the men in exchange for their leader, and everyone else could go. But he knew they'd want to see the boys and decided against it.

"They're dead," Love shouted. "They started shooting at us."

One of the women in the group wailed. Brother or husband, Love guessed. He was too old to be a son. The woman in front translated for the leader, Joaquin, who said something back.

"All they wanted was freedom, not bloodshed," the woman shouted. "That is all any of us want!"

"You shoulda thought of that before you started warrin' on ranchers and deputies," Love replied.

"We defended ourselves, that is all!" she yelled.

"Ma'am, I don't know what happened and I couldn't change it even if I did," Love replied. "All I *do* know is what will be. I *will* be takin' this fella Joaquin back to Los

Angeles."

The woman translated. Love waited. He noticed David Peel off to his left, listening to what was said as Joaquin and the woman swapped words, some of them sharp-sounding. He wrote things down. Love wondered if those would be useful at Joaquin's trial before the man hanged.

Finally, the woman faced Love again. "He said he will go with you," she replied. "But only if he has your word that the rest of the group may leave."

"He's got that," Love said.

She told Joaquin. He said something.

"He asks that your men put down their weapons," the woman said. "He's afraid someone may shoot or be shot by accident."

Love looked out from under his wide brim. None of the bandits or their women had guns drawn that he could see. He put his own weapon away, extended his arms, and lowered them. The deputies lowered the barrels.

"They're as down as I'm gonna allow," Love replied.

Joaquin didn't need to have that translated. He didn't look at the companions to his left or his right. He nudged the horse and it moved forward. The rider circled the field as an agitated Father Santiago came from the chapel. The padre hurried to the deputy's side.

"Please reconsider what you are doing," the clergyman said. "This boy is the heart of these people."

"I think that woman's got some iron in her," Love said. "They'll be fine."

"What does this gain you?" Father Santiago asked. "He is not a violent man."

"He's gotta answer for what he's done," Love told him. "You should understand that. We all do that one day."

"And he will if you give him a chance to atone."

"I'm not God. I can't do that."

"You are bringing him back to hang."

"I am bringing him back to be tried where he'll have his say," Love insisted.

"In a court of white men, presided over by a white judge."

"I'll be there to say what needs to be said on his behalf," Love assured him. "But the man is still a killer. So were his friends in the mission and maybe some of those others out there. I am tryin' to be as fair as I can be."

"They murdered his family," the padre said. "What would you do?"

"Prob'ly the same as him," Love admitted. "Then I'd swing an' Peel here would write about it."

"All of which accomplishes what?" the padre asked.

"Maybe gives the next fella somethin' to chew before he spills blood."

Joaquin cleared the field and turned toward the deputy. Love looked to both sides to make sure the men were still aiming at the ground. The world around them was quiet save for the crunch of the horse's hooves on the dirt and the heavy breathing of the padre. Love was calm, hopeful that the bandits were sincere.

And then a shot from behind the deputy broke the silence and rolled across the plain.

# 10
## JUSTICE

The first shot hit Joaquin in the left thigh. He listed to that side but managed to hold onto Libertad's mane. The second shot struck him in the right arm. The limb tingled painfully for a moment and then went numb, as though it had vanished. The young man toppled from Libertad. As he did, he saw Veehall dragging himself from inside the chapel. The rancher's mouth was twisted in anger as smoke curled from the barrel of his gun.

The weapon coughed a third time. This bullet missed the man, but grazed the horse in the flank. The animal reared and came down on the wounded Mexican's chest before bolting away. Kunga rode after it, throwing a rope to capture the animal, then dismounting to check its wound. Beatrisa galloped to Joaquin's side. Several of the deputies raised their rifles.

"Don't shoot!" Love yelled.

The deputy was also running toward Joaquin. So was the padre. One of the deputies had gone to restrain Veehall.

Joaquin lay on his back, sucking hard to draw breath through lungs that had been raked and stabbed by his shattered rib cage. Of all the wounds, the one from Libertad was the gravest. In a way, that made this easier. Joaquin did not mind so much receiving a mortal stroke from a friend, if that was what had happened.

Except for the center of his chest, Joaquin felt very little pain. He was surprised. He knew that he had been shot. He had heard the gun and felt the punch of the bullets. But he always thought gunshot wounds would be hot and terrible. These burned a little, but not much.

The young man discovered that his chest hurt less when he took small, shallow breaths. Doing so put him in a dreamlike state. He looked up at the deep blue sky and enjoyed the sun's warmth. It was strange but Veehall's attack seemed farther away than things he had done long ago — working and playing with Carlos, deciding to come to California, meeting Juanita. Those memories were all happy ones and he felt himself smile.

Suddenly, faces appeared where the sky

used to be. They were dark, featureless, but sharp-edged shapes and they made him feel cool. He wanted to tell them to move away from the sun, but it was easier to think than to speak. Joaquin was touched and jostled. The poking caused his chest to hurt, and he wished they would stop. He tried to ignore the commotion and continued to gaze up at the crisp sky.

"Joaquin?"

There was a soft voice just above him. Only his eyes would move, and he moved them to look at the face of Beatrisa. He still couldn't see her expression. That was all right, as long as he could hear her.

"They are getting a blanket to cover you and Father Santiago is getting water," she said. "Then we will move you inside."

*I like it here,* he thought.

"Kunga is beside me," the woman said. "He wants to thank you for showing us a better way to live. We both do."

*I had anger. You had courage.*

Kunga said something in Pechangan. It was a chant of some kind. Joaquin had heard Kunga sing softly a few times, in the mornings, when they were certain no one was nearby. The native did not have a very good voice. Yet Joaquin found this chant soothing.

Someone else came over. She laid a gentle hand in his, leaned close, and kissed his cheek very softly. Joaquin recognized the newcomer by the mint leaves she chewed. It was Polly.

"Thank you for everything you did," she said.

*Don't go back with the deputy, Polly. Go north, the way we planned.*

The faces moved away, but the sky remained darkened. There were swirls of red on the edges of his vision. Joaquin closed his eyes. It was suddenly too difficult to keep them open. He felt himself being lifted. He gasped as the motion caused a stabbing sensation in his chest. After that it was also too difficult to breathe. He stopped. The blood-colored eddies appeared inside his head now.

Amidst the flashes of red Joaquin saw his wife and brother again, on the mountain-top, above those morning clouds, looking bright and expectant as he returned with water. This time he did not descend alone, but stayed with them.

He looked around.

It was a good place to stay.

# 11
## DEPARTURE

Joaquin's followers laid him on the floor of the chapel. The padre administered the last rites while Deputy Love made sure the man was dead.

He was not breathing and there was no pulse. His face quickly turned a pale olive hue. Kunga, who was still chanting softly, covered the young Mexican with the blanket on which he had been carried. Joaquin's mask had slipped around his neck when he fell. Love reached under the blanket and yanked it off.

"You saw where this came from," Love said to David Peel.

The journalist nodded.

"No sense bringin' the body back. I'm gonna leave it with his people," Love told him.

"I'll vouch for what happened," Peel said. "This was a doubly good day for you, Deputy."

Love stood and stuffed the mask in his gun belt. He looked at Peel. "How d'ya figger that?"

Peel jerked his pencil over his shoulder, toward the front of the mission. "One of the men killed back there is Three-Fingered Jack. He's wanted for robbery and murder, among lesser crimes."

"We'll leave him too."

"His wife already took him so *you* wouldn't," Peel said. "Though I did get this as proof." He opened his notebook to a center page. There were smudged prints from three fingers that had been touched in blood. There were also two bloody patches from the stumps.

"That could be anyone's fingers," Love said.

"We'll clarify the picture a little when we etch the plate, show some bone in the stumps. Anyway, people will believe the story when I tell it."

Love shook his head as he looked out the open door toward the garden. Veehall was sitting against the trunk of an oak. One of the deputies was beside him, patching the man's leg.

"What are you gonna write about that murderer, Mr. Peel?" Love asked.

"Edison Veehall is a powerful man," Peel

replied. "He's also a brave one. He returned fire even though he was wounded in the shootout with the outlaw."

"The shootout? The man didn't even have a gun!"

"That's because you shot it from his hand before he could kill Mr. Veehall," Peel said. "Two wanted men, heroics — you'll be a full-fledged sheriff after this story runs, Deputy Love."

"Even if I don't wanna be?"

"Don't you?"

"Pay's better," Love agreed. "I guess I just wish the facts made me one and not your story."

"The truth is you pursued these men with single-minded purpose, not knowing what you'd be facing," Peel said. "The public needs to understand the kind of courage that takes."

"So you dress it like a pig at a roast."

"What I do to make the story read shorter and better doesn't change the fact that the pig's still a pig and that you stopped two menaces."

"Three," Love said after a moment's reflection.

Peel frowned. "Excuse me?"

The deputy strode from the chapel. Peel followed, folding over a fresh page in his notebook. The deputy looked down at Vee-hall. The rancher looked pale and spent. He was obviously in pain from the wound he had suffered. Love reached down with both hands, grabbed the man by the front of his dusty vest, and pushed him hard against the tree. Veehall winced.

"You interfered with justice," Love said. "That man was coming in."

"That was an animal, not a man."

Love drew back his big right fist and drove it hard into Veehall's face. The rancher cried as blood spilled from his nose and along his gums. Love pulled his fist back and hit the man again, this time in the mouth. Several teeth came loose. Blood streamed freely over Veehall's lower lip and down his chin. The deputy wiped his bloody knuckles on the rancher's vest.

"That was a man you turned *into* an animal," Love said. "Just be glad you ain't turned me into one. Otherwise, you'd be offering your explanations to the devil and not to me."

Love let the rancher go. Veehall dropped heavily to the ground, barely conscious, his arms reaching blindly, his mouth moving without offering up anything but blood and dislodged teeth.

"You forgot the part about how Mr. Veehall struggled with the dying bandit and took several hard blows," Love said to Peel. "Or you can tell the truth. I want everyone to get credit for what they done."

The deputy walked back to the front of the mission where his men were gathering. Though it was still early, they would camp in the plain before starting the long journey home. The men had earned a rest. Love was confident that David Peel would stick with his fiction and that Veehall would back it. Both men had too much to lose by telling the truth.

Love took some consolation from the fact that the boy would have been hanged. He felt bad, though, because this wasn't like a war. Nothing had been accomplished by all the killing.

*Except for possibly becoming a sheriff,* he thought. The one result that no one had sought.

It was a strange and curious life. Love couldn't wait to get back to his wife's side where the world made sense.

Where the truth didn't need explaining and interpreting.

Where he could put his arms around what mattered most.

# 12
## PARADISE

The grieving mix of men and women were of different faiths and nationalities, different ages and skills. But they were all of one heart as they buried their leader and his companions in holy ground. Though Joaquin might have preferred to be taken north and interred in the community he had hoped to found, his followers felt that he belonged here, among the other saints.

The padre felt it was also important that he be here. Moses had killed too, and Father Santiago would never judge the patriarch; why should he judge Joaquin? That was the task of the Almighty. However, the clergyman did feel that people passing through, those who may have heard of Joaquin's activities, should hear of him from one who knew him even briefly.

Thanks to men like Peel, legend had a way of overtaking truth. The truth of what had happened here was worth holding onto.

Before the immigrant group headed north led by Kunga and Beatrisa, the newspaperman asked the young woman to tell him about their leader. She said that Joaquin Murrieta was quick to defend those who could not defend themselves and to sacrifice himself so that others might live.

"You have witnessed all that there is to know about this man," Beatrisa told the journalist.

"Were you hoping to marry him one day?" Peel asked eagerly.

"Joaquin was already married," she said.

"I thought his wife —"

"She was always with him." Beatrisa smiled, a little sadly. "She always will be."

"Would you say he rode to his death to *be* with her?" the reporter asked.

"No," she replied. "But I heard what you told Deputy Love and I suspect you will say exactly that."

The group left the mission that afternoon. Kunga did not trust the deputies to keep their word about letting them go. They traveled through cold snowy mountain peaks and through flat, torrid plains, across treacherous valley floors and open stretches of beach. Few of the group had ever seen the ocean before, including Beatrisa. She missed Joaquin even more when they finally reached a fertile and isolated valley. It was situated just north of the town that had been known as Yerba Buena until the Americans won California from Mexico. Now it was called San Francisco.

Kunga left to return to his people. He felt it was important to tell them what had happened. He believed that while the deputy had been sympathetic to them, law alone would not stop Veehall from oppressing men and women who were not white. They would have to defend themselves, as Joaquin had taught.

Beatrisa called the settlement Sueño de Joaquin. Perhaps one day the Americans would change that too. For now the valley was Joaquin's Dream. She and Maria Garcia, the widow of Three-Fingered Jack, established a school amidst the fertile farmland. There they taught the children language and history, as well as tales from the places that gave them their blood — Mexico and Ireland, the Carolinas and the Orient. They were taught to farm and they were taught to ride.

Some of the older children were also taught how to use a knife and a whip.

One day Kunga returned with members of Joaquin's family, his parents and grandmother as well as young cousins. He had gone to Mexico to get them. They had visited the mission and then settled where Joaquin always wanted them to live.

They also lived *how* he wanted them to live — free. It wasn't an end but a start, and Beatrisa knew that Joaquin would have been content with that.

The employees of Thorndike Press hope you have enjoyed this Large Print book. All our Thorndike and Wheeler Large Print titles are designed for easy reading, and all our books are made to last. Other Thorndike Press Large Print books are available at your library, through selected bookstores, or directly from us.

For information about titles, please call:
(800) 223-1244

or visit our Web site at:
www.gale.com/thorndike
www.gale.com/wheeler

To share your comments, please write:
Publisher
Thorndike Press
295 Kennedy Memorial Drive
Waterville, ME 04901